"You s... Annie ..., ... absolute truth. I haven't felt like this in a long time, and I'm not quite sure what to do about it."

Annie turned her hand and cupped his cheek gently. "If it helps, you frighten me, too. I'm still in the middle of an ugly divorce. I'm not ready to have feelings for someone else."

"So, what do we do about this?"

Annie shook her head and dropped her hand from his cheek. "I don't know. If we were smart, we'd agree to be friends and leave it at that."

Her answer disappointed him, but he knew she was right. "I agree, that would be the smart thing."

"Neither of us can afford to get involved," Annie went on quickly. "You have the Eagle's Nest and Tyler to worry about. I have to focus on Nessa while I still have her. And I'm leaving for Seattle in a couple of months. We can't forget that."

He groaned low in his throat and forced himself to remember what she'd said. She was leaving. Getting involved with her would be foolish. And yet...

Dear Reader,

One of the questions authors are frequently asked is where we get ideas for the stories we write. As a reader, I'm always fascinated to hear about those snippets of conversation, moments glimpsed from the train or the car, stories on the evening news and songs on the radio that spark other imaginations and turn into the seeds from which stories grow.

Mr. Congeniality got its start about three years ago. I was halfheartedly watching a cooking show on television, trying to take my mind off the fact that I had to pay bills. I don't remember what was on the menu or even which show it was. But I do remember glancing up once to see a chef (who was quite obviously from the city) standing along the bank of a stream in the mountains of the American West. As I watched, the chef began pulling tin containers, linen napkins and assorted trinkets from a saddlebag—things she'd hauled up the mountainside by horseback so she could create an artistic arrangement of hors d'oeuvres along the trail. By the time she cheerfully assured her viewing audience that presentation is vitally important even in the mountains, my bills were forgotten, Annie Holladay had come to life and Dean Sheffield had crept into the shadows of my mind.

Mr. Congeniality is a story about forgiving and healing, about loving and laughing, about letting go and hanging on. It's about life with teenagers and all the joy—and occasional pain—that comes with the territory. I hope you'll enjoy reading it as much as I did writing it.

I love hearing from readers. You can contact me c/o Harlequin Enterprises Ltd., 225 Duncan Mill Road, Don Mills, Ontario M3B 3K9, Canada, or visit me at http://www.slbwrites.com.

Sherry Lewis

Mr. Congeniality
Sherry Lewis

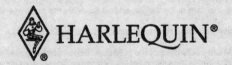

HARLEQUIN®

TORONTO • NEW YORK • LONDON
AMSTERDAM • PARIS • SYDNEY • HAMBURG
STOCKHOLM • ATHENS • TOKYO • MILAN • MADRID
PRAGUE • WARSAW • BUDAPEST • AUCKLAND

ISBN 0-373-71072-0

MR. CONGENIALITY

Copyright © 2002 by Sherry Lewis.

Printed in U.S.A.

This one's for the best guy cousins around...
Gary, Ted, Bart,
Tony, Ray,
Carter, Chris, Jay, Todd,
Blaine, Brad, Garth, Clay, Clint, Blake,
Mike, Steve and Sam
Thanks for a lifetime of laughter and memories

CHAPTER ONE

DISASTER.

That was the only word to describe the scene that greeted Dean Sheffield when he walked into the main lodge of the Eagle's Nest Dude Ranch. He stared, open-mouthed, at scaffolding climbing one wall, boards for bookshelves stacked against one another, and rocks for the fireplace heaped on a tarp near the chimney.

He turned slowly toward Gary Parker, his best friend and right-hand man. "Tell me I'm dreaming."

Gary's dark eyes narrowed slightly and he stroked the thick handlebar mustache that bracketed his mouth as he took in the mess in front of them. "I wish I could, buddy. But I think this is for real."

Dean lowered the toolbox he'd been carrying to the floor. "Any guesses where the construction crew might be?"

Gary followed a trail of muddy footprints across the polished hardwood floor with his gaze. "On break or taking an early lunch? I didn't notice any of their trucks when we pulled up, so they might even be through for the day."

In spite of the warm spring sun hitting Dean's back and the call of a meadowlark in the distance, a chill worthy of a Montana winter inched up his spine. "The foreman promised they'd be finished yesterday," he said, instinctively checking his watch. "We only have two weeks until we're supposed to open for business."

"They've almost finished." Gary pushed back the brim of his cowboy hat and took another long look around the room. "It just doesn't look like it. Why don't you try to relax? There's plenty of time to finish everything before Memorial Day. I'll look for the foreman and find out what the holdup is."

Dean reached to pick up the toolbox. Worry and frustration almost made him forget to use his left hand, but the warning flash of discomfort he felt as he stretched reminded him in a hurry. "Thanks, but I'll talk to him myself. I'm just glad you're still optimistic, because I'm having trouble staying upbeat. The furniture's not here yet, none of our food or supplies have arrived, and unless I'm mistaken, nobody's heard from Miles in days."

Gary's cowboy boots echoed on the wooden floor as he trailed Dean across the room. "Barry said the furniture would be here tomorrow and I checked with our other suppliers yesterday. We should start receiving things in the next couple of days. As for Miles, he's a good friend and reliable as the sun. He'll deliver the horses before we open, guaranteed."

Dean shoved through the swinging doors that led to the kitchen and stopped just inside. In spite of Gary's reassurance, the sight of the renovation crew's sawhorses and temporary workbenches made him very nervous.

Was he making a mistake to think he could run a dude ranch? The business courses he'd taken in college were a distant memory and the research he'd done on the vacation industry suddenly felt skimpy rather than extensive. But it was too late to back out now. His savings account was almost depleted, and he'd borrowed heavily against the money in his retirement plan. Besides, Dean didn't back out of commitments—at least not willingly.

"Maybe I should ask Les and Irma if I can store the furniture in their barn in case it arrives before the crew clears out."

Gary took the toolbox from Dean and carried it toward the bank of windows overlooking the wide clearing behind the lodge. "Good idea. And if they don't have room, they'll know someone who does. That's one thing there's no shortage of in Whistle River—storage space."

In spite of the turmoil his life had been in lately, being surrounded by good friends helped keep Dean grounded. He'd met Les and Irma just four years earlier on his first visit to Montana. Two years later he'd met Gary, and now Dean felt as if he'd known them all forever. He counted himself lucky that they'd all offered to help him get back on his feet.

Gary pulled two scrapers from the toolbox and handed one to Dean. "Now, how about we wait and see if something actually goes wrong before we start coming up with solutions?"

Dean stared at the tool in his hand. "I'm not trying to sound pessimistic. It's just that life's thrown me a few curveballs lately."

Sitting on his heels in front of the window, Gary started working on a label stuck to the pane of glass. "Things are finally looking up for you. Why can't you just accept that and be grateful? Everything's going to be fine. Trust me."

Dean let his gaze linger on the broad sweep of landscape outside the window. He could see the red-roofed stables at the bottom of the hill, the shadow of forest separating the lodge from the fire pit, the slow slope of tree-covered hills rising toward snow-capped mountains.

"This land is the first thing I've allowed myself to want since the accident. And renovating this lodge is the first risk I've let myself take." He took a deep breath and brought up a subject he usually refused to talk about. "Sometimes it's hard to be grateful when you're only thirty-eight and the only career you've ever wanted is a distant memory."

Gary peeled a long strip of paper from the window, shrugging as if they were discussing something inconsequential. "Try looking at it this way—you're only thirty-eight and you've been given a chance to start over. How many people get that?"

"I'm grateful," Dean said, stretching toward a label high overhead. "I'm downright giddy when I can go a whole day without taking a pain pill, or when I get a full night's sleep." Agitated by their conversation, he reached too far and pain blazed through the muscles in his right shoulder. Before he could stop it, the scraper tumbled uselessly to the floor at his feet.

Frustrated and angry, he grabbed his shoulder and fought back the unwelcome tears that still came with the pain. Turning away from Gary, Dean headed for the sink, pulled a prescription bottle from his pocket and shook a capsule into his hand. He scooped water into his mouth, swallowed the pill and swabbed his chin with his sleeve.

Gary kept working as if nothing had happened. His tactfulness was one of the things Dean liked best about him.

When Dean could breathe easily again, he leaned against the counter and took up the conversation. "I know I was lucky to even have money after the accident. I had great insurance, too. Most people would be buried under a pile of medical bills and fighting just to survive and here *I* am with a piece of the most beautiful country in the world and a new business on top of that. I keep telling myself how lucky I am, but I can't shake the feeling that something major will go wrong before we open."

"You worry too much," Gary said with a grin. "Fortune's getting set to smile on you. I can feel it."

Dean returned the smile halfheartedly and started toward the window again, determined not to let the pain immobilize him for long. The sound of rapidly approaching footsteps caught his attention just as he bent to retrieve his scraper, and Jill Beck, the woman he'd hired as cook for the ranch, burst through the swinging door.

Her short blond hair was tousled as if she'd just climbed out of bed, her blue eyes were as round as silver dollars, and her wrinkled white shorts and bright pink halter top looked as if she'd slept in them. She was young, flighty and inexperienced, but without a reputation to back him Dean had been damn lucky to find her. He'd tried for months to lure a more experienced cook away from one of the other lodges, but none of them had been interested in taking a chance on a completely unknown establishment.

"You're never going to believe what's happened," Jill gushed before the door could even begin to swing shut. "Never in a million years."

Dean picked up the scraper and nudged the toolbox out of his way. "Whatever it is, please tell me it's good news."

"It is…in a way." Jill ran her fingers through her hair and shifted her weight onto one thin leg. "I'm getting *married!* Can you believe it? Scotty *finally* asked me— after six long years."

Dean grinned at her. "I'd say that qualifies as good news. Congratulations."

Gary covered the distance between them in three long

strides and swept Jill into a bear hug. "It's about time that guy of yours pulled his head out. When's the big day?"

Jill's smile faded slightly and she glanced sideways at Dean. "That's where things get sticky." She clasped her hands in front of her and twisted her fingers. "The thing is, we want to have a real small wedding. Just immediate family and a few close friends, you know? And we want to do it before Scotty's brother leaves for basic training. The fifteenth of June is, like, the only day we can do it and have everyone there."

The explanation tumbled out of her mouth in such a rush, Dean felt a tingle of apprehension in his scalp. "That's quick, but nothing we can't work around. Any idea how much time you'll want off for your honeymoon? I should probably start trying to find a temporary replacement right away."

Jill's smile disappeared completely and the knuckles of her tangled fingers turned white. "Well... That's another problem." Her gaze danced around the room, never landing anywhere for more than a second and touching everything except Dean's face. "The thing is, Scotty's been doing a lot of work in Cheyenne the past few months. I told you about that temporary job he's got...."

Dean nodded, but he was starting to get an uneasy feeling in the pit of his stomach.

"Well, anyway," Jill continued, "he's making a whole lot more there than he can here, and he just got offered a permanent position, so that's why he finally proposed." She took a deep breath, shot a glance at Gary, and then finished at top speed. "The thing is, with his job and everything, we've decided we should live there. In Cheyenne, I mean."

The tingles on Dean's scalp turned into ice. Gary kept

his gaze locked on Jill's face so he wouldn't have to make eye contact with his friend. "When are you going?" Gary asked.

"Next week."

Dean raised both eyebrows but his heart sank. "I guess this means I'm not looking for a *temporary* replacement."

"No. And I'm sorry." Jill's hands sprang apart and her fingers fluttered nervously. "I know this is a horrible thing to do to you at the last minute. Do you hate me?"

"I'd be lying if I said this wasn't a stumbling block," Dean said, forcing a smile. "But that's my problem, not yours. And I'm not the kind of guy to begrudge someone a little happiness just because it inconveniences me. I'm happy for both of you."

Jill let out a sigh so heavy and filled with relief, Dean thought she might fall over. "Oh, thank you. Scotty kept telling me everything would be okay, but I was still so worried. I didn't know how you'd react because, you know, sometimes—" She broke off, tittering, and flapped a hand between them. "Well, anyway, I just *know* you'll find someone to take my place. Someone a whole lot better than me, I'll bet." She turned toward the door, obviously anxious to be away. "If I can help, just let me know."

Dean sighed heavily as the door closed behind her, and turned toward his friend.

Gary held up both hands defensively. "Don't say it."

"Say what?"

"That you told me so."

Dean rotated his shoulder gently. "I don't need to say it, do I?"

"No, but you want to. I can see it in your eyes." Gary stared at the door, still swinging gently behind Jill. "It's not the end of the world, you know. There's a solution out there. All we have to do is find it.''

Dean rolled his eyes, exasperated that nothing seemed to shake his friend's optimism. ''Just for the record, if this is your idea of *good* luck, I'd rather have fortune smile in another direction.''

''Joke if you want to. I'm dead serious.'' Gary gathered the small pile of paper shavings he'd accumulated and carried it across the room. Dropping it into the trash can, he stood for a few seconds without moving, then turned back with a grin. ''In fact, I'll bet a hundred dollars I can have a replacement for Jill before the day's out.''

Dean took a couple of steps toward him. ''What do you have in mind?''

''It just so happens, I have a cousin who's a gourmet chef. I haven't seen her in years, but my mom mentioned her when she called the other day.'' Gary dusted off his hands on the back of his pants. ''Apparently, she and her husband are splitting up and she's been applying for jobs all over. Mom said she's accepted a teaching position at some cooking school this fall, but she's at loose ends until then—or was three days ago.''

Dean shook his head with a laugh. ''Great idea,'' he said sarcastically. ''I could barely afford the salary I promised Jill. There's no way I can afford a gourmet chef. And that's assuming she'd even *want* to come here.''

Gary glanced around in surprise. ''Why wouldn't she?''

''For one thing, we're pretty isolated. For another, we're not a gourmet restaurant or a four-star hotel, or a spa, or a country club. And let's not forget that the people who have made reservations so far are coming because they want a rustic experience. You think your cousin would be interested in fixing meat and potatoes for a bunch of weekend cowboys?''

Gary shrugged. "Why not?"

"I can't imagine that any gourmet chef would find our setup even slightly interesting."

"Oh? And how many gourmet chefs do you know?"

"A few," Dean lied without batting an eye. "I haven't always lived in Whistle River, and I used to eat at plenty of high-class restaurants."

Gary waved his explanation aside. "Well, you haven't met Annie. She's completely down-to-earth."

"If you say so."

Gary leaned on the counter and looked Dean square in the eye. "Do you want me to call her, or would you rather give up before you try?"

"I'm just trying to be realistic."

"Well, stop. We only have fourteen days until we're supposed to open, and I don't see a whole lot of options out there. This isn't the time to be practical and realistic. It's the time to be bold and daring."

Dean held up both hands in surrender. "Okay. Fine. Call her if you want to but don't get your hopes up. When she hears what I can afford to pay, she'll laugh you off the phone."

"She might. But she also might be willing to do a favor for her favorite cousin. We won't know unless we ask."

"Then ask."

"And if she *is* interested?"

Dean sat on the floor to work and smiled for the first time that morning. "If a gourmet chef is willing to work on a dude ranch in Whistle River, Montana, for a fraction of what she could make anywhere else, I'll eat crow. And *she* can cook it.''

''*MONTANA?* You've got to be kidding.''

"Montana," Annie Holladay repeated. "And I'm completely serious." She scooped pieces of diced mango into a saucepan and tried not to let her daughter's reaction dampen her own high spirits. Fifteen-year-old Nessa might not agree, but to Annie, Gary's phone call couldn't have come at a better time.

Nessa kicked her feet onto the chair next to her and a lock of the straight brown hair she'd inherited from her father fell into her eyes. She blew it off her forehead, pushed another lock from her shoulder and pulled the stack of CDs she was sorting a few inches closer. "I'm serious, too, Mom. This is a horrible idea." She flipped open the expensive CD holder her dad had given her during their weekend visit and shook her head. "I can't believe you're even *thinking* about saying yes."

Annie turned away from Spence's most recent attempt to buy Nessa's forgiveness and pulled an onion from the refrigerator. She put her frustrations into peeling and dicing as she talked. "Well, *I* think that getting away from Chicago is exactly what we both need."

"Maybe it's what *you* need, but the whole point of me moving in with Dad is so I can *stay* in Chicago—remember?"

Annie stopped chopping and tried to ignore the emptiness that filled her whenever she thought about moving to Seattle and leaving Nessa behind. Her heart and her head had been at war since the first time Nessa had suggested staying, and she was no closer to truly accepting their decision than she'd been the first time they'd discussed it.

"Of course I remember," she said, forcing a smile. "Just like you remember promising to spend this summer with me. It wouldn't be fair to back out just because I've decided to do a favor for my cousin."

From beneath her bangs, Nessa shot her mother a sullen look. "Yeah, but aren't you the one who's always telling me that life isn't fair?"

With just a little over three months until September, Annie didn't want to waste precious time arguing with her daughter. She managed a grin in spite of the ache in her heart. "Yes, but it's easier to accept that when life's being unfair to someone else." She swept the onion into the pan with her knife and blinked back the tears caused by the onion's pungent aroma. "It's going to be hard enough to leave you here when I move. I'm not ready to let you go yet."

Nessa dug through the stack of CDs and found the one she wanted. "Well, I don't want you to move to Seattle. As far as I'm concerned, things are fine the way they are."

"Things aren't fine," Annie said firmly. "The culinary world isn't big enough for your dad and me to stay in the same town. I'm constantly running into him and Catherine, and it's still hard for me to see them together." She put a red pepper on the grill and turned up the flame. "I don't like feeling hurt and angry all the time. That's why I have to leave."

Nessa's gaze flickered across the room, then back to the stack of CDs in front of her. "I know that, but *I* don't want to move, and I *don't* want spend the summer in Who Cares, Montana."

"Whistle River."

"Whatever." Nessa slipped another CD into her new case. "It sounds awful."

"It sounds kind of fun to me." Annie kept her voice light as she turned the pepper over. "My cousin and his friend need help, and I'm in a position to give it to them. You don't really want me to turn them down?" She held up one finger and tried to change the tone of their conversation. "Only answer that if the answer is no."

The corners of Nessa's mouth curved and Annie's heart soared. "I guess I wouldn't want you to. But I *can't* go, Mom. Not *this* summer."

"And why not?"

"Because Tracee says Brian likes me. *Really* likes me. He's thinking about asking me out—and you know I've liked him forever."

Annie knew how important friends were to teenagers, but it hurt to think that Nessa would consider trading their last few months together for time with a boy. "You won't be gone that long," she said. "Brian won't forget you, I promise. And by the time you get back here, you'll almost be old enough to date."

Nessa frowned, sinking back into her chair. "So you're going to make me go?"

"If that's the way you want to put it. I'd rather have you agree to go, but either way I want you with me for the summer."

Nessa kicked one heel against the leg of her chair and studied the table. "Fine," she said after what felt like eternity. "But this totally stinks."

"I'll remember that."

"My whole summer could be ruined."

"Try to keep an open mind, okay? It could also turn out to be the best summer of your life."

Nessa rolled her eyes and stood up. "Yeah. I'm just *sure* it will be," she said over her shoulder as she left the room.

Annie watched until Nessa disappeared into the living room, then turned back to her dinner with a sigh. A year ago, she'd been happy and contented with her life. She'd had a loving and generous husband, a gentle and caring daughter, and the career of her dreams. At least, she thought she had. Since the day she'd walked in on Spence and Catherine eight months earlier, she felt as if she was walking in a stranger's shoes.

Sometimes Annie believed that her life was on the mend; at other times, she felt as if she was free-falling from some great height toward a bottomless valley. On those days, there was nothing to do but grit her teeth, close her eyes and pray that she'd eventually land on solid ground.

Her relationship with Nessa had been strained for weeks—months even. She hadn't expected that her divorce from Spence would be easy on Nessa, but she also hadn't stopped hoping that Nessa would change her mind about staying in Chicago. She hoped this trip to the Eagle's Nest would help to strengthen the bond. It would give them three months away from friends, family and other distractions—and that's exactly what they both needed.

BATTLING EXHAUSTION, Dean turned on the stereo in his office and dragged the day's mail across his desk. He'd been working since sunrise and every muscle in his body ached, but he didn't want to go to bed until he checked to see whether or not any new reservations had come in.

At least a few things were finally looking up. The furniture he'd been waiting for had been delivered on schedule three days earlier. One of their suppliers promised delivery by truck the following day. The crew had actually finished renovating the fireplace and building the bookshelves. And for the first time in weeks, Dean was starting to believe the Eagle's Nest would actually be ready to open for Memorial Day.

Yawning noisily, he tossed bills onto his desk and junk mail into the garbage can at his feet. He fought the sinking sensation that swept over him when he finished sorting without coming across any new business. He knew that some of his old teammates were planning to come after baseball season ended, but that guaranteed business was months away, especially if the team made the playoffs. Anyway, Dean had put some distance between himself and his old friends after the accident and he was nervous about seeing them again. He couldn't even talk to them on the phone without painful memories of the past coming back to haunt him. They were all living a life Dean had been forced to leave behind—a life he preferred not to talk about and tried not to think about. He wasn't exactly looking forward to a week's worth of baseball talk—no matter how much he needed the money.

He shoved the bills into a basket on the corner of his desk and walked across the room to the window. Leaning his shoulder against the window frame, he watched the sun setting over the snow-capped mountain peaks and tried to convince himself that Gary was right about everything working out in the end. He'd been right about his cousin, hadn't he? And though he'd taken great delight in rubbing that in Dean's face over the past few days, Dean couldn't deny a strong sense of relief.

What they'd do with a gourmet chef on a dude ranch remained to be seen. He worried a little that she'd turn out to be temperamental or full of big ideas about what kind of food should come out of the kitchen. But he had plans to keep that from happening, and he'd know soon enough if Annie Holladay was going to fit in. If she didn't…well, he'd soon know that, too.

There wasn't anything he could do about it now.

At least he'd have company at the Eagle's Nest soon. Tomorrow, Gary would move into one of the dormitory-style rooms on the second floor so he could be on-site all summer. Annie Holladay and her daughter would arrive by late afternoon.

Much as Dean liked the quiet evenings, there were times when he had too much time to think, letting his doubts and fears get the best of him. A little company would be a good thing—as long as they didn't make him lose his focus. It would take everything he had to make the Eagle's Nest turn a profit in its first year.

The CD player changed to a Toby Keith song. Dean aimed the remote at the stereo, turned up the volume, and sang along until the telephone on his desk rang. He stopped singing, left the window reluctantly and picked up the receiver.

"Somebody's got to do something with this boy," a woman shrilled when he answered. "I'm about to kill him."

Hearing his sister's voice at such an unexpected moment jolted Dean out of his reflective mood. He aimed the remote at the stereo again and muted the sound. "Carol? What's wrong?"

"Tyler's what's wrong. I swear, Dean, I can't take any more of this."

Sixteen-year-old Tyler had been a trial to Dean's younger sister for most of his life. Carol had gotten pregnant in high school—long before she was emotionally ready to be a mom. She still hadn't grown into the role.

Dean hadn't been around for much of Tyler's life, but it seemed to him that every scraped knee and cut finger over the years had reduced Carol to tears. Now that Tyler was older, signs of normal teenage rebellion sent her into hysterics.

"Any more of what?" Dean asked. "Give me a specific problem, okay?"

"You want specific? How's this? Your nephew is completely out of control." Carol's heels clicked as she paced the floor and ice rattled in a glass as she drank something. Dean's stomach knotted at the sound, even though Carol had been sober for years. There was nothing to worry about. "You know that PlayStation you sent him a couple of Christmases ago? Well, it's gone."

"What do you mean, gone?"

"I mean *gone*. Tyler claims he doesn't know where it is, but I know he's lying."

Dean tried not to fuel Carol's hysterics. "Maybe he really doesn't know."

"Of course he knows." Carol's voice rose a couple of decibels. "He's doing this to torment me."

Dean kept his voice steady. "Maybe someone moved it, or—"

"This isn't the first thing that's gone missing around here," Carol broke in before he could finish. "You remember Mama's pearl ring? Well, it's disappeared, too."

That made Dean feel slightly sick, but he still had trouble believing his nephew was responsible. "Are you sure you haven't just misplaced the ring?"

"No, I haven't. I always put that ring back in my jewelry box when I'm not wearing it—and I hardly ever wear it. Tyler knows that."

Dean rubbed his forehead with his fingertips. "Maybe, but that doesn't prove he took it."

"Who else would?"

"Who else has been in your house?"

"Randy, of course. And Tyler's friends. Randy wouldn't steal from me, but I wouldn't put anything past those kids Tyler hangs out with."

The mention of her new boyfriend made Dean sit up straighter. He hadn't met Randy yet, but Carol's taste in men had always been a source of concern. Every time she brought a new man into her life, Dean worried that she'd gone back to the same kind of loser she'd once found so attractive.

He might have suggested Randy as the possible thief, but questioning Carol's judgment when she was in this mood would be like tossing gasoline on an open flame. He decided to save himself the grief and focus on the other possibility she'd named. "You can't hold Tyler responsible for what his friends do."

"Oh, can't I?" Carol laughed harshly. "Tyler knows how I feel about his friends being here, but he doesn't care. He doesn't care about *anything* I say. If his friends are stealing from me, Tyler is at least partially to blame."

Dean used the remote once more and turned off the stereo. He had the feeling this conversation would take a while. He rubbed his eyes and stifled a yawn. "What does he say when you bring up his friends?"

"What do you think he says? He defends them, of course. He refuses to believe that they're as bad as I tell him they are."

Tyler must have learned that trick from his mother, Dean thought, then immediately felt guilty even though Carol *did* habitually defend the deadbeats she dated.

Rubbing the back of his neck, Dean ignored the grit of exhaustion in his eyes and tried to steer her toward the point of her call. "What do you want me to do, Carol? Would it help if I talked to Tyler?"

"Talking doesn't do any good. I've talked myself silly, and so has Randy. Tyler tunes out everything we say."

"Then why are you calling me?"

"Because I'm at my wit's end. I need your help." Carol took a deep breath and let it out again in a rush. "I called because I want you to take him."

CHAPTER TWO

THE REMOTE SLIPPED from Dean's hand, hit the desk and fell to the floor by his foot. He stared at it while he tried to process what Carol had just said. "What do you mean by *take?*"

"Just what I said." Carol sucked in another deep breath and let it out all at once. "I want you to let him come there to stay. He needs to get out of here and away from his no-good friends."

Dean struggled to remember how long it had been since he spent significant time with Tyler. Far too long, he knew that. He fought to remain rational, but it wasn't easy. Carol's hysteria had always been contagious. "You want Tyler to *move* here from California? You want him to *live* with me?"

"Not permanently. Just for the summer."

Dean sighed with relief. "That's a little different, but—"

Carol cut him off before he could finish. "I need your help. I have to work and Randy's always busy, so Tyler would be here alone all day with nothing but time on his hands. He needs someone to keep an eye on him. I think he's punishing me for being with Randy, and he'd be happy if I never had another date in my life."

"You and Randy aren't exactly dating," Dean pointed out. "And you only knew Randy for a few weeks before he moved in. Maybe Tyler just needs more time to adjust.''

"He doesn't *want* to adjust. He likes making me miserable."

Dean winced at the bitterness in her voice. "What about Brandon? If you're going to send Tyler away, shouldn't he have first chance?"

The ice in Carol's glass rattled again. "I've called Brandon half a dozen times, but he won't return my calls."

Dean didn't blame Carol's ex-husband for being tired of the constant melodrama that seemed to fill Carol's life. And Brandon wasn't Tyler's biological father. But he was the closest thing to a father Tyler had, and he'd be a hands-down better choice than Dean. "I'm just not sure that sending Tyler away is the best solution," Dean said again. "It sounds like he's looking for attention. If so, it's yours he wants, not mine."

"He gets *all* my attention," Carol said with a sniff. "That's part of the problem. Did you know that I've had to miss work to deal with the stunts he pulls?"

"No, of course not. But—"

"Don't say no." Tears filled her voice. "I'm at my wits' end. But he'll listen to you. I *know* he will. You know how he admires you."

"He hardly knows me."

"But he still looks up to you. You're his famous uncle."

She sniffed again and Dean felt like a jerk for hesitating. His former career had consumed his life for so long, he knew next to nothing about kids. But he'd be a lousy big brother and a worse uncle if he refused.

"Maybe you're right," he said when he realized that she was still waiting for his answer. "It can't hurt to try.

But only if he's willing to work. There's too much to do around here to give him a free ride."

"Of course he'll work. It'll be good for him." Carol blew her nose and laughed softly. "You're my hero, you know that, don't you?"

"That's what big brothers are for," Dean assured her. "You'd do the same for me if our situations were reversed."

"As if they would be. I'm *always* the one in trouble and you're always the one bailing me out. Speaking of which, there's one other tiny thing I need to ask you. Do you think you could loan me enough for Tyler's ticket? I'm a little short of cash, but I'll pay you back as soon as I can."

"No problem." Dean made a note to himself on a scratch pad and tapped the pencil's eraser on his desk. His personal bank account was nearly empty, but he could juggle the money from somewhere. "He'll have to fly in to Billings and then take a bus to Whistle River. It makes for a long day. Do you want to come with him?"

"Not now. Maybe later. I need some time with Randy to work things out between us."

"You and Randy are having problems?"

"Nothing that getting Tyler straightened out won't solve. If I can play my cards right, I'll be wearing a wedding band again before Christmas."

In spite of his concerns, Dean tried to sound enthusiastic, and they soon shifted into a discussion of travel arrangements. It wasn't until Carol rang off a few minutes later that Dean realized he'd forgotten to ask what Tyler thought of their plan.

LATE THE NEXT AFTERNOON, Annie leaned against the truck's headrest and clenched her teeth as the truck hit a

patch of washboard ruts in the dirt road. A groan floated
up from the back seat and Annie glanced back to see
how Nessa was faring.

They'd been traveling most of the day, and Nessa's
mood had been growing worse by the hour. Annie longed
to soak away her weariness in a hot bath, but the farther
they traveled the less likely it seemed that the Eagle's
Nest would even have running water.

Trying hard to keep her spirits up, Annie watched the
landscape as they bounced along the bone-jarring dirt
road. A dense forest of aspen and pine grew right to the
edge of the road, and behind the trees, white-capped
mountains cut into a cloudless blue sky. The scents of
nature—weeds and flowers, trees and soil—mingled with
dust kicked up by the truck's tires.

The breeze coming in through Gary's open window
teased a lock of her hair from its clip at her neck. She
smoothed it back into place and rested her hands on the
legs of her casual linen suit. She'd thought her clothes
were perfect for the country until she caught a glimpse
of Gary's straw cowboy hat, dusty jeans and leather
boots. If everyone else dressed like him, Annie and
Nessa—with her baggy jeans and hair done up in tiny
braids—would stick out like sore thumbs.

Not that there were likely to be many people around.

They'd been driving for what felt like forever since
leaving the tiny town of Whistle River, and they hadn't
seen another car in all that time. "It seems a little se-
cluded way out here," Annie worked up the courage to
say. "Does the dude ranch do much business?"

Gary grinned across the seat. "We're only five miles
from town as the crow flies. And we don't know about
business yet because this is our first season. But don't

worry, I'm sure we'll do just fine. Plenty of folks pay good money to stay in places like the Eagle's Nest.''

Her dark-haired, dark-eyed cousin had grown tall and muscular over the years. Hours in the sun had weathered his skin and a new mustache added to his rugged appearance. His movements were unhurried, his speech leisurely and tinged by a slight drawl. If Annie hadn't known him as a child in Chicago, she'd have sworn he'd been born in a saddle.

"I'm not worried," she said, unsure whether she was trying to convince him or herself. "I'm just glad I can help, and grateful for the chance to get away from the city for a while. Your offer was perfectly timed."

Gary took his eyes off the road for a second. "Well, you can thank the family grapevine for that. If Aunt Shirley hadn't told Mom about your situation, I never would've known."

Annie shook her head in wonder. "I know they're sisters and they talk almost every day, but the speed at which they circulate information still surprises me."

"Which is why I'm selective about the information I share. If you think my mother knows all the details about *my* divorce, you've got a screw loose." He grinned lazily and added, "You know they're not being malicious."

"I know, I know. They're being helpful. If I had a nickel for every time Mom's told me why it's necessary to broadcast someone's misfortune, neither of us would need to work again."

Gary's mustache twitched around another broad grin. "My mom's excuse is the embarrassment you'd suffer if you ran into someone and said the wrong thing because you didn't know they were having trouble."

Annie laughed. "It would be a tragedy for sure."

Gary's gaze drifted toward the rearview mirror and the

twinkle in his eye grew more pronounced. "Speaking of trouble—you doin' okay back there?"

"Oh, yeah." Nessa's voice drifted up between the seats. "Just great."

Annie sighed softly and hoped Nessa wouldn't offend Gary with her attitude.

Luckily, Gary seemed to find Nessa's answer amusing. He shot a conspiratorial glance at Annie before addressing the rearview mirror again. "Look, I understand how you feel, but you really shouldn't worry about your hair. I knew a lady who used to go to church like that, and nobody ever said a thing." His expression grew almost serious as he turned to Annie. "You remember old Bessie Marshall, don't you?"

Annie glanced at the myriad of tiny braids Nessa had plaited the night before and smiled at the memory of the old woman who'd frequently come to Sunday service with her hair in pin curls. "Yes, but I haven't thought of her in years."

Nessa ticked her tongue and shifted slightly in her seat. "You *wish* you could look as good as I do."

Gary hooted as they bounced over another series of ruts. "I might have an ugly mug," he shot back, "but I do okay for myself."

"I'll bet you do." To Annie's surprise, Nessa didn't appear quite so bored when she leaned into the space between the two front seats. "So tell me what there is to do around here."

"I'm sure the ranch has lots of activities available," Annie said, looking to Gary to agree.

He pursed his lips, shook his head and steered around a hole in the road. "Nope. Nothing. Sorry." He let a few seconds lapse then acted surprised to find they were both waiting for an explanation. "You don't believe me?"

Nessa shook her head. "Should I?"

Pulling one hand from the wheel, Gary chucked Nessa under the chin. "Shucks, young lady, we're just country folk clear out here. We don't do anything but whittle and spit."

Nessa laughed and put her arms on the back of Annie's seat. "What do you spit at?"

Gary's brows knit in mock confusion and his drawl deepened. "Well, now, isn't that just like a city person, trying to complicate everything? Spitting *at* something would take too much energy."

Nessa put her chin next to Annie's ear. "Okay, I get it. Sorry."

Gary nodded with satisfaction. "All right, then. Guess I'll confess that Dean's bringing in a string of horses for trail rides. He's had Les and me working for months re-cutting some old hiking trails, and we'll be putting up the net for volleyball and badminton tomorrow. And a tetherball pole. He's planning ice-cream socials when the guests start coming. You name it, we'll try to provide it. Dean's even talking about putting in a swimming pool, but we won't see that this year."

"It sounds nice," Annie said, relaxing in her seat. "How did you get involved with the Eagle's Nest, anyway?"

Gary steered around a muddy patch of road. "It was a fluke, really. I met Dean a couple of years back. It was like meeting up with a long-lost brother or something— like we'd known each other all our lives." He shook his head and grinned at the memory. "Then circumstances changed for both of us and he decided to open the Eagle's Nest, so I decided to throw my lot in with his."

"So are you partners?"

"Not technically. He offered, but I couldn't see it. Between my divorce and helping my sister and her kids when her husband died, my nest egg was nothing but a memory. And I couldn't see Dean giving me half of his place just because I'm so good-lookin'. Maybe in a few years, after I earn my keep awhile, things'll be different.''

He slowed and nodded toward a wooden sign on the side of the road. ''Would you look at that? We're here already.'' He turned onto an even narrower road and began a steep uphill climb. ''Don't be too disappointed, Nessa. It's not as bad as it seems.''

At the top of the hill, the truck emerged from the forest into brilliant sunlight, showing off a wide green meadow dotted with white, blue, yellow and red flowers. A clear blue stream wound across the valley floor and circled behind a cluster of cabins next to a large log building. To the south, several buildings were scattered around the field, and mountains climbed into the sky on every side.

When Gary drew to a stop, Annie slipped out of the truck, arched her back to work out the kinks and took a deep breath of clear air scented with pine and sage. They might be standing in the middle of nowhere, but Annie had never seen scenery to equal what lay in front of her.

''Oh, Gary,'' she whispered as he came around the front of the truck. ''This is beautiful.''

''We think so.'' He turned to Nessa and added in a stage whisper, ''Outhouses are in back if you need 'em.''

Annie gaped at him and prayed he was just teasing again. Even in a valley this lovely, she couldn't spend three months with an outdoor toilet.

Nessa's wide eyes filled with a horror that matched Annie's. ''No *way!*'' she said, whipping around to face Annie. ''That's it. We're going home. I am *not* using an outhouse.''

Gary kept a straight face for a few seconds before

breaking into a belly laugh. "You ought to see your faces," he said when he could talk again. "Don't worry. We have modern plumbing for people who require that kind of luxury."

Annie managed a relieved smile.

Nessa nudged Gary with her shoulder. "Luxury? You're insane. You know that, don't you?" She tugged her duffel bag from the truck bed and slung it over her shoulder. "Where do I go?"

"Head on up to the lodge if you want." Gary pushed the brim of his hat back and nodded toward the two-story log building that seemed to be the center of this universe. "Look around until you find Irma. She's housekeeper, earth mother and undisputed queen of the castle. If you don't believe me, just ask her. She'll show you where to put your things, but don't give her any guff. She's tougher than a bear and twice as mean."

Nessa gave her eyes one more enthusiastic roll, then scuffed off toward the lodge. Annie took her place at the tailgate beside Gary and pulled her garment bag from the pile of luggage. "Thanks for being so great with Nessa. She's been having a hard time adjusting to all the changes in our lives."

Gary unloaded two heavy bags and followed Nessa with his eyes. "I don't suppose it's easy for a kid to watch her parents split up."

"I'm sure it's not. But it's not like it's easy being the parent y'know."

"Yeah, but you two at least have some say in what happens. She just has to go along for the ride."

"She doesn't realize that *I* didn't have any say either," Annie said as Nessa disappeared through the lodge's open door. "I've worked with Spence at Holladay House since his dad died and Spence took over the restaurant.

I've practically killed myself making it into what Spence wanted. Now I have to start over and Spence is the one who's been making all the decisions—starting with his affair, right on down to telling Nessa she can stay in Chicago with him.''

''She's not going to Seattle with you?''

''She doesn't want to leave her friends.'' Annie stretched to reach her overnight case and set it on the ground at her feet. ''I don't like the idea of her staying in Chicago. In fact, I hate it. But she's so upset about leaving all we did for weeks was argue. It was beginning to ruin our relationship. So I'm getting out of Chicago for my sanity, and she's staying with Spence for hers. And I spend every day just trying to convince myself that it'll be okay in the long run.''

Gary's brows knit in concern. ''He's a good father?''

''Yes, for the most part. Sometimes he gets his priorities mixed up.'' Annie forced a grin. ''He's a lousy husband, though, that's for sure!''

Gary chuckled and pulled the last two bags from the truck bed. ''I'm sorry you've been through a rough time, but you're here now. I have a feeling the Eagle's Nest is going to be good for both of you.''

Annie glanced toward the long front porch of the lodge where several pine rocking chairs interspersed with ferns and baskets of flowers seemed to beckon, promising comfort. ''I sure hope you're right.''

''The first thing to remember,'' Gary said with a wink, ''is that I'm *always* right.'' He loaded himself with bags and jerked his head toward the lodge. ''Ready?''

Annie trailed him across the patch of mown wild grass that took the place of a front lawn. He climbed the steps two at a time and stood on the broad veranda, waiting for her to catch up. With every step she took her nervousness grew stronger.

She'd worked at Holladay House with Spence for a lifetime. She wasn't used to new jobs, new situations and new people. But that was just one more reason why this summer was a good idea. It would help with her adjustment when she got to the culinary institute in September.

Taking a deep breath for courage, she stepped through the double doors that had been propped open to catch the breeze and gazed at the huge room in wonder. Honey-colored wood gleamed from the floors, the walls and the ceilings. The scents of wood and polish filled the air. A huge braided rug lay in front of a massive stone fireplace, and another in front of a two-story window that took up one long wall and framed a breathtaking view of the meadow and mountains. Several groupings of chairs formed conversation pits centered around Native American art and western sculptures, and shelves filled with books covered an entire wall.

Slowly, Annie lowered her bags to the floor and turned toward Gary. "I thought you said the Eagle's Nest was rustic."

"It is."

She ran her fingers along the arm of a chair and shook her head. "It's beautiful. I didn't expect this."

"That's exactly the reaction we're hoping for." Gary propped his hands on his hips and followed her gaze with a gleam of satisfaction in his eye. "If we can just get people here to see it once, I think the word will spread and we'll do okay."

Annie agreed. "How are bookings for the summer?"

"We have reservations staggered through all three months and some friends of Dean's may come later in the fall, but we're not full by any means. I've been trying to convince Dean to advertise more…you know, make the most of having a gourmet chef on staff. But he's not interested. I think it would be a great gimmick since none of the other lodges around here serve world-class cuisine. But Dean doesn't want to start out that way and change midstream.''

Annie slanted a glance at him. ''That makes sense from a business perspective. But if he doesn't want gourmet, what does he expect of me?''

Gary seemed ready to answer, but the sound of footsteps nearby changed his mind. Annie turned just as a man wearing jeans, boots and a chambray work shirt rounded the corner.

He was probably around Annie's age, but that was the only similarity between them. He looked as rough and rugged as Gary, with his sleeves rolled up to reveal deeply tanned arms, a cowboy hat capping sun-bleached hair, and his face and neck sporting the same deep tan as his arms.

He drew to a stop and his dark gaze wandered across her face, her unkempt hair and travel-wrinkled clothes. He extended one hand reluctantly. ''You must be Annie.''

Annie felt surprisingly ill at ease under his scrutiny, but she slid her hand into his. ''I am.''

''Dean Sheffield.'' He gripped her hand just long enough to shake once and then release. ''Glad you made it.''

So this was her new boss? Annie started to respond to his greeting, but he'd already turned away. She glanced at Gary uncertainly, but he merely scooped up a load of bags and headed toward a broad staircase on the far side of the cavernous room.

Before Annie could decide whether to stay or follow,

Dean pulled a notebook from a polished wood table and thrust it at her. "You might want to study this so you can see what I want you to make for each meal."

Stunned, she took the notebook and did as he suggested. When she found that he'd already come up with a spectacularly unimaginative weekly meal plan she glanced back at him in dismay. "You want me to make meat loaf and mashed potatoes *every* Monday?"

"I do," Dean said without glancing at her. "Most of our guests will be staying for a week or less. They won't care what we serve after they're gone."

Annie took another look at the menu plan. Spaghetti on Thursday, roast beef every Saturday and fried chicken on Sundays. She closed the notebook slowly and tried to hide her disappointment. "I don't mean to sound impertinent, Mr. Sheffield, but if this is what you want to serve, why did you offer me this job?"

"The name's Dean." He took the meal plan from her and put it back on the table. "And I offered you this job because I was between a rock and a hard place. I thought Gary told you that."

Annie flushed. "He did, but—"

"So, is there a problem?"

The sharpness of his tone and the deep frown curving his mouth stunned Annie. If he didn't show a different personality to his guests, he'd need more than wood polish and art objects to keep them coming back.

She squared her shoulders, determined not to let him intimidate her. "There's no problem," she said firmly. "It's just not what I was expecting. I'm not used to cooking family style."

Dean motioned her toward the staircase and fell into step beside her. "That's what I've advertised, and we have guests arriving in a week. I don't plan to change everything just because you're here.''

Annie's step faltered and she glanced up the stairs, wishing Gary would come back. Dean claimed to need help, but he acted like a man who'd been coerced into something he didn't want.

''I understand why you don't want to change,'' she said, dragging her eyes away from the empty staircase. ''I was expecting something slightly different, that's all. But don't worry, I'll adjust.''

''Well, that's good.'' Dean's gaze traveled across her face, but when their eyes met, he turned away. ''All I need is someone who can throw a few simple meals together. You don't need to knock yourself out trying to impress people.'' He nodded toward the stairs again. ''Have you met Irma yet?''

''Not yet.'' Gary's description of the woman made Annie wonder how many other unpleasant surprises she had in store. ''I'd be happy to introduce myself. Do you know where I can find her?''

''She's probably upstairs getting your rooms ready.'' Dean moved strangely and touched one shoulder gingerly. His mouth was pinched and tiny white lines formed around his lips. ''I'm sure she'll be happy to show you around and fill you in on the rest. If she can't, Gary will.'' He turned away, making it clear that he considered the conversation over.

The dismissal ignited a spark somewhere deep inside of Annie. ''Gary hasn't told me what my duties include,'' she said before Dean could get away. She was through letting someone else call the shots while she reacted, and she wasn't about to let Dean Sheffield—or anyone else— think she could be pushed around. ''According to your meal plan, you'll want three meals a day for staff and guests. How many people will that be?''

Dean turned back reluctantly. "That will vary. We have twelve cabins. Each can hold up to four people. If we're full, that's forty-eight guests and a staff of seven, counting you and your daughter. But we won't always be full."

"So I'll be feeding between seven and fifty-something people on any given day?''

"That's right. You'll know in advance, of course.''

"Fine. And who do I see if I encounter a problem?''

Dean's gaze lifted to hers and locked there for the first time. The expression in his dark brown eyes startled her. It seemed aggressive and vulnerable at the same time. "You can see either Irma or Gary.''

His gaze was so disconcerting, Annie's gaze was the one that faltered this time. "Perfect. Thank you.'' She started up the stairs, then turned back. "One last question. Where do I find you if I need to discuss something with you?''

He looked at her for a long moment, and she could have sworn she saw uncertainty flicker in his eyes. But the expression disappeared in a heartbeat and his eyes grew distant. He turned away and tossed his answer over his shoulder.

"You won't.''

CHAPTER THREE

IT TOOK ALL THE SELF-CONTROL Dean had not to check behind him as he strode away from Annie. That anyone could look so much like another person was uncanny. Unbelievable. And one of the worst shocks he'd ever received.

Nothing Gary had said had prepared him for meeting Annie Holladay. Her blond hair had been pulled back, but he knew those barely controlled curls would cascade beyond her shoulders if they were turned loose. She was the right height—or the wrong one, depending on your point of view—reaching barely to his shoulder. And those sky-blue eyes...

It had taken several seconds for Dean to realize that he wasn't staring at Hayley. He didn't think his heart had realized it yet.

It wasn't just her looks that left him shaken. She moved with that peculiar grace that he'd only found before in women who'd been raised with a sense of taste and culture. Women like Hayley. The kind of woman who was used to eating—and apparently cooking—gourmet food. She even wore the same scent, for hell's sake...or something close to it.

His hand trembled as he opened the door to his office, and the shaking spread to his legs as he shut himself inside. He sank into the chair behind his desk and ran a hand across his face while he tried to process what had just happened.

He'd reacted badly. He knew that, but he hadn't been able to stop himself. He'd been doing a lot of physical work lately, pushing himself too hard. The resulting pain in his shoulder served as a constant reminder not just of the car crash, but of her. So even though logic had told him he was talking to a stranger, he had felt the old hurt, anger and frustration in every word he'd said.

Gary should have warned him...but, of course, Gary had never met Hayley. He couldn't have known. But there was no way Dean could spend the summer with that woman under his roof. Every time he looked at her, he'd remember the three years he'd spent with Hayley. Every time she spoke, he'd think about their disagreements and he'd relive the pain of Hayley walking out on him just two months after the accident.

Those memories were better left in the past.

He closed his eyes and tried not to see Annie Holladay's image as it swam in front of his eyes. But over and over again, he relived the kick in the gut he'd received when he came around the corner and saw her standing there.

He didn't want Annie underfoot all summer, but he couldn't send her away. Gary was one of the few friends he had. Dean didn't want to offend him. And the ranch was already running on a skeleton crew. He couldn't afford to lose even one person.

Well, he'd been good at separating his personal and professional lives before. He'd just have to dredge up those old skills and put them to use again.

As far as he was concerned, the less time he spent around his new chef, the better off he'd be.

ANNIE STARED AT THE LUGGAGE piled against her wall and tried to figure out how she could possibly survive for an entire summer in the tiny room she'd been assigned. The room was clean and bright, but it was barely large enough to hold a single bed, a wooden chair in front of a minuscule writing table, and a narrow four-drawer dresser that doubled as a nightstand. Then again, with that incredible room downstairs, she probably wouldn't be spending a whole lot of time up here.

Determined not to let disappointment throw her off track, she concentrated on figuring out where Gary had put the bag that held her cookbooks. Not that she'd need them. If she followed Dean's meal plan, she could probably find every recipe she'd need all summer in one good women's magazine.

As Annie leaned over to pick up her heaviest suitcase, the door to her room flew open. She glanced up in surprise to find Nessa glaring at her from the doorway.

The girl strode inside and flopped onto Annie's bed with a sigh that seemed to have come up from the soles of her feet. "I think Gary's right about the whittling and spitting. Do you realize they don't even have a TV here?"

Annie yanked the suitcase free of the pile. "Are you sure? Maybe they have one downstairs."

"I checked. Dean doesn't want one." Nessa shoved a hand beneath her head and frowned up at the ceiling. "This is going to be one boring summer."

Annie straightened and tried to catch her breath. "I know you're disappointed, but we just got here and I'm exhausted. Let's get through today and worry about the rest tomorrow, okay? I'll ask Gary to take us into town in the morning and maybe we'll find some things there to keep you occupied."

Nessa lifted her head slightly. "Like what?"

"You brought your boom box, didn't you?"

Nessa nodded miserably. "I can lie on my bed and listen to CDs, but I don't have that many with me."

"Then we'll try to find some new ones in town. I'm sure we'll find other things, too. Have you checked out the bookshelf downstairs?"

Nessa shook her head. "Not yet."

"Well, maybe there'll be some books you'll enjoy there. And we'll buy paper and pens so you can write letters to your friends...." Annie let her voice trail away as if the list were endless, but the truth was she couldn't think of any other possibilities off the top of her head, and she didn't want to suggest something they wouldn't be able to find in Whistle River.

"I can write letters and tell them what?" Nessa rolled onto her side and propped her chin in her hand. "That I'm lying on my bed listening to cowboy music and counting the holes in the ceiling?"

Annie tried to hang on to her rapidly fraying patience. "Tell them whatever you want to. When they write back, you'll have things from home to talk about."

"They'll be too busy having fun to write," Nessa predicted dourly. "Please tell me you aren't going to make us stay here all summer. We don't even have our own bathrooms."

Annie didn't want Nessa to see the disappointment she'd felt when Irma showed her the facilities a few minutes earlier. "I'll admit it's not as convenient as having a bathroom of our own, or even one on the same floor. But Irma told me that she and her husband live in town, so you and I will be the only staff members using the women's room."

"Yeah, but it's the principle of the thing. These rooms

are like…'' Nessa waved a hand through the air, searching for the word she wanted. "They're like barracks."

"At least they're clean and so is the bathroom."

Nessa let out another overly dramatic sigh. "That's not the point."

Their long day of travel and her encounter with Dean had frazzled Annie's nerves. Nessa's complaint snapped the last thread. "And what *is* the point? If you're trying to convince me to send you back to Chicago, save your breath. I'm not going to let you throw in the towel after only a few minutes."

Nessa fell back on the bed and flung an arm over her eyes. "I want to go home. I want *both* of us to go home."

"I'm not leaving, and neither are you." Annie scowled at her determined daughter, at the stubborn lift of her narrow chin and the set of her shoulders. She took out her frustrations by opening her suitcase and busily filling the dresser with socks and underwear. "Try to view this as a new experience. Take walks. Learn about nature. Practice volleyball. Do *something* besides complain all day, honey, or you'll end up making us both miserable and I won't be able to do my job."

"Come on, Mom. You don't need this job."

"We need money to live on until I start teaching at the culinary institute," Annie reminded her. "And I need some time with you." She slammed the drawer shut and turned back to face her daughter. "You might think that letting you live with your dad is no big deal, but it's the hardest thing I've *ever* been asked to do. Harder than finding out that your dad was seeing Catherine. Harder than watching the court dissolve my marriage after sixteen years. Harder than applying to the culinary institute and starting over with a new career." She dashed tears from her eyes angrily and turned back to her suitcase.

"Maybe you're ready to say goodbye to me, but I need a little more time before I'm ready."

Nessa sat up quickly, eyes wide. "Then stay in Chicago. I'd rather live with you, anyway. I'd *rather* live with you and Dad together than with either of you alone."

Annie sank to the foot of the bed and grabbed her daughter's hands. "That's not going to happen, sweetheart. The divorce will be final by the end of the summer and you're going to have to accept it." She squeezed Nessa's hands gently. "I know how frightening it is to make changes, but wishing won't bring back the life we had. Your dad's with Catherine now, and I've told you how hard it is for me to work around them."

Nessa dropped her head. "I know. But he isn't going to stay with Catherine. I know he won't. He loves you, not her."

Annie shook her head firmly. "Love can't exist without respect and trust." And the way Spence had handled the affair, his complete lack of remorse, had killed both. "Even if he broke up with Catherine tomorrow," Annie said, "our relationship is over. I could never trust him again. But let's not argue, okay? There's not enough time for that. Can't we just forget about everything that's wrong with the Eagle's Nest and have a great summer together? Even if there are some things we don't like. Even if we have to share a bathroom, and go outside to shower, and get along without a TV while we're here?"

She held her breath while Nessa pondered that suggestion. After only a few seconds Nessa sent her a lopsided grin. "I'll try. But it'd sure be easier if you'd chosen a dude ranch with cute guys on it."

Annie let out a relieved laugh and pulled her daughter close for a hug. "Sorry. You'll have to talk to Gary about that." She held Nessa at arm's length. "Who knows? Maybe getting rid of *all* the distractions for one summer will be good for both of us. It'll give us a chance to concentrate on each other before we have to say good-bye."

"I guess you're right."

"So it's a deal? No distractions?"

"Sure."

Annie suspected Nessa wasn't one-hundred-percent committed, but she didn't care. As long as Nessa was still here, she had time. And that's all she cared about.

THAT EVENING, DEAN PUSHED open the kitchen door and checked the dining area of the lodge's great room. Since Annie had arrived only a few hours earlier, Irma had volunteered to fix dinner, and Dean had to admit that she'd done a bang-up job. The aromas in the kitchen were making him almost sick with hunger, and he hadn't ever imagined the lodge could look so spectacular.

Irma had set the long pine table with a white tablecloth and napkins. Candles in tin holders alternated down the table's center with Mason jars full of wildflowers. The soft glow of candles filled the room with golden light and shadow.

He inched the door open a little wider and found Annie and Nessa sitting in matching wing chairs near the window. Annie sat primly, hands in her lap, speaking softly to her daughter. She wore silk pants and an expensive-looking pink sweater—exactly right for dinner with friends in a high-rise apartment but all wrong for the mountains of Montana.

Nessa wore baggy jeans and a gray hooded sweatshirt. She'd curled in the chair beside her mother's, wearing an expression that was either bored or irritated, Dean couldn't tell which.

He turned back into the kitchen and let the door swing shut behind him. Irma had stopped working and stood near the sink, frowning at a piece of lettuce over the rims of her wire glasses. In all the years he'd known her, Dean had never seen Irma wearing anything but jeans rolled up at the cuff and plaid shirts—cotton in the warm months, flannel when it was cold.

She was the kind of low-maintenance woman he'd come to appreciate since leaving Baltimore. She kept her salt-and-pepper hair cut short, and Dean doubted she'd ever worn makeup—a far cry from Hayley, who wouldn't even check the mail without first spending an hour in front of the mirror. Judging by that getup Annie Holladay was wearing, she probably wouldn't, either.

Not that Dean cared. All he needed was for Annie to do her job without bothering him. The rest would take care of itself.

He crossed the kitchen and filched a radish from the relish tray. "Everything looks great and smells better," he told Irma. "Are you almost ready?"

"Ready as I'll ever be." She pushed a lock of hair out of her eyes with the back of her hand. "I've never cooked for a gourmet chef before. Hope this is good enough."

"It's fine," Dean assured her. "*More* than fine. If she doesn't like it, she can fix her own dinner." He took another radish and would have followed it with a carrot if Irma hadn't slapped his hand away.

"Quit snitching my food," she snarled. "And quit being such a sourpuss. You've been in a foul mood all afternoon."

Reflective, not sour. But Dean didn't want to explain

the difference. "Only because I waited too long to take a pain pill," he fibbed. "I'm fine now."

"Uh-huh." Irma gave him a quick once-over and turned back to her dinner. "We'll see."

Dean stole a piece of cauliflower from the salad and popped it into his mouth. "Before you serve dinner, let me load a plate, okay? I'm going to eat in my office."

Irma stopped working. "Oh?"

"I have a ton of paperwork to do."

Irma motioned for Dean to hand her an oven mitt and bent to pull a pan of biscuits from the oven. "If you don't stop picking at the food, you won't need a plate at all. And you *can't* take a plate into your office. You have guests."

"They're not guests, they're employees," Dean reminded her. "And they're doing fine without me."

The heat from the biscuits made Irma's glasses slide down her nose. She nudged them back with one finger. "They're new folks under your roof. You shouldn't be ignoring them."

"I've met them both, what more do you want me to do?" Dean knew he'd spoken too harshly. He softened his voice and forced a smile. "All I want is to eat dinner in my office while I finish some paperwork. What's wrong with that?"

"It's an excuse." Irma set the biscuits aside to cool and pulled a basket from an overhead cupboard. "I don't know what it's an excuse for, but it is one." She leaned against the counter and stared into his eyes. "What's your problem, anyway? Annie and her daughter seem nice enough."

"I'm sure they are."

"So, why are you avoiding them?"

"I'm not. I'm busy."

"You had time to shoot the breeze with Les for an hour this afternoon, but you're too busy to sit down for dinner? I don't believe it. Whatever's on your mind, I suggest you *un*-busy yourself and get your hindquarters into the other room. There'll be no plates anywhere but the dining room tonight."

Dean pushed away from the counter. He should be used to her bossing him as if he were one of her own sons, but tonight it rubbed him the wrong way. "I'm not a child, Irma. I'll eat wherever I like."

"Not while I'm in charge of the kitchen, you won't."

"Are you forgetting who signs the paychecks around here?"

She planted her fists on her hips and straightened her spine. "Are you going to let me forget?"

"I hadn't planned on it."

"Well then, I guess I won't." She turned away and flapped a hand as if she'd lost interest. "Fire me if you want to. Makes no difference to me. But you and I both know there's nothing that needs doing so badly that you can't take time for dinner. So unless there's some other reason you don't want to sit down with the rest of us, I suggest you try acting civilized and get out there."

Dean could have given her a reason, but he knew what Irma would say if he did. He'd already endured one too many of her lectures about holding on to painful pieces of the past.

Grumbling under his breath, he shoved through the door into the main room. When every head turned toward him, he pasted on a smile and headed toward the bar, where Gary was already mixing a drink for him.

"Thanks," he mumbled when Gary slid a glass toward him.

Gary wiped his hands and tossed the towel onto the bar. "Nice of you to join us."

Dean glared at him. "Save it, okay? Irma's already given me enough grief for one night." He sipped and set his glass down. "Why are you playing bartender?"

"Just trying to be hospitable."

"That's commendable, but there aren't any guests here. We can all take care of ourselves." Dean tried to keep his voice light, but he could tell by Gary's look of reproach that he'd failed.

"Well, aren't you a bundle of laughs tonight? What are you doing, running for Mr. Congeniality?" Gary pulled a beer from the minibar and opened the bottle. "When's the last time you took a pain pill?"

"Last time I needed one." Dean reached for his glass again and caught a glimpse of Annie from the corner of his eye. She looked so wistful, he froze with his glass halfway to his lips. When he realized that Gary was watching him, he took a quick drink and nodded toward her. "Is she all right?"

"I think so. She's been going through a rough patch for the past year, and things are a little tender with Nessa because of it. But I'm sure it's nothing some peace and quiet won't cure."

Dean shot a sharp glance at him. "What are you trying to do, send me on a guilt trip?"

"Nope. You got a problem with my cousin?"

"Of course not. But she's not exactly dude ranch material, is she?"

"Underneath that glossy exterior, she's just down-home folk. And if you keep thinking of her as a burr under your saddle, you'll regret it."

"I'm not thinking of her as anything," Dean said firmly. He could have explained her resemblance to Hayley and what it did to him, but he couldn't find a way that didn't make him sound shallow and childish. Instead, he picked up his glass, slid from the bar stool and changed the subject. "I'm going to talk to Les. Let me know if there's anything you need from town. I'll be leaving before breakfast in the morning."

Gary nodded and rolled down one sleeve. "I'll tell Annie. She might want you to pick up a few things."

Dean's gaze traveled involuntarily toward the window where the setting sun created a backdrop of purple, orange and red behind Annie's chair. Her pale hair gleamed in the fading light and the soft curve of her cheek set his heart beating a little faster. Putting her firmly out of his mind, he crossed the room and sat beside Les, where conversation, if there even was any, wouldn't be so irritating.

He managed to avoid looking at Annie again until Irma came in from the kitchen and announced dinner. Even then, in spite of Irma's efforts to engage everyone in conversation, Dean managed to avoid all but the briefest of exchanges with Annie through dinner, ignored the mannerisms that brought Hayley uninvited to their table, and shut himself inside his office as soon as the meal was over.

He stayed there, trying to focus on what needed to be done, until the sun had completely disappeared behind the mountains and he heard Les and Irma driving away. He stayed longer, until the footsteps overhead faded away and he was convinced that the others had gone to bed.

By the time the noises faded and silence took over the lodge again, he'd managed to stop thinking about Annie. But only because he'd given other worries free rein.

He'd learned the hard way not to expect too much. *Want nothing, lose nothing* were words he'd come to live by. But in spite of his efforts, his expectations for the Eagle's Nest were taking giant leaps forward by the day and his fears were growing just as fast. One minute he'd tell himself that the Eagle's Nest was sure to succeed; the next, he was absolutely certain the project was doomed to failure.

He thought about pouring himself another drink, but decided to take a hot shower instead. After checking to make sure the doors and windows were shut and locked, he climbed the stairs to his room, peeled off his shirt and grabbed soap and a towel, then headed to the other end of the hall where a set of stairs on the outside of the lodge led to the showers.

Even on the hottest and stillest of days, evening brought a welcome breeze from the mouths of two nearby canyons, and the temperature always dropped sharply when the sun went down. Dean stood at the bottom of the stairs and listened to the canyons breathing life into the valley—to the leaves overhead and the brush of grass in the meadow. And he told himself that even if the Eagle's Nest failed, he hadn't been wrong to buy this land.

He was lost in thought when a door opened behind him and light spilled out onto the darkened ground. Surprised, he pivoted in the loose gravel and found Annie standing in the door to the ladies' room, toothbrush in one hand, cosmetic case in the other, a towel draped over the shoulder of her knee-length terry-cloth robe. A pair of bright pink flip-flops adorned her feet and her hair hung in damp waves past her shoulders, just as he'd known it would. She was so startlingly beautiful, Dean had trouble catching his breath.

Annie seemed equally surprised to find him there. Even in the dim lighting he could see her eyes grow wide and color flood her cheeks. She put a hand to her breast and laughed nervously. "You startled me."

"Sorry." Dean tossed the towel over his shoulder to cover the hated scars. "I didn't realize anyone was still awake."

Annie ran a hand through her wet hair and glanced toward the darkened windows on the second floor. "I tried to sleep, but I guess we spent too long traveling. I couldn't wind down." She gestured weakly at the towel on her shoulder. "I hoped a shower would help."

Dean swallowed convulsively and tried not to notice the smooth legs peeking out from beneath the hem of her robe. "Yes. Well." He couldn't find anything to say, and that made him feel like an awkward kid. He cleared his throat and tried again. "I had the same idea."

Annie smiled uneasily, pulled the towel from her shoulder and clutched it in front of her. She lifted her chin and seemed to steel herself to talk to him. "I'm glad I ran into you. Gary said you were planning to go into town tomorrow. I wonder if Nessa and I can tag along?"

She didn't seem to mind being caught without makeup in place and hair done, and Dean battled one brief pang of guilt over the way he'd been acting. He nodded slowly, even though the idea of riding into town with Annie wasn't a welcome one. "Sure. But I'll be gone most of the day. If you'd rather, you can give me a list. I'll be glad to pick up what you need."

"Thanks, but I need to go myself. I can't guess what Nessa might want, and I need to do some personal shopping. Irma suggested that I might benefit from a more appropriate wardrobe."

Dean felt better knowing he wasn't the only one who'd been treated to Irma's opinion that evening. "She's probably right. Those clothes you've been wearing won't last long around here.''

"So, is it okay?"

"It's fine, but be ready early. I want to leave by eight."

"That's not a problem. I'm always up early." Annie reached behind her to turn out the light.

Dean's eyes readjusted to the dark within seconds...and he immediately wished they hadn't. Her physical resemblance to Hayley was stronger than ever in the moonlight. To make matters worse, it had been a long time since he'd been alone with a beautiful woman who'd looked at him with eyes so wide or an expression so vulnerable. Far too long since he'd felt the unwitting physical reaction that he felt now, and even longer since he'd done anything about it.

He wanted to turn away, but he couldn't seem to move. He willed her silently to go upstairs and leave him alone. The last thing he wanted was for her to get a good look at him in the moonlight and come away with the wrong impression.

She smiled gently and wrapped her towel around her neck. And when she spoke again, her voice felt like a warm breeze. "Thank you. I promise, we won't be a bother. You can just drop us somewhere when we get to town and then tell us where and when to meet you later."

"Sounds fine."

When at last Annie turned toward the stairs, Dean let out a breath thick with relief. But as he watched her climb the stairs and felt himself responding again, this time to the gentle sway of her hips beneath the terry-cloth robe, he knew Annie Holladay was going to be more of a bother than she could possibly imagine.

CHAPTER FOUR

AT A LITTLE BEFORE four-thirty the next afternoon, Dean leaned against his truck on the side of the highway, holding a warm can of iced tea and watching for the Greyhound bus to arrive from Billings. What had started as a soft breeze that morning had stiffened noticeably as the day wore on, and enough dust and pollen floated through the air to make anyone's eyes red. Adding to the discomfort, the temperature was unseasonably warm. The sun beat down on Dean's shoulders and baked the earth beneath his feet.

He sipped from his can, grimaced and set it on the tailgate beside him. He'd kept himself busy all day picking up supplies, having his shoulder checked at Dr. Mills's office and refilling his prescription at the drugstore. He'd managed not to waste time anticipating Tyler's arrival or dwelling on his brief conversation with Annie the night before. He was just glad Nessa had been there that morning to act as a buffer. Being around Annie was a whole lot easier when other people were around.

He wondered if he should have mentioned that Tyler was coming to Annie, but he dismissed the doubt immediately. She needed to know how many to cook for, but Dean didn't want to risk anyone asking questions about his personal life. That was one door Dean liked to keep firmly shut.

It was just ironic that the past should come back to

haunt him now, when he needed his concentration to be at its peak. When he needed to stay tightly focused on the present in order to carve out a future for himself. He downed the rest of his drink, crumpled the can and checked for a garbage bin. When he didn't find one, he tossed the can into the truck bed and paced the side of the highway until he heard the bus coming.

Suddenly, he found himself jumpy as a cat. He hadn't seen Tyler since the boy was ten and Dean had finally worked his way onto the Orioles' starting lineup. There'd been a lot of changes since then. Dean wasn't the same person, and Tyler wouldn't be, either. It would be nice to spend time together and get reacquainted, and Tyler was certainly old enough to understand that business had to come first this summer.

The bus drew to a stop a few feet from him, kicking up a cloud of dust and emitting diesel fumes into the pine-scented air. A few seconds later, the door swished open and one lone passenger climbed down the steps carrying two heavy-looking duffel bags.

Dean told himself that he would have known Tyler anywhere, but he wasn't sure it was the truth. The kid had nearly doubled in size since Dean last saw him. Tall and lanky, broad-shouldered and narrow-hipped, the boy had almost turned into a man, and Dean's nervousness took a sharp upswing.

Tyler's naturally dark hair was cut into short spikes and bleached blond at the tips. A pair of baggy jeans rode low on his hips and a tight T-shirt accented the muscles in his shoulders and arms. He glanced up the street, then down through a pair of mirrored sunglasses, and stood still for a long time, as if he didn't recognize Dean, either.

That wasn't surprising. The last time they'd seen each

other, Dean had been caught up in his career and all the trimmings that had come with it. The hand-tailored suits, silk shirts and Italian leather shoes he'd worn then were a far cry from the straw cowboy hat, dusty jeans and boots he wore today.

Eager to get the awkward part out of the way, Dean strode forward. "Tyler?"

The kid curled his lip and dropped his bags into the dirt at his feet. "Oh, great. Now he's a cowboy. What next?"

In spite of Carol's phone call, Dean hadn't expected hostility—especially not directed at him. It took him a couple of heartbeats to recover and ask, "How was your trip?"

Behind the sunglasses, Tyler's expression oozed insolence. "Fine, I guess. Why?"

"I'm just curious. How's your mom?"

Tyler glanced away and nudged his glasses up on his nose. "Her? She's just peachy."

Dean decided to ignore the sarcasm. "Well, I'm glad you made it. My truck's over here. We're just a few minutes from the ranch." He reached to pick up one of Tyler's bags, but Tyler jerked the duffel out of Dean's reach.

"Don't bother. I can take care of my own stuff."

Maybe Carol hadn't exaggerated. Dean kept his expression neutral and pulled his keys from his pocket. "Fine with me. I've been talking to my foreman about what we should have you do this summer. Gary suggested letting you work in the stables. What do you think?"

Tyler tossed one bag into the truck bed and leveled a glance at Dean over the tops of his glasses. "Shoveling crap?"

That might be better than dishing it out. Dean shook off the uncharitable thought and nodded. "Cleaning the stables would be part of the job, but you'd also help with feeding and grooming. After you and the horses get used to one another, we can give you more responsibility."

Tyler stared at him for a few seconds, then hoisted the second bag into the truck. "Whatever."

"You don't have to work in the stables if that doesn't interest you. But I do need you to work while you're here. There's too much to do this first season for anyone to have a free ride. So check things out at the ranch when we get there and tell me if there's something else you'd rather do."

Tyler kept his gaze straight ahead. "Whatever, dude. It doesn't matter to me." He stood that way for a beat or two, then shifted his mirrored gaze to Dean's face. "If I had my way, I wouldn't even be here."

At least Dean didn't have to wonder any longer how the kid felt. He leaned against the truck and tried to nip Tyler's unexplained hostility in the bud. "Look, I understand how you feel—"

"Really? So you're a cowboy *and* a mind reader?"

"I didn't say that. I only meant that I know you'd rather be home with your mom—"

Tyler cut him off again, this time with a bitter laugh. "Oh, yeah. I *really* want to be there." He wrenched open the passenger door and climbed inside the truck.

Dean slid in behind the wheel, but despite his efforts to stay positive, Tyler's attitude was beginning to grate on his nerves. He ground the engine as he started it and had trouble shifting into gear. Finally, he had the truck running and a better handle on his own temper.

He glanced across the seat at the young man he barely

knew. "If you don't like my suggestions, why don't you tell me what you *do* want?"

"From you? Not a damn thing."

Dean didn't know much about teenagers, but it didn't take a child psychologist to see that this one wanted to provoke a reaction. But Dean wasn't about to let the kid call the shots. He nodded as if Tyler hadn't said anything unusual and turned on the radio. "You want to pick the station?"

A couple of different expressions flickered across the kid's face. "Do you have any decent stations in this hick town?"

"Depends on your definition of 'decent.'" Dean nodded toward his CD case on the seat. "You can pick a CD if you'd rather."

Tyler started to reach for the case, then pulled his hand away quickly and turned back to the window. "What's the point?"

Dean tried to match the kid's cool and keep his own reaction hidden. He turned onto Whistle River's main street and drove slowly through town. A few years ago, Tyler had been a friendly kid with an engaging smile and an infectious laugh. A boy who'd adored his mother and had been anxious to win his uncle's approval. When had he turned into this surly, angry young man?

More importantly, why?

Dean felt a momentary pang of guilt that he didn't know more about his nephew's life, but he pushed it away. He wasn't to blame for Tyler's attitude, he'd merely promised Carol that he'd help change it.

Unfortunately, that might be a far bigger job than he'd first anticipated.

ANNIE SLID INTO A WINDOW BOOTH at the Whistle River Café and settled a dozen bags and her purse on the bench beside her. The scent of hot grease and fried food made her stomach slightly queasy, but this was where Dean had said he'd meet them at five o'clock, so she had to tolerate it for a little while.

Nessa sat across the chipped Formica table with her chin in her hands, staring out at the spotty traffic and nearly empty parking lot. They'd been searching for things to interest Nessa all day, but Whistle River's sparse shopping district hadn't offered much variety.

They'd stumbled across a small crafts store that had filled Annie with hope for about three seconds. Nessa hadn't been even slightly interested in anything they'd found there, but Annie had picked up two counted cross-stitch kits just in case. The only real luck they'd had all day was finding clothes for Annie that were suitable for this rugged country.

With her remaining energy, Annie dredged up a smile and leaned back in her seat. "Okay, so you were right. There wasn't much to pick from."

Nessa sighed unhappily. "That's an understatement."

"I'm not defeated, though. There's always mail order and shopping over the Internet."

Nessa's gaze trailed slowly from the window to Annie's face. "If Dean even has a computer."

"He *must*. How can he do business without one—especially way out here, so far from everything?"

Nessa almost smiled. "I thought the same thing about a TV, and look how that turned out."

Annie sipped water and trailed her finger along the condensation on the side of the glass. "You have a point, but I'll ask him, anyway. I'm determined to find some way to make this summer fun for you."

"I know how you can do that."

Annie held up a hand to stop her. "We're *not* leaving."

"Okay, then. How about letting Brian and Steve and Tracee come and stay here for the summer?"

Annie laughed. "Nice try, but I don't think that's a good idea."

"Why not?"

"Because Tracee's parents can't afford to send her here, and I certainly can't pay her way. And believe it or not, it won't hurt you to spend three whole months without boys."

"They're *guys*, not boys, and life's boring without them."

Annie had once felt that way, but since separating from Spence she was enjoying the emotional peace of being single—at least for a while. "Life without guys doesn't have to be boring," she said. "There are so many other things to think about, to do and to try...."

Nessa rolled her eyes. "I'm fifteen, Mom. I don't *want* to think about anything else." She grinned and sat back in her seat. "Being totally obsessed with guys is, like, my job."

Annie loved seeing her smile. "And *my* job is helping you know when enough is enough. This summer may turn out to be a great experience for you." She pulled two menus from behind a napkin holder and passed one to her daughter. "We'll just have to keep searching until we find something to interest you. There has to be some way to convince you that guys aren't everything."

Nessa's eyes sparkled with mischief. "You could talk Dean into getting a TV for the lodge. If he had cable or a satellite dish, I could at least keep up with the new music videos as they come out."

Annie shook her head, decided to order a strawberry

milk shake and set the menu aside. "We've been here less than twenty-four hours, and I haven't done a bit of work yet. I don't think this is the best time to be asking for changes. Especially since Dean doesn't seem inclined to *make* changes."

Frowning slightly, Nessa tucked her menu back into place. "Come on! It doesn't hurt to ask. I'll bet *I* could convince him to put in a dish."

Nessa could probably break through Dean's crust if anyone could, but Annie shook her head and linked her hands together on the table. "Let's wait awhile, okay? I haven't figured out his moods yet, and I'm not entirely convinced he doesn't bite."

Nessa giggled and leaned back in her seat. "Come on, Mom. He's not *that* bad."

That was the first positive thing Nessa had said since they arrived, but it was one thing Annie couldn't agree with her about. "You weren't there when I met him yesterday."

"Well, Gary likes him. And so do Irma and Les, so how bad can he be?"

"Not bad at all when he's like he was this morning." *And last night.* A waitress approached their table and Annie realized it wasn't smart to be gossiping about her new boss, so after they placed their order, she changed the subject. "You haven't told me what you think of Gary."

Nessa twirled a spoon on the table and took her time answering. "He's funny. I like him."

"I'm glad. I like him, too. I'd forgotten how much fun he is to be around. I'd also forgotten what teases some of my family are. I guess it's safe to say that you come by your love of teasing naturally."

Nessa started to answer but stopped when something outside captured her attention. Annie followed her gaze and recognized Dean's black Dodge in the parking lot. She tried to decide which mood he was in, but he'd pulled the sun visor down in the windshield and she couldn't see his face.

"Who's with him?" Nessa asked.

"I have no idea. Let's hope it's someone who knows how to keep him happy."

Dean jumped from the truck and started toward the restaurant. A tall young man about Nessa's age followed more slowly. Even from a distance, and in spite of the boy's platinum-tipped spikes and mirrored sunglasses, Annie could see a striking resemblance between the two.

When Nessa saw Dean's companion more clearly, she straightened in her seat, the boredom flew out of her eyes, and a flush painted her cheeks. "Who's *that?*"

"I don't know."

"Do you think he's going back to the ranch with us?"

"I think we're about to find out."

Nessa moved her shake to the center of the table so that it appeared as if Annie had ordered two for herself. She checked the front of her blouse as if she was afraid food had jumped onto it by mistake. "He's hot, isn't he?"

Annie pretended not to understand. "Who? Dean?"

"No." Nessa scowled deeply. "The other guy."

She shrugged casually. "I guess so—for someone young enough to be my son."

Nessa darted a glance at her. "He's *hot*, Mom."

"Okay. He's hot." The fact didn't exactly thrill Annie, but guys seemed to be the only subject that sparked any real interest in Nessa.

Nessa ran her hands across her hair and frowned slightly. "Do you really think Dean's hot?"

He *was* pleasant to look at, but Annie knew her daughter still had high hopes that her parents would get back together. She also knew that Nessa wasn't ready for even a lighthearted discussion of Dean's charms. Glancing at Dean's broad shoulders and muscular thighs, she filled her mouth with strawberry ice cream. "I was joking."

Nessa relaxed slightly as Dean noticed them and started toward their table. Annie's heart gave a strange little skip of anticipation. She told herself it was dread, stood and picked up her purse.

"Let's not keep him waiting. It might bring back the bad Dean."

Nessa slid out of the booth and Annie bent to retrieve her bags as Dean stopped beside their table. He glanced at their full glasses and waved them back to their seats. "You're not finished."

"We're ready to leave," Annie assured him. "We were just killing time."

"We're not in that much of a hurry. Sit down and finish."

Nessa sank back in her seat without arguing, but she seemed shocked to find a milk shake in front of her. Annie dropped back onto the bench and slid toward the window. When Dean showed no signs of leaving, she remembered her manners. "Would you like to join us?"

Dean glanced at the young man who had pushed his glasses to the top of his head and was trying hard not to stare at Nessa. The kid's gaze drifted across the top of Nessa's head and glanced off her face. He lifted one shoulder and tried to give the impression that he didn't care. "Sure. Why not?"

Dean slid in beside Annie and left the opposite bench for the kids. Annie ignored the soft brush of his thigh and the feel of his arm grazing hers as he moved. "I'm

Annie Holladay,'' she said to the young man. "And this is my daughter, Nessa.''

The boy's eyes flicked across Nessa's face again. "I'm Tyler.''

"My nephew," Dean added. "Tyler Bell.''

That certainly explained the resemblance. Annie pulled her milk shake toward her and stirred it slowly with her straw. "Do you live nearby, Tyler?''

The kid's gaze drifted across the tabletop and landed for less than a heartbeat on Nessa's cheek. "California.''

Nessa's eyes widened as if she'd never heard anything more brilliant. "What part of California?''

"San Diego.''

Annie tried not to let their mutual awareness disturb her, but it wasn't easy to ignore. "So, you're here for a vacation?'' *Please say yes. Please, please, please.*

Tyler toyed with the wrapper from Nessa's straw. "Not exactly.''

Once again, Dean filled in around Tyler's answer. "Actually, Tyler's here for the summer.''

Annie's stomach dropped.

Nessa sat up straight and positively glittered. "The *whole* summer?''

Tyler nodded, and this time his gaze actually locked on Nessa's for a full second. "Afraid so.''

"I know what you mean. My mom's the cook, so we have to stay until after Labor Day.''

The *cook?* Annie could have sworn she felt a headache coming on. Dean stiffened beside her and Annie realized how insulted he must feel to hear the kids complaining. She forced a light laugh and sent a look full of meaning at her daughter. "Listen to you two. You make it sound like staying here is a death sentence.'' She turned to Tyler and added, "The ranch is beautiful. I'm sure you'll love it."

Tyler glanced at Dean and rolled his eyes toward Nessa. "Yeah, well since there's somebody else my age around maybe it won't be so bad."

A flattering pink flush stained Nessa's cheeks and her eyes glistened. She appeared more interested in life than she had in a year. But that only made the pounding in Annie's head worse.

Yes, she'd been hoping to find something that would interest Nessa here in Montana...but this was *not* what she'd had in mind.

By six o'clock, Annie was back at the lodge and in the kitchen. She'd been pleasantly surprised by the spacious room, with its huge windows overlooking the west side of the valley. The kitchen was well stocked with professional-quality appliances that were as good as any Annie had used in Chicago. It was a shame Dean wouldn't let her use the kitchen to its full potential.

She worked quickly, keeping one eye on the clock while she fixed barbecue ribs with her signature sauce instead of the bottled stuff Dean had provided. She wanted her first meal at the Eagle's Nest to be special— as special as it could be considering the menus Dean had planned.

As she finished peeling and slicing potatoes, she turned toward the sink and caught sight of Nessa sitting with Tyler on a log across the clearing. Annie tried not to be concerned about the obvious attraction between the two. Tyler was a distraction Annie hadn't planned on having to compete with. She just hoped their interest in each other wouldn't go too far.

Tyler's arrival might explain why Dean had been so

snappy the day before. The tension between the two of them had certainly been thick. Dean might also have been edgy about meeting her. After all, he'd hired her sight unseen, based only on Gary's word.

The fact that Dean trusted Gary so much said a lot about their friendship, but Annie still wasn't ready to relax completely around him.

"Are you okay?"

Irma's question brought Annie's head up with a snap. She let out a thin laugh and scanned the room to get her bearings, embarrassed that she hadn't heard the other woman come in. "I'm fine," she said, pulling a bell pepper onto the chopping block. "Just thinking."

Irma's glasses seemed to ride perpetually halfway down her nose, giving the impression that she was in charge of the world and keeping an eye on it. "About anything special?"

Annie shrugged casually. "I wouldn't say that."

"How was your visit in town? Did you find what you needed?"

"Almost," Annie fibbed, tossing seeds into the trash. "I found several new outfits, including this one." She untied her apron and held out her arms so Irma could get the full effect of the jeans and sleeveless western-cut shirt she'd picked out.

"Looks perfect to me." Irma nudged her glasses ineffectually. "How do you like it?"

"The blouse is cool and comfortable, but I'd forgotten how stiff new jeans can be. It's been years since I wore a pair. I'll get used to them, though."

"They'll be better after a few washes." Irma checked the recipe Annie had left on the counter and pulled a casserole dish from a cupboard. "What about that girl of yours? How did she make out?"

"Not so well." Annie resisted the impulse to refuse Irma's help. She preferred working alone, but she didn't want to offend the only other woman at the Eagle's Nest. And once guests started arriving, Irma would probably be too busy cleaning and keeping up with laundry to spend much time in the kitchen. "Are there any stores besides the ones we saw on Main Street?"

"Not in Whistle River." Irma buttered the dish and set it aside. "Guess we must seem small to you."

"Well, the town *is* a little smaller than we're used to," Annie admitted, "but it has a nice feel. I liked it."

Irma bobbed her head in satisfaction. "It's a good town. Nice, friendly folks—at least most of 'em. There's a few who aren't, of course. One town's like another that way. How'd Nessa like it?"

"It's a little small for her taste, I think. She's used to having whatever she wants at her fingertips. But experiencing a different kind of life will be good for her. For both of us, actually."

"Life's quiet here, but you'll get used to it, eventually." Irma wiped her hands on her apron and leaned against the counter. "Even Dean did, and that took some doing."

Annie cut open a head of cabbage and rinsed it under the tap. "Dean hasn't lived here forever? That surprises me."

"Does it? I guess Gary didn't tell you, then?"

"Tell me what?"

"What brought Dean to Whistle River."

Annie shook her head and set the cabbage on paper towels to drain. "I don't even know much about what brought Gary here, except that he married a girl who lived around here. And *we're* related. Gary's an open book in some ways, and very private in others. And he *never* talks about other people."

Irma sent her a lopsided smile. "You're right about that. Most of the time, I agree that a person's stories are their own to tell. But Dean's past spills over into the present at times, and if you're going to work here it's only fair that you know about it."

Annie laughed uneasily. She *was* curious, but it didn't seem right to encourage Irma to share Dean's secrets. "Maybe I should ask Dean..." she said hesitantly.

"I wouldn't suggest it." Irma pulled a towel from a drawer and patted the cabbage dry. "I don't know if you noticed Dean acting peculiar last night...?"

"He was a little standoffish yesterday," Annie admitted. "But he seemed okay today."

Irma laughed and began shredding the cabbage for coleslaw. "*Standoffish* is a gentle term for it. He was being a mule, and you know it." She stopped working and wiped her hands on her apron. "Don't get me wrong, I think the world of Dean. He can be one of the nicest men you'll ever meet. Kind. Generous. Always willing to lend a hand or help someone in need."

Annie glanced at the door to make sure no one had come in behind her. "If you'd told me that yesterday, I'd have thought you were crazy."

"It's the pain that makes him act a little different sometimes." Irma wiped her hands on a towel. "I guess Gary also didn't tell you that up until two years ago, Dean played baseball for the Baltimore Orioles."

"Professionally?" Annie wasn't sure why that stunned her. He certainly had the body of an athlete, but he had the look of a lifelong cowboy. "He's not very old. Why did he stop?"

"Car accident." Irma eyed the mound of cabbage on

the counter. "He and a friend were hit by a drunk driver on the way home from a party."

Annie's hands stilled. "And he was hurt?"

Irma nodded. "His shoulder was mangled. The damage was too severe for him to keep playing."

"What about his friend?"

Irma's mouth pursed with disapproval, and Annie felt the heat of embarrassment creeping into her cheeks. She hadn't meant to pry, but she must have stepped over an invisible line.

"She escaped with only minor injuries, and that's another story entirely. I'm only telling you this because it still affects him at times."

Annie nodded quickly. "I understand."

"Starting about four years ago, he came here for vacations during his off-season," Irma continued after a brief pause. "Les met him on a trail ride he was guiding into the backcountry and he found out that Dean's girlfriend was in Europe with her parents and Dean was planning to spend the holidays alone. We invited him to join us, and since then he's become almost like another son to us. Our own boys live so far away and they're busy with their own lives. Poor Les was having a tough time getting used to not being needed. And then Dean showed up and he was anxious to learn the things Les knew about roping and riding and such. Dean gave Les a new lease on life, and that's no lie. But he's been a different man since the accident, and sometimes he's not so pleasant to be around."

Annie pulled the coleslaw bowl closer. "I had no idea he'd been through all that."

"Dean keeps quiet about his troubles for the most part. Doesn't want anyone feeling sorry for him. He never talks about his career. I don't think he lets himself even think about it.''

"I can understand that," Annie said. "I just wish Gary had told me." Maybe their mothers' excuses for spreading family news wasn't so off the mark, after all.

"The two of 'em have gotten close as brothers in the past couple of years," Irma said. "Dean was recovering from his accident and Gary had just been through his divorce when they met. They can bicker like cats and dogs, but in the end they'll stick together. Dean doesn't want people to know about his past, so Gary doesn't tell. But there's no way you'll be here the whole summer and not encounter one of Dean's bad spells. I thought you ought to know why it happens beforehand.''

Annie nodded slowly. "Thank you. You said the pain makes him edgy. Does medication help?"

"Not near enough." Irma sent her a lopsided smile. "It'd help a whole lot more if he'd take the pills like the doctor orders. But he won't, and there's nothing anybody can say to convince him."

"That's good to know, too."

Irma found a knife and pulled a bunch of scallions onto the chopping block. "You want my advice for how to deal with him?"

Annie nodded quickly. "Absolutely." They were going to be spending the entire summer together. She might as well find a way to get along.

"Don't feel sorry for him. Even more important, don't ever let him get the best of you. Just give back as good as you get and I guarantee the two of you will get along fine."

CHAPTER FIVE

THE FIRE IN DEAN'S SHOULDER woke him long before his alarm was set to go off the next morning. He groaned and lay in the dark, willing the pain to recede as the sky slowly turned from ink to charcoal. Eventually, he admitted defeat, clenched his teeth and began the agonizing ritual of getting out of bed.

Starting the day in agony meant he'd be useless before noon. With only six days until their first guests arrived, he couldn't afford to lose even one. He swore under his breath and felt around in the dark for his prescription. He slid a pill into his mouth and gulped water from the bottle he kept on his nightstand, then leaned his head against the wall and waited.

Last night's dinner had been one of the best meals Dean had ever eaten, but pain curdled what was left in his stomach this morning. His medicine left a bitter taste in his mouth, taking away the memory of the sweet tang of Annie's barbecue sauce and the pleasant sourness of his first-ever gourmet coleslaw. Still, he refused to cave in to his physical limitations. The driver who'd caused his accident had stolen almost everything; Dean wouldn't hand the rest over without a fight.

After a long time the pain began to recede. He rose to his feet and forced himself to dress. It took a while and it hurt like hell, but just as the sky began to turn a pale blue-gray he was ready to leave his room.

He stood in the hall for a minute, studying Tyler's door and wondering what new challenges the kid would have for him today. No doubt he'd soon find out. It had become increasingly obvious that Tyler was trying to provoke a reaction. He was determined, Dean would grant him that. But Dean was just as intent on proving that not everyone reacted to provocation with hysterics.

He turned away and his gaze skimmed across Annie's door. Maybe he should tell her that last night's dinner had been truly worthy of a world-class restaurant, but he couldn't decide whether she'd been challenging his authority by changing his planned menu, or simply trying to introduce herself to the rest of them. He'd been too busy trying not to stare at her tight-fitting jeans and bare arms, and had struggled to keep her gaze from completely disconcerting him during dinner. He had been unable to keep his mind from repeatedly noting the similarities, as well as the differences, between Annie and Hayley.

This morning, it all seemed unimportant.

Putting her out of his mind, he clutched his boots in one hand and tiptoed down the stairs and out onto the porch. He sat on the wide front steps and looked out over the land that would be his home for the rest of his life. He spent far too many mornings awake when the rest of the world was still asleep, but there were times when he enjoyed the solitude.

Birds and squirrels never passed judgment, told him how to feel or offered opinions on what he should do with his life. They didn't pout when he had a bad day or expect more than he could give. They were, in short, the perfect companions.

Boots on at last, he stepped into the gathering sunlight, circled the lodge slowly and gave everything a once-over. Soon, the day's work would get under way. There was still a lot to do, but if he could convince Tyler to help, the workload for each of them would be cut considerably.

As Dean rounded the corner to the back of the lodge, an unfamiliar scent made him stop and scan the area. It only took a second to realize he was smelling smoke—not from a forest fire but from the bitter scent of a cigarette. He pivoted in his tracks and followed the smell to the back of the shed, where he found Tyler sitting on an overturned bucket, eyes closed as he inhaled.

Dean snatched the cigarette before the kid even had time to get his eyes open. "What the hell do you think you're doing?"

Tyler was on his feet in a flash, fists clenched, eyes shooting fire. "Give that back. It's mine."

"Not anymore." Dean tossed the cigarette to the ground and crushed it beneath his heel. "Where did you get it?"

"None of your damn business."

"As long as you're living here, it *is* my business. You're not even old enough to buy cigarettes in this state."

Tyler's nostrils flared. "So? What do you care?"

"You're my sister's kid. You're my responsibility as long as you're here." Dean reached into Tyler's shirt pocket, pulled out the pack he could see outlined against the fabric and crushed it in his fist. "You're not doing something this dangerous and stupid as long as you're living under my roof."

Tyler looked as if he wanted to hit him. Instead, he curled his lip and jerked his head toward Dean's hand. "Go ahead. Take them. I can always get more."

"Not from anyone who lives here." Dean threw the crushed pack into the trash barrel beside the door.

"What's your problem, Tyler? Aren't you in enough trouble? Your mom says—"

Raw emotion flared in Tyler's eyes. "What do I care what she says? She thinks I'm a worthless piece of scum, anyway."

The burning pain in Dean's shoulder ate through the thin veil of relief his medication had created, but the sudden spiny knot in his stomach was almost as strong. He remembered his vow to remain calm with Tyler and did his best to pull himself together. "I know your mother's excitable," he admitted, "but she doesn't think you're worthless."

Tyler laughed bitterly and took a couple of steps away. "Well, that just shows how much *you* know."

Staying calm in the face of Tyler's hostility wasn't easy, but Dean wasn't about to give up. "Okay. Fine. Then why don't you tell me what's going on between you and your mom?"

"Like you really want to know."

"I wouldn't have asked if I didn't."

Tyler shrugged and glanced away. His eyes darted from one end of the clearing to the other and his shoulders remained tense, his legs taut and ready to spring. "She doesn't want me, that's what's going on. Big surprise, huh?"

Such agony filled the boy's voice, Dean couldn't stay angry. He poised on the balls of his feet, ready for anything. "Of course your mom wants you. She loves you."

"Yeah? Then I guess I'm a liar, too, aren't I?"

"I didn't say that. I only meant maybe you're mistaken."

Tyler rolled his eyes as if Dean's naiveté exasperated him. "Yeah? So, then, what am I doing *here?*"

Dean wondered what reasons Carol had given Tyler

for this visit. She'd been pretty tightly wound when she called him, but he wanted to believe she'd showed some restraint when she explained her plans to her son. "You're here," he said evenly, "because I want to spend time with you this summer."

"Bullshit." Tyler snatched a rock from the ground and hurled it at a nearby tree. "Don't lie to me, okay? I'm not stupid."

Dean could have kicked himself for stretching the truth. "I'm not lying. I *do* want you here. But your mother did call me first to ask if you could come."

"I *heard* my mom call you. I know what she said, and I *know* you didn't want me here."

The knot in Dean's stomach took a painful twist. He felt about an inch tall. "You heard her part of the conversation," he said in an effort to dig himself out of the pit he'd created. "I never said I didn't want you here. I just thought you might prefer to go somewhere else."

"Yeah, well, why do I have to go anywhere?"

Good question. Dean wasn't sure he had the answer. "Your mom's upset," he said. "Some pretty expensive stuff has gone missing at home."

"Yeah, and she thinks I took it."

Dean looked at him head-on. "Did you?"

The question seemed to catch Tyler off guard, but he recovered quickly and hid behind his tough-guy mask. "Why ask me? I'll probably just lie. Besides, everybody else *thinks* I did, so it doesn't matter what I say."

"I'm asking because you're the only one who knows the answer. I don't know what's going on between you and your mom, but sometimes when two people are clashing a lot the smartest thing to do is put some distance between them. By the end of summer, you'll both have had time to think—"

"*She* won't be thinking," Tyler snarled. "Not about anything Randy doesn't want her to think about."

Now they were getting somewhere. Dean plucked a stalk of wild grass from the ground and turned it between his fingers. "I take it you don't like him?"

"That's an understatement."

"You want to tell me about him?"

Tyler shrugged. "What's to tell? He's got my mom wrapped around his little finger. Whatever he says, goes. Whatever he wants, he gets. She's a puppet and I hate it."

"It's that bad?"

"I'm here, aren't I?" For the first time since he arrived, Tyler stared Dean straight in the eyes. "He's been wanting to get rid of me since the day he met my mom. He finally got his way and he used you to do it. How does *that* make you feel?"

There was such pain, such self-doubt, such anger and bitterness in Tyler's eyes, Dean felt as if someone had gut-punched him. How had this happened? Why had Carol allowed things to get so out of control?

"For the record," Dean said, "Randy didn't use me. If I hadn't wanted you here, I wouldn't have said yes. And this is only temporary. Your mom wants you home at the end of the summer."

"You wanna bet?" Tyler pushed to his feet, picked up another rock and tossed it into the clearing. "You wait and see. Randy'll come up with some excuse to leave me here or send me somewhere else." Picking up a handful of small stones, he hurtled one after another against the side of the shed, his movements becoming shorter, harsher and more tense with every throw. After firing off a few more, he whirled to face Dean. "Just forget it, okay? None of it matters. Not to you. Not to her."

"You're wrong about that. It matters to both of us."

Tyler let another rock fly. "You don't even *know* my mom. You don't know what she feels, or what she thinks, or why she does what she does. And I'm not stupid. I know damn well why *you* wanted me here. So just do me a favor and quit pretending." He threw another stone hard enough to chip the wall of the shed, and set off across the clearing.

Dean scowled at the wall and thought about following, but he recognized the expression in Tyler's eyes and he knew the feelings behind it. If he tried to reason with Tyler now, he'd only be wasting his breath.

DEAN WAS STILL RATTLED when he let himself into the back door of the kitchen a few minutes later. Things at Carol's house must be worse than she'd told him. If he was going to help Tyler, he needed more information about their life at home. He had to call the bank in a few hours, anyway. He'd take a few extra minutes to call Carol while he was at it.

Lost in thought, he forgot that Irma wouldn't be the one putting coffee on and getting ready for the day. When he saw Annie standing behind the counter, his step faltered enough to bring her head up.

She sent him a warm smile. "Good morning."

Caught unaware, he wasn't prepared to resist her. The slim fit of her jeans made his mouth dry and the curve of breast beneath a soft peach tank top made his pulse jump. In sharp contrast to the woman of his past, Annie's face was freshly scrubbed and she wore minimal makeup. Her hair floated around her shoulders and framed her face gently.

He managed to hide his reaction by tugging down the

brim of his hat and making sure he didn't have a goofy smile on his face. "Morning."

"Coffee's about ready if you're interested."

He nodded once and headed toward the coffeemaker. "That's what I came in for."

"What time would you like me to serve breakfast?"

He avoided her gaze while he found his mug and kept his eyes from straying while he waited for the coffeemaker to stop gurgling. He didn't want to look at that skimpy blouse—the same color as clouds at sunrise—her slim, bare arms, or the narrow piece of bare midriff that showed whenever she moved.

"It doesn't matter what time we eat today," he said. "When the guests arrive, the crew'll need to be finished eating and ready to work by seven. Breakfast for the guests will be between eight and ten."

Again, he thought about commenting on last night's dinner, but it was easier for him to avoid the subject. One argument per morning was enough for him, and complimenting her might give her the wrong idea.

Annie reached into the cupboard for a mug just as Dean started to pour his coffee. Her blouse skimmed up one side and exposed a hand-width of bare skin. He tried to decide if she was teasing him on purpose, or if she was so naive she didn't realize what a sight like that could do to a man first thing in the morning.

Hayley would have known. She never made a move that wasn't calculated for effect. But Annie's eyes were so clear and bright, so completely guileless, he made up his mind that she had no idea what she was doing.

He shook his head to clear it, realized he'd stopped pouring when his cup was only half-full and made himself top it off. "So, are you all settled in?"

"I think so." She moved closer and Dean swallowed thickly...until he realized she only wanted the coffeepot.

He tried not to notice the warmth that spread up his arm when their fingers brushed. "And Nessa? Is she adjusting to the fact that I'm not going to put in a satellite dish so she can watch MTV?"

A slow blush crept into Annie's cheeks. "She *asked* you about that?"

"She did."

"I am so sorry. I told her not to, but her philosophy of life is that it doesn't hurt to ask."

Dean sipped and tried to ignore the effect that blush had on him. "No harm done—as long as she can take no for an answer."

Annie leaned against the counter and crossed one foot over the other. "That's the problem. She doesn't easily, and she rarely gives up on anything she wants."

"Yeah?" Dean grinned, grateful for something else to think about. "Well, I was born stubborn. I never give in without a good, long fight."

Annie's eyes met his and he felt as if someone had sucked the air from his lungs. "Don't let Nessa know that. She loves a good fight."

"So do I. And I'm very good at it."

A slow smile curved her lips. "I'll bet you are."

She seemed different this morning. Dean couldn't put his finger on what had changed, but whatever it was he liked it. "Now, how could you know that? Has someone been telling on me?"

Her smile widened a little more. "Nobody had to tell me anything about that. I met your argumentative side the first day I got here."

Dean grimaced with embarrassment and lowered his mug to the counter. Her straightforward reaction surprised him. Hayley had hated his moodiness—and with good reason. But he'd hated the way she'd tried to manipulate him out of it just as much.

"Yeah," he said to Annie, "I guess you did. I apologize for that. I'm not usually such a bear—at least I try not to be."

"That's good to know. Any other personalities I should be aware of?"

Dean *had* recently reencountered one, but he didn't think Annie would appreciate meeting it just now. This personality couldn't seem to remember his vow to forget the fair sex for a while. It didn't even worry about making another mistake.

In fact, this personality didn't seem to think at all.

Silence fell between them and Dean saw the sudden shift in Annie's expression, the astonished and unexpected awareness of what was happening reflected in her eyes. Even then he couldn't make himself move. He would have sworn the clock had stopped ticking, the birds had stopped chirping and the breeze had stilled. Not even a whisper of sound broke the silence.

He didn't know how long they stood that way before the sound of heavy footsteps sounded on the back porch and Gary's familiar whistle cut through the stillness. Annie's startled gaze flew to the door, and that was all it took to get Dean moving.

He hurried across the kitchen and pushed past Gary into the rapidly warming morning, muttering the briefest "good morning" in history as he did.

What had happened in there?

Scratch that. How had he *let* it happen?

He didn't want to become involved with a woman, especially not an employee. That was a surefire one-way road to disaster. He didn't want to become involved with a woman who reminded him so much of Hayley—although, if he was a hundred percent honest with himself, he'd admit that the resemblance had all but evaporated over the past couple of days.

A sudden surge of anger with Gary curled in Dean's chest as he headed toward the stables. A true friend would've warned him about Annie. Would have told him what she looked like and mentioned that she could bewitch even the most cynical of men with a smile. He sure as hell wouldn't have let Dean be alone with her. Because the images flashing through Dean's mind right now were *not* the kinds of things most guys wanted people thinking about their cousins.

He reached the stables and wrenched open the door, taking out his irritation, frustration and surprise on the innocent piece of wood. The unexpected pain that tore through his shoulder knocked him to his knees and tore a cry from his throat.

He dropped his coffee and, through the haze of agony, felt it soaking into his jeans. He gulped air and tried to blink away the sudden blinding tears. Cradling his shoulder with his good arm, he gritted his teeth to keep from crying out again.

What was wrong with him? How had he forgotten, even for a moment, that he couldn't use that arm to open the heavy stable door? What had he been thinking?

He sat back hard in the dirt and turned slowly toward the house. He knew what he'd been thinking, but it was absolutely unbelievable. It made no logical sense at all. And yet…

For the first time since the accident, he'd had a few minutes without even a flicker of pain. And all because of Annie Holladay.

ANNIE WORKED HARD to keep Gary from seeing how flustered she was after that moment with Dean. It had been a weird moment, and completely unexpected, but she wouldn't pretend it had actually *meant* anything. She wasn't even sure that she was attracted to him. She might just be responding to his human side now that she knew he had one. Or she could have been overreacting since Dean was the first man who'd looked at her in eight long months. The first man who'd *really* looked at her in years.

Yes, that's all it was. That's why her cheeks were warm, her hands shaking, and her heartbeat had taken a moment to return to normal. She slanted a glance at Gary, who was leaning on the edge of the counter sipping coffee and chattering about something. She poured another cup for herself and cradled the mug in both hands, struggling to pay attention, to forget those deep brown eyes and the play of golden hairs on tan, muscular arms.

She shook herself and lifted her cup to her lips again, hoping another jolt of caffeine would drag her foolish head out of the clouds. She tuned into the conversation just as Gary said, "The horses should be here by Tuesday afternoon. You should come down to the stables and watch us unload them."

Annie had the feeling she'd need things to keep her mind occupied while she was here. "I'd love to," she said. "Just remind me that morning, okay?"

"Sure, but unless you're on another planet, you'll hear the ruckus. Horses and cowboys aren't exactly a quiet combination." He took another long drink and glanced around the kitchen. "Mind me asking what's for breakfast?"

Annie set her cup aside and decided she'd dropped out of the clouds enough to start cooking. She pulled the notebook Dean had given her from the cupboard and checked the day's menu. She could have sworn her cholesterol level rose just reading about what he expected her to fix.

"Eggs, bacon, sausage, hash browns..." Annie shook her head and stared at Gary in amazement. "Do you really eat like this every morning?"

"Pretty much."

"And you're all still alive?"

"Pretty much." Gary grinned and slid from the counter. "It's a different world out here, Annie. A bowl of cereal or a fruit cup might work for people who have to pay money to get a little exercise, but it doesn't carry you very far through the day when you're chopping firewood and rounding up horses."

Annie pulled a handful of potatoes from the basket she'd put on the floor after dinner. "Well, I'm *not* a ranch hand and I'm almost positive my blood will stop flowing if I eat like this every day. Don't you think most of your guests will be used to eating lighter?"

"Maybe. But some folks pay to forget about cholesterol and fat grams for a week."

Annie rinsed the potatoes and set them aside to drain. "It would still be nice to give people a choice, don't you think?"

Gary shrugged. "I suppose. You'll have to talk to Dean about that, though. I'm not the man in charge."

Annie's heart gave a traitorous leap of anticipation. "What do you think my chances are of getting him to agree?"

"I'd say that depends on the kind of day he's having and how you ask." Gary turned to rest his arms on the counter. "I'd give him a little time if I were you. Tyler's

going to need a little more attention than Dean anticipated.''

Annie started toward the refrigerator for eggs and milk,
but movement just outside the window caught her attention. She stopped and took a closer look and realized that
Nessa was walking with Tyler along the edge of the
clearing. Their heads were bent close together until Nessa
laughed at something Tyler said.

Gary crossed the room to stand beside her and bent to
see what she was watching. ''Something wrong?''

''Not really.'' She smiled and turned away from the
window.

''Not really, or not at all?''

Annie wasn't sure she liked being so easy to read.
''Not really,'' she said again. ''It's just that I've only got
three months left before Nessa moves in with Spence,
and I seem to be moving down a few notches on her list
of priorities.''

Gary's smile faded. ''You want me to talk to Tyler?''

''No. Of course not. It's not surprising that the only
two young people around would gravitate toward each
other. I'm just being selfish.''

''I'm not sure that's the word I'd use for it.''

Annie waved his concern away. ''It's no big deal.
They're just walking together. It's not as if they're doing
anything wrong. And I do have to learn to let go before
September.''

Gary turned away from the window. ''So, are you really okay letting her move in with her dad?''

''Do I have a choice?'' The question came out a little
too harshly. Annie tried to relax before she spoke again.
''Nessa's as much Spence's daughter as she is mine.
There's no logical reason not to let her stay.''

''Who the hell cares about logical?''

Annie let out a tight laugh and leaned against the cupboard. "*I* have to. If I fight this too hard, I'll end up losing her and I can't bear that." She smoothed a stray hair away from her forehead and repeated the words that had become a mantra over the past weeks. "I'll learn to live with her being a thousand miles away. I don't think I could survive if she hated me."

"Those are the only two options?"

"They seem to be. I really don't mind that she's enjoying Tyler's company. Maybe she'll stop talking about going back to Chicago." Annie tried again to glimpse the kids, but they'd already disappeared. "But there are times when I wish she wasn't quite so crazy about boys."

Gary smiled softly. "Correct me if I'm wrong, but weren't *you* boy crazy at her age?"

"Yes, and look at all the problems I caused myself. Married right out of high school. Pregnant before the first year was up... Not that I regret having Nessa. But I sometimes wonder if things might have turned out differently if Spence and I hadn't been so eager to become adults."

"That's one of those questions with no answers, isn't it?"

"Maybe."

"Don't 'what-if,' Annie. It's a dangerous game and you can eat yourself alive with it."

"I'm not trying to second-guess the past." She turned away and pulled a mixing bowl from an overhead cabinet. "I'm trying to make the future better. I don't want Nessa to make the same mistakes I did."

"And you think you can control that?"

"Not for long. Any influence I might have will disappear in September."

Gary turned a comical expression on her. "Are you

kidding? I don't know about your mother, but mine still has *plenty* of influence over us kids.''

Annie smiled reluctantly. "It's not the same, though."

"Well that's true. But Nessa's going to be an adult before long. No matter where she lives or who she lives with, your relationship is going to change. That's just life."

Annie cracked eggs into the bowl and put her frustrations behind the wire whisk. "I know that. But do you have any idea how hard this is for me? Letting her go to live with her dad? Leaving her a thousand miles behind? Being across the country, too far away to go to her if she's having a bad day?"

All the emotions she'd been struggling to keep in check came rushing to the surface, and she whipped the whisk even faster. "I hate Spence for having this idea and I'm furious with Nessa for wanting to go along with it—and I can't do anything about it because the more I say, the more determined she becomes to go through with it."

Gary moved closer and slipped an arm around her shoulders. "I know this probably doesn't help much, but Nessa seems like a smart girl. Steady and reliable. I'm sure she'll be okay."

Annie blinked back tears and nodded. "I know that, too, or I wouldn't have said yes. Maybe I'm just jealous because Spence's new girlfriend is going to be taking my place, doing things with Nessa that *I* should be doing. Taking her shopping, talking about boys..."

A lump formed in her throat and she had to stop whisking the eggs to dash tears away. "That's the worst part, you know. Being expected to relinquish *my* role to some other woman—and the fact that it's *that* woman is just more than I can stand."

"This is the woman you found him with?"

"The one and only."

"Ouch."

Annie glanced at the froth she'd worked up and made a face. "How did we get on this subject, anyway? If I start thinking about Spence and Catherine I'll ruin breakfast completely."

"Then don't think about them." Gary gave her a quick squeeze, crossed to the refrigerator and pulled out an apple. "Feed me before I waste away completely."

Annie had released enough tension to manage a laugh. "I will if you'll get out of here and let me concentrate."

Gary started to close the refrigerator, changed his mind and took a second apple, then crossed to the back door. "You going to be okay?"

"I'll be fine. Thanks for caring."

He took a bite from an apple, pushed the door open with his back and gestured toward the counter. "Don't forget the sausage and bacon. I'm a growing boy, you know. I need sustenance."

Annie tossed an orange at him and laughed as he caught it before ducking out the door. The release of emotion had worn her out, but the familiar acts of moving through the kitchen soon gave her a second wind. She found her rhythm so that every movement flowed into the next. As always, she lost herself in the process.

She loved creating new dishes and she wondered whether or not she could possibly enjoy teaching as much. Resolutely, she pushed the doubts aside and reminded herself that she was moving forward, not looking back.

She couldn't afford to start doubting herself now.

CHAPTER SIX

BY TUESDAY MORNING, the air pulsed with excitement over the horses' arrival. Les had taken an extra cup of coffee at breakfast. Dean and Gary jumped at every sound from outside, and Irma kept looking out the windows, just in case. Even Nessa and Tyler seemed more animated.

Annie didn't feel the same level of anticipation, but she wanted to join the fun. Besides, creating a party atmosphere would give her an excuse to cook something special for lunch.

She spent the morning stirring together bread dough, which she left to rise in a sunny corner of the counter, then pounded chicken breasts, diced tomatoes, garlic and herbs, and grated the fresh Parmesan cheese she'd been stunned to find in Whistle River's small grocery store.

With the chicken Parmesan ready to stick in the oven at the right time, she dug through closets, where she eventually found a stack of bright yellow place mats, several mismatched vases and half a dozen brandy glasses. Wandering outside, she strolled along the edge of the meadow and filled a basket with sunflower buds, which she placed in the brandy glasses down the center of the table and arranged in the vases with a few white lacy flowers and some greenery she couldn't identify.

She cooked bow-tie pasta to the al dente stage and stirred in olive oil, a handful of different herbs, olives and fresh vegetables, then stuck the bowl into the refrigerator so the salad could cool. She carefully tufted crisp, white napkins in stemmed goblets at each place setting and stepped back to view her handiwork, but the joy she felt in the creative process only reinforced the doubts she'd been trying to dodge about teaching at the culinary institute.

She was so deep in thought the shrill ring of the telephone tore a surprised shriek from her. She spun toward it quickly, knocking over a glass, and by the time she'd righted it again the ringing had stopped. Irma's voice drifted down from upstairs a few minutes later.

"Phone's for you, Annie."

Annie wiped her hands on her apron, crossed to the phone on the wall and answered uncertainly. She'd left this number with her mother and with the director of personnel at the institute, but she hadn't expected anyone to call so soon.

"Annie."

The familiar male voice sounded out of place in the sunny kitchen of the Eagle's Nest. "*Spence?* Is something wrong?"

"That's what I'd like to know. Nessa left a message on my voice mail a couple of nights ago. She didn't sound happy."

Annie sank into a chair at the table, certain that the cloud suddenly shadowing the room was a purely emotional one. "What did she say?"

"Just that she needed me to call her."

"She called you two days ago and you're just getting around to finding out why?"

"Don't start, Annie. I've been busy, and I knew that if anything was seriously wrong, you'd take care of it."

The vote of confidence didn't help. Annie couldn't

help comparing how he'd have reacted if their situations were reversed. "So, why are you calling me? Why not talk to Nessa?"

"Curiosity, I guess. I wanted to know what's really going on before I talk to her. And, frankly, I'm a little afraid of stepping on your toes."

Annie let out a tight laugh. "I was ready to believe you until you said that."

"What's that supposed to mean?" Spence asked, his voice suddenly cool.

"Just that it's been a while since you showed any concern about my toes."

"That's not true."

"Really? How concerned were you when you convinced Nessa not to come with me when I move?"

Spence sighed heavily. "I had nothing to do with her decision."

"She couldn't have made it without you."

"I offered to let her stay with me, Annie, but only because she was so determined not to move away from Chicago. I'd like you to tell me what you'd have done differently."

Annie knew she was letting hurt feelings cloud her judgment, and she hated when she did that. She forced herself to return to his original question. "Nessa's fine, Spence. There's no need to worry about her. I don't know why she called you, except that things are a little different here than in the city and she's facing an adjustment. But she'll be fine. It's only temporary."

"That's what I figured." Spence let out a deep breath and Annie imagined him sitting at his desk, his ever-present cup of coffee at his elbow, his dark hair softly spiked from running his fingers through it.

She knew more about Spence than anyone alive, and

there were times when she missed knowing someone so well. Times when she missed having a second half to herself, another person whose ins and outs she knew as well as her own. That was probably another reason she'd imagined herself attracted to Dean.

"I should still talk with her, though," Spence said, breaking into her thoughts. "Is she around?"

Annie pulled herself back to the conversation with effort and craned her neck to see outside. "I think she's down at the stables, but there's no phone down there. Should I have her call you when she comes back?"

"If she wants to. I don't want to intrude on your summer together."

Annie closed her eyes and kneaded her forehead with her fingertips. "I'm trying to decide whether I appreciate you being thoughtful, or whether I resent it."

Spence laughed softly. "If my vote counts for anything, I'd pick the former. I'm not trying to be a jerk, you know. I regret hurting you after all the years we were together. I don't want to do it again."

Annie didn't trust herself to respond to that. She'd either cry or say something sarcastic, and she didn't want to do either.

When Spence realized she wasn't going to speak, he changed the subject. "So, what's it like working at a dude ranch?"

She cleared her throat and managed to answer. "Fine so far. I haven't been here long enough to form an opinion."

"You're serious about spending the entire summer there?"

"Why wouldn't I be?"

"It's just that you belong here, not off in the middle of nowhere."

Annie traced one finger along a beam of sunlight on the table. "You know I can't stay in Chicago, Spence."

"I don't mean just Chicago. You helped make this restaurant after Dad died. It's not the same without you."

He'd been so determined to retain sole ownership of his family's restaurant when they initiated their divorce proceedings, his admission stunned Annie at first, then made her uneasy. "What are you getting at?"

"Nothing, really. Or maybe I'm worried about you. You've worked too hard to throw your career away now."

"You don't need to worry," Annie assured him, purposely relaxing her grip on the receiver. "I'm not throwing my career away. I'm taking it in a different direction."

"The wrong direction. You're a certified chef, Annie, not a cooking instructor, and certainly not a trail cook. What you're doing is so far beneath you, I can't even find the words to verbalize it."

His judgment irritated her. Even worse, it magnified the doubts she'd already been battling. "I don't consider it beneath me," she said firmly. "I like it here."

"Come on, Annie. You thrive on challenge. You'll stagnate without one. And you can't convince me that there's anything out there putting your skills to the test. For heaven's sake, don't ruin your career to spite me."

"I'm not ruining my career, and I'm certainly not out to spite you. This may surprise you, Spence, but you don't figure into the decisions I make now."

"You aren't leaving Chicago to get away from me?"

The more he talked, the more exasperated Annie became. "I'm leaving to start over."

"Believe what you want. But after sixteen years and

one child together, you'll always be part of the decisions I make.''

Such a blatant attempt to make her feel guilty was the final straw. ''Does that include the decision you made to sleep with Catherine while we were still married?''

''This isn't about Catherine. It's about you. I'll always be concerned about you.''

Annie laughed harshly and stood to look out the window. ''Thanks, but no thanks. I walked in on your concern and saw it with my own two eyes, remember?''

''It must be convenient to blame me for everything,'' Spence said, his voice tight and angry. ''But *you* have to shoulder a little of the responsibility for what happened to our marriage, too. It was over a long time before I met Catherine, and that's as much your fault as mine. I made a mistake sleeping with Catherine before the divorce, but that's not what ended our marriage. So can't we please put this episode behind us?''

Despite Annie's efforts to remain calm, the familiar hurt and anger boiled to the surface. ''It was a little more than an 'episode,''' she snapped. ''It was an affair. That's not so easy to forget. If you found our marriage so horrible that you just *had* to sleep with Catherine to feel better, it might have been a good idea to share that information with me first. Now, unless you have something important to say about Nessa, I'm through talking.''

She gave him about five seconds to respond, then broke their connection. As soon as she did, a fit of trembling overtook her and forced her back into her chair. She put her head down and gulped air in a vain attempt to calm herself, but her emotions were too raw and confused.

She was furious with Spence, but other feelings were tangled up with the anger as well, and those were the ones that bothered her the most. She didn't know if she hated him, or if he made her so furious because a part of her still loved him.

She stood to hang up the phone and saw Dean pass by outside the window. His long legs churned up the dirt as he walked toward the stables. His shoulders strained against his worn denim shirt.

Her heart beat a little faster at the sight of him, but she closed her eyes quickly to stop it. She might not know exactly what she felt about Spence, but she was absolutely certain that she had no business thinking about Dean. There were too many issues she needed to resolve first.

TWO LONG, CONFUSING HOURS after hanging up on Spence, Annie followed a slow-moving caravan of trucks and horse trailers to the stables. Excitement pulsed through the air all around her, and though she still didn't share the others' enthusiasm, she would have watched grass grow if it would take her mind off Spence's phone call.

She found Les, a short, stocky man with thinning gray hair, wearing his usual starched white shirt under striped bib overalls and standing to one side of the clearing. He waved his arms and shouted continually as he directed traffic. Through the billowing dust she could see Gary on the other side of the yard, and Nessa standing with Tyler across the paddock.

Dean oversaw the activity only a few feet from where Annie stood. He was perched on the bottom fence rail and leaned into the corral, shouting directions to the men who'd brought the horses. It was hard to believe the story Irma had told her. No matter how hard Annie looked, she couldn't see any but the faintest signs that he'd ever been hurt.

One shoulder was as broad and strong as the other. He'd taken off the denim shirt and now muscles bunched and flexed beneath the sleeves of his cotton T-shirt, and his thighs strained against the faded fabric of a worn pair of jeans. Annie had always considered Spence physically fit, but if he'd stood beside Dean, there would be no comparison.

Dean turned, saw Annie watching him and motioned for her to join him. Embarrassed at having been caught and still determined to keep her thoughts in check, Annie hesitated—but only until two men began to back a huge horse out of a trailer directly in front of her. The sight of those powerful hooves and haunches spurred Annie to action.

Trying not to choke on the dust, she hurried toward the corral and hopped onto the fence rail beside Dean. When she gripped the top rail with both arms to keep her balance, Dean raked his gaze across her face. "You okay?"

"Fine, thanks. Just a little overwhelmed by the size of those animals." The slightly off-center smile on his lips and the unexpected twinkle in his eyes made her heart jump—or maybe she was just out of breath. "I hope you don't mind me being here," she said, dragging her gaze away. "Gary suggested I might like to watch."

"Why should I mind?"

"You didn't hire me to hang around the stables."

"I didn't hire you to spend all day in the kitchen, either." He shifted slightly and his arm grazed hers, leaving a trail of gooseflesh on her skin. "As long as the meals are served on time, you can go anywhere or do anything you want."

Annie smoothed a hand across her arm, trying to re-store normal feeling to it. She really was a piece of work, questioning her feelings for her ex-husband one minute and going gaga over her boss the next.

Dean turned an odd look on her, but his gaze flickered away the second she made eye contact. He took a deep breath and let it out slowly. "Lunch was great, by the way."

A flush of pleasure made her internal temperature climb about twenty degrees. "Thank you. I wanted to do something special."

"Well, you did." His gaze trickled to hers again. "A little different from the poor-boy sandwiches and chips I included on the menu plan, though."

This time, Annie looked away first. "I know. I'm not trying to be difficult. I just wanted to make something nice today since today seems to be so special to the rest of you."

Dean nodded slowly and fell silent. He motioned a couple of the men toward the corral, shouted directions to a few others and hopped down to help steer a partic-ularly stubborn horse the right way. Even so, Annie could tell that he was only partially focused on the job and she couldn't help wondering if she was a distraction for him.

She stood there while men and horses stirred up a thick cloud of dust. For someone who'd only recently become a cowboy, Dean certainly seemed to have the part down pat. He moved with precision and seemed as familiar with the routine and the horses as any of the others. Les had obviously been a good teacher.

When Annie realized that she'd been watching him exclusively for several minutes, she forced herself to fo-cus on something else. But no matter where she turned her attention, it always drifted back to Dean. His voice seemed slightly louder than the rest, his presence more commanding. It had been a long time since Annie'd felt such an intense physical reaction to another person—not since she'd been falling head over heels with Spence. And that worried her.

Spence's affair had left her feeling insecure and unattractive. She might have reacted the same way to any man who gave her a second glance. That meant she had to be careful. She'd seen friends on the heels of a heartache become involved with men entirely wrong for them, and she wasn't going to make the same mistake.

When things settled down again, Dean climbed onto the fence beside her and turned another of those lopsided grins in her direction. "Well, what do you think?"

Lunch was obviously forgotten. In a weak moment, that smile could easily undo her resolve, but Annie forced herself to ignore it. "About the horses? They're magnificent."

"Do you ride?"

"Afraid not." Annie watched a lanky cowboy lead a seemingly sedate brown horse past her and suppressed a shudder at the horse's size. "Before today, I've never even come close to a horse—unless you count taking a carriage ride in the park when I was a girl."

"Would you like to learn?"

"I don't think so. They're about three times bigger than I thought they were."

Dean chuckled. "They have to be big for the work they do. But these horses have been trained to carry novices, and most of them are extremely patient."

"*Most* of them?"

Dean reached for a length of rope coiled on a nearby fence post. "Gary and I like our horses to have a little spirit, but the trail horses are as docile as lambs." He nodded toward a brown horse near the stable door. "If you're interested, I'll make sure you get a gentle old lady like Maisie over there."

While other horses shied this way and that, nothing seemed to faze Maisie. But Annie still wasn't convinced that climbing on the animal's back was a good idea. "I don't know," she said with an uneasy laugh. "I won't be much good to you if I end up with a broken arm or leg."

"Well, think about it." Dean tossed the rope over his shoulder. His eyes skimmed her face and his gaze locked with hers before she could steel herself. "Old Maisie's as gentle as a horse can get, and I promise that we'd take it slow and easy. I wouldn't leave you alone with her unless you were ready."

Annie held her breath while his eyes lingered on her face. The thought of spending time with Dean was almost enough to make her throw herself on Maisie right then and there, but common sense eventually returned and she nodded slowly. "I promise I'll think about it."

One of the hands shouted for Dean and his gaze slipped from hers reluctantly. He said something Annie couldn't quite understand and strode away, leaving her gulping air as greedily as if she'd been smothered.

She clutched the fence rail and watched him, amazed that such a big man could move so gracefully and still be so completely masculine. She'd never been attracted by athletic men before. Even in high school, when all of her friends had been vying for the attention of the football quarterback or the star forward from the basketball team, Annie had set her sights on the quieter types. But there was something about the way Dean moved that held her attention and wouldn't let her look away.

She reminded herself again of the countless reasons

why being attracted to Dean wasn't a good idea. He was her boss. She was only here temporarily. She was on the rebound and not officially divorced yet. Even if this attraction had been real and right, there was no future for them. Their lives were on different tracks. And Annie wasn't interested in a summer fling.

If all those reasons weren't enough, she had only three months left to spend with Nessa. Annie couldn't let anything distract her from making this the best summer she and Nessa had ever had together.

She glanced around until she found Nessa and Tyler again. Even from a distance she could see the fascination on her daughter's face and the sparkle of excitement in her eyes. Nessa said something to Tyler, and Tyler leaned slightly forward, watching closely as two cowboys unloaded another horse and led it into the corral.

As Dean had predicted, most of the horses seemed quite docile, but there were two with more spirit than the others, and those were the horses that had caught Tyler's eye. Dean must have noticed Tyler's interest at the same moment Annie did because he made his way to stand beside his nephew.

Tyler's countenance changed immediately. Nessa turned toward Dean and spoke. Tyler hopped from the fence and started away. When Dean took a step after him, Tyler rounded on him and shouted something. His words were lost in the noise, but his animosity was crystal clear. Even Nessa seemed stunned.

Dean stood frozen in the midst of the activity. Annie felt as if she'd stepped into something private and painful.

She kept her attention on the paddock and tried to put the moment out of her mind. But the noise and dust couldn't wipe Tyler's anger from her mind or make her forget the hurt and confusion on Dean's face.

It seemed that Dean needed a distraction just about as much as she did.

HOPING TO CATCH NESSA before the day got under way, Annie woke early the next morning and hurried down the outside stairs to the ladies' shower room. The sun was just beginning to peek over the mountains, but the valley still lay in shadow and the chill made Annie shiver.

She closed the door behind her, grateful for the slight warmth of being indoors. She and Nessa might be the only two using this shower room, but it still felt like being back in a high-school physical-education class to Annie.

Three shower stalls lined the far end of the room. Three plain mirrors hung on the wall above three sinks with tiny counters. Beneath a row of high windows, a long shelf and several electrical outlets provided places to plug in curling irons and blow dryers.

Annie slipped into the corner stall, showered quickly and was cinching herself into her robe when Nessa came in. Nessa's hair was tousled gently around her face, and her eyes were still puffy. She wore one of Spence's old shirts over her pajamas and yawned loudly as she scuffed toward an empty shower stall.

"Morning, sweetheart." Annie pulled the towel from her head and began patting her hair dry.

Nessa's step faltered. She blinked as if the sound of a human voice had surprised her, squinted in confusion, then finally nodded. "Morning."

"You seem tired."

"I am." Nessa scratched one arm lazily. "Getting up this early in the summer is whacked."

Annie laughed at her choice of words. "You'll get used to it, I promise." She draped the towel over her shoulder and pulled her hairbrush from her cosmetic case. "What are your plans for today?"

Nessa shrugged, caught a glimpse of her reflection in a mirror and leaned in close to inspect her face. "Nothing special. Why?"

"Dean said I could do whatever I want in my spare time, so I was thinking maybe you and I could hike one of the trails after I'm through with breakfast."

"Oh." Nessa glanced toward the door and frowned slightly. "I guess that would be okay."

"It's just a suggestion," Annie said. "If there's something else you'd rather do, I'm game."

Nessa turned on the faucet, wet her finger and scrubbed at something on the side of her cheek. "It doesn't matter."

"It wouldn't hurt for you to pretend to be a little more enthusiastic."

"Sorry. It's just that I was sorta planning to hang out around the stables with Tyler."

"Then you *do* have plans."

"Not really *plans*. It's just something I wanted to do, that's all."

Annie nodded slowly and tried to decide how much Nessa would resist if she asked her to change her mind. "I won't be able to spend more than an hour or two," she said. "Maybe you could hang out at the stables afterward."

Nessa turned away from the mirror and lifted one shoulder. "Maybe. Except that Gary promised to start teaching us how to ride this morning so we can help exercise the horses."

Annie lowered her brush to the counter. "Those sound like firm plans to me."

"I guess maybe they are." Nessa grinned sheepishly. "I just don't want you to feel bad."

"Watching out for my feelings is nice, but I'd rather you be honest with me. Go ahead and do what you want this morning. We can hike the trails another day."

Nessa pulled her bottom lip between her teeth. "Are you sure?"

"I'm positive."

"Cool." Nessa leaned into the shower and turned on the spray. "Now that the horses are here, it's a lot less boring."

Annie knew the horses weren't the only factor contributing to Nessa's change of heart. She put toothpaste on her toothbrush and ran it under the tap. "Speaking of being bored, I forgot to mention that your dad called yesterday. He said you'd left a message for him a few days ago."

Nessa rolled up one sleeve and held her hand under the spray to check the temperature. "Yeah, I did. Are you mad?"

"No. Did you think I would be?"

"Maybe." Nessa turned the hot water a little higher and tested again. "I mean, I know you don't want me staying with him when you move...."

Annie turned to face her. "It's not that I don't want you staying with your dad," she said for what felt like the hundredth time in two months. "It's that *I* don't want to live without you. That's very different."

Nessa nodded as if she understood, but Annie knew she didn't. She wouldn't really be able to understand until she had a child of her own. "I know, Mom. I'm going to miss you, too."

Annie smiled at the concession even though it felt a little lacking. "I told your dad that I'd have you call if you still need to talk to him."

Nessa shook her head and stepped into the dressing cubicle outside her shower. "I'm okay now. What else did he say?"

Annie thought back over their conversation. "Nothing, really."

"Did he say whether or not he's decided to let me paint my room?"

Annie tried not to let the question bother her. She couldn't dissolve into a puddle of hurt feelings every time Nessa mentioned living with Spence. "No, he didn't."

"What about the new comforter for the bed? Did he say if Catherine got it yet?"

Hearing Nessa drop that name into conversation so casually was a little harder to take. Annie clutched her toothbrush so tightly, her fingernails dug into her palm. "He didn't mention it." The sound of water changed, and Annie knew Nessa had stepped under the spray.

"She probably won't get it. She promised she would, but she'll forget."

Annie refrained from commenting. There was something not quite right about standing in a public shower, discussing her husband's mistress with her daughter.

The shower curtain opened a few inches and Nessa's face appeared in the opening. "If Dad got smart and broke up with Catherine, would you take him back?"

The question caught Annie by surprise and she nearly dropped her toothbrush. "I'm afraid it's not that simple, honey."

"Well, what *would* he have to do?"

Annie lowered her toothbrush to the counter. "There's nothing he can do, Nessa. He made a decision that destroyed my trust in him. That's something that just can't be repaired.''

Nessa's eyes shadowed. ''What if he tried?''

Annie turned to face her and leaned against the counter. There were times when Nessa's bulldog nature seemed like an asset. This wasn't one of those times. ''The point is, he's not interested in trying,'' Annie said, ''so that's not an issue. But even if he did try to repair the trust I once felt for him, it's too late.''

''It's never too late.''

''In this case it is. A marriage is like a house. You can break a window or put a hole in the wall, and when you fix those things the house is good as new. But if you knock down one of the support beams, the house will eventually collapse. Your dad's lack of remorse over this has done almost as much damage as the affair itself.''

''Yeah, but—''

They'd had this discussion so many times, Annie was losing patience with it. ''You can't have a good marriage without trust, Nessa. After what your dad has done with Catherine, I could never trust him again. Every time he worked late or went somewhere alone, I'd wonder what he was really doing. I'd be suspicious of every move he made, and that would eventually destroy us.''

Water dripped from Nessa's hair onto her cheek. She wiped it away. ''But other people stay together. Jodie's parents did. Why can't you?''

''Because I know myself, honey. I know what I feel now, and I know how I'd react if I were with your dad. And since he's still totally besotted with Catherine—and living with her—this really isn't an issue you and I need to worry about.''

''But I don't want to end up like Tracee, bouncing

from house to house and parent to parent, split down the middle on holidays. It's not right.''

"No, it isn't. But it's what we've been dealt and we have to live with it. So why don't we drop the subject and you tell me more about those riding lessons you were talking about?''

Nessa gave that a moment's thought before disappearing into the shower again. "Gary says he can have me riding like a pro before the end of the summer,'' she said after a long time.

Annie let out a silent sigh. "And you want to learn?''

"Yeah, I think it'll be cool.''

Annie shuddered at the thought of climbing on the back of one of those huge animals, but she loved hearing the enthusiasm in Nessa's voice. "Dean offered to teach me, too.''

Nessa's face appeared again, this time scrunched with concern. "Why don't you let Gary teach you?''

"Dean offered.''

Nessa's frown deepened. "Are you going to do it?''

"I haven't decided yet.''

"Well, if you do, you should have Gary teach you. He's a whole lot better than Dean. And nicer, too.''

"*If* I decide to do it," Annie said, turning back for one more try with the toothbrush, "I'll keep that in mind. But why are you suddenly anti-Dean? Weren't you the one who said he wasn't so bad just a few days ago?''

"He stares at you too much for one thing.'' Nessa slipped back behind the curtain. "For another, Tyler thinks he's a jerk. And Tyler ought to know, don't you think?''

Annie nodded slowly, but she hadn't moved past Nessa's first objection. And it took a long time for her to get her toothbrush into her mouth after that bombshell.

CHAPTER SEVEN

WEDNESDAY MORNING, DEAN pretended to be hard at work on a stack of firewood beside the kitchen door while he waited for Tyler to finish breakfast. The first wave of guests were scheduled to arrive on Friday, and Dean wanted to lessen the hostility between Tyler and himself before they got here.

This seemed like the perfect time to do it. Gary had already gone down to the stables. Les had taken the truck to pick up another load of firewood in town. Irma and Annie were both busy inside, so it looked like he wouldn't have any interruptions.

Dean shifted another couple of logs into place and stopped to run his sleeve across his forehead. According to folks in town, the temperature had been running unusually warm for this early in the season. He just hoped that would eventually translate into increased bookings during the summer.

When the sound of chairs scraping against the floor warned him that the kids had finally finished eating, Dean turned toward the door to make sure Tyler couldn't slip past him. Nessa came outside first, wearing a pair of baggy overall shorts over a pink tank top. She'd twisted her hair away from her face and secured each twist with a hot pink elastic.

Tyler stepped onto the porch behind her. The blond tips on his spikes caught the morning sunlight. His mirrored sunglasses reflected it. He wore a pair of black biker boots, black jeans and a tight black T-shirt under a black leather vest.

Dean smiled, wondering if there were two more unlikely candidates to work in the stables. Surprisingly, even Tyler seemed eager to get busy. He shot a glance at Dean as he jumped from the porch, then turned his back and swaggered down the hill toward the stables.

Nessa spared Dean a smile before heading the other way, but the smile was thin and tight and Dean wondered if Tyler's attitude was beginning to rub off on her. Suddenly nervous, Dean called out before the kids could get more than a few feet away.

"Hey, Tyler. Come here for a minute, okay?"

Tyler drew to a reluctant halt and turned partway around, but he made no move to actually retrace his steps. "What?"

Dean ignored the challenge in his voice and kept his own tone neutral. "I'd like your help with something."

Tyler glanced at the stables as if they might disappear if he didn't get there. "What?"

"I need you to give me a hand with this firewood. Nessa can tell Gary that you'll be there in a little while."

Nessa nodded and started on her way again, but Tyler still made no move to come back. He gave the stack of wood a long, slow once-over and trailed his gaze back to Dean's as if he recognized the excuse. "What do you need me to do?"

"If you'll come here, I'll show you."

Tyler hesitated for a few seconds more, then closed the distance between them—but he sure took his time doing it. "Okay," he snarled as he drew closer. "I'm here. So, show me already."

Dean refused to let the kid's hostility get to him. "We

need to straighten this stack so that when Les brings in the next truckload of firewood, we can get it unloaded quickly.''

Tyler shrugged, watched Dean move a couple of logs, and nudged his sunglasses farther up on his nose. ''Looks to me like a waste of time.''

''You won't think so when Les gets here.''

Tyler's lip curled slightly. ''Yeah?''

A trickle of perspiration ran down the side of Dean's face. He swiped a sleeve across his forehead, rested his arm on a log and decided not to push his luck by lying. ''Okay. You're right. It's a bunch of busy work. I just wanted a chance to talk without anyone else around.''

Tyler's shoulders stiffened. ''Why?''

''Because you've hardly said two words to me since I caught you smoking and we need to discuss what's going on here.''

Tyler nudged a log with the toe of his boot. ''Oh, yeah. Like you really want to hear what I have to say.''

''Well, I do.'' Dean sat on a log and motioned for Tyler to join him. ''I want to know why you think Randy wants to be rid of you.''

Tyler folded his arms and held his ground. ''Why? So you can tell me I'm wrong?''

''No, because I'm curious. I've been trying to call your mom, but there's no answer.''

''Big surprise.''

''Your mom sounds pretty happy with this guy. You seem to dislike him a whole lot. I've never met him, so I can't form my own opinion. So why don't you tell me what you don't like?''

''Gee, I don't know,'' Tyler quipped. ''Maybe it's because he hates *me* so much.''

In spite of Tyler's sarcasm, Dean felt a ray of hope.

At least they were talking. "Randy hasn't been around that long," he pointed out. "Maybe you're still getting used to each other."

"Dude, I *told* you. He wants to get rid of me. He knows what a pushover my mom is when I'm not around and he wants me outta there. So far he's doing a good job of getting what he wants."

Dean didn't like to admit it, but men had always been able to manipulate Carol without much effort. "What does he want from your mom that he can't get when you're around?"

Tyler snorted a laugh and pushed his sunglasses onto the top of his head. "Everything." He paced a few steps away and jerked one arm toward the west end of the valley. "The thing is, I know the truth about him. I *know* what he's been doing—and he knows that I know. He's afraid that my mom will actually listen to me one of these days and kick him to the curb. Not that he has anything to worry about. She hasn't believed anything I say for a long time."

Dean stretched his legs out in front of him. "Maybe you should tell me exactly what you know about Randy."

Tyler's gaze shot to Dean's, lingered for a split second, then darted away again. "Well, for one thing, I know he's not faithful to her."

"Are you sure?"

"Positive. I've seen him with a couple of different women since he and Mom got together." Sweat beaded on Tyler's nose and his cheeks flushed. "But don't worry about her. She won't be faithful to him for long, either."

It sounded as if some things in Carol's world hadn't changed, after all.

"And I know what *really* happened to Grandma's

pearl ring,'' Tyler continued. ''And to the other stuff that's missing. Randy's the one stealing from my mom. I don't know what he's doing with the money, but Grandma's ring is in a pawnshop down the street from my friend's house. I saw it a couple of weeks ago.''

The knot in Dean's stomach grew spikes. Stealing was bad enough under any circumstances, but taking a family heirloom made the offense unforgivable in Dean's book and he hoped like hell Tyler wasn't the one responsible. ''Have you told your mother that you saw the ring?''

Tyler laughed bitterly and took a couple of steps away. ''I've tried, but she won't believe me.''

Dean squinted into the glare of sunlight and tried to keep his anger in check. ''Do you know the name of the pawnshop?''

Tyler's gaze narrowed. ''Yeah. Why?''

''It's my mother's ring, too,'' Dean said. ''I'd rather pay to redeem it than let some stranger walk away with it.''

Tyler hooked his thumbs in the back of his waistband so that his elbows stuck out from his sides at right angles. ''And then everyone can be grateful, right?''

The question jolted Dean. ''I have no idea. That's not my first concern.''

''Really? So you get the ring back and then what?''

''Then maybe I'll talk with your mom and tell her what you've told me. She deserves to know the truth.''

''She won't believe you. She won't believe anything bad about Randy. She's *in love*.'' He said the last two words as if they left a sour taste in his mouth. Considering the constant upheaval Tyler had lived through, Dean supposed they did.

''Oh, she'll believe me,'' he assured the kid. ''Don't worry about that.''

Tyler laughed sharply. "If you think that, you really *are* deluded." Tyler pulled his thumbs out of his waistband and shoved a hand through the air. "Okay. The ring's at Arrowhead Pawn Shop on Mariposa. The guy who runs the place is a drinking buddy of Randy's, so don't expect him to tell the truth about how it got there." He kicked a log hard enough to send several others sliding off the stack, then strode off toward the stables.

Dean watched until he disappeared over the hill, then let out a heavy sigh and wondered what was really going on at Carol's house. Both Carol and Tyler seemed absolutely convinced that they were right. Maybe the truth was somewhere in the middle.

DEAN SLIPPED AWAY after dinner that evening and climbed the stairs to his bedroom. He'd been itching to call Carol all day, but he'd made himself wait until the long-distance rates went down and he was reasonably sure she'd be home from work to take his call.

It had been a long time since he'd had to watch his wallet this closely and he hated doing it, but with his shaky bank balance he had to think twice about every penny he spent. He just hoped it wasn't long before money started rolling in and he could live normally again.

Once upstairs, he shut himself inside his bedroom and turned on the radio to prevent anyone—especially Tyler—from overhearing his conversation. He wasn't anxious to confront Carol, but he couldn't ignore Tyler's accusations. Carol answered on the third ring and Dean could tell immediately that she'd been drinking.

So that had started again, too.

Fighting disappointment and an inexplicable sense of failure, Dean dropped onto the edge of his bed. Talking to Carol when she was in this condition never did any good. But if she'd started drinking again, there probably wouldn't be a good time for their conversation.

A dull ache started in the back of his head and his shoulder twinged painfully. "It's me, Carol," he said quietly.

"Dean?" Something clattered near the telephone, and when she spoke again he could tell she was making more of an effort to sound coherent. "I din't know you were going to call. Whatsup?"

"We need to talk about Tyler. How much have you had to drink?"

Carol hiccuped softly into the phone. "Drink? I've only had iced tea after work. Honest."

Dean kneaded his forehead and bit back a growl of frustration at the obvious lie. He could call her on it, but they'd played this game too many times before. He knew the drill. He'd accuse and Carol would deny, and they'd end up dancing around the real issues and losing track of what was really important.

He closed his eyes and took a couple of deep breaths in an effort to remember the reason for his call. "I'm worried about Tyler," he said at last.

Carol sighed heavily. "What's he doing, stealing from *you* now?"

"No. He's angry and showing a little attitude, but he's not doing anything wrong. Did you know that he's been smoking?"

"Yeah, I knew that."

She sounded so matter-of-fact about it, Dean had trouble remaining calm. "What are you doing about it?"

"What *can* I do about it?"

"You can stop him. He's not an adult."

Carol laughed harshly. "If you think it's so easy, why don't *you* stop him?"

"I will. Believe me." Too agitated to sit, Dean stood and paced as close to the window as the cord would stretch. "Tell me what you've tried to get him to quit."

"We've tried everything." Ice rattled in a glass near the phone. Carol swallowed and sighed softly. "We've grounded him from the phone and from his friends. We've grounded him from TV and his stereo. We've told him again and again that he's not old enough to smoke, but he still takes Randy's cigarettes whenever he feels like it."

Dean stared out the window at the mountain peaks. "It might be easier to convince Tyler to stop if Randy didn't smoke."

"Oh, so it's Randy's fault?" Carol voice changed so quickly and sounded so protective, Dean knew that Tyler had been telling the truth about that, anyway. "Randy's an adult," she said in a cold voice. "Tyler's not. There's a world of difference."

If she'd been sober, Dean might have argued that point, but there seemed little reason to waste his breath. "I'll take care of the smoking issue," he said firmly. "The real reason I called is because Tyler said something today that concerns me."

"Oh?" Carol's voice cooled considerably. "What was it?"

"He says that Randy's the one who's been taking your things, that Randy pawned Mom's ring and Tyler knows where it is."

"Well, of *course* that's what he'd say. I *told* you how he feels about Randy. He'll do anything to break us up."

"I want to check on his story, Carol. And if the ring's there, I'm redeeming it."

"You will? Thank you."

"I'll redeem it and have the guy ship it to me. You

can get it later, when everything's sorted out.'' Listening to the distinct slur that only alcohol or drugs could produce made Dean nauseous. ''Does Randy know that you're a recovering alcoholic?''

The question seemed to catch Carol off guard. She hesitated for a breath, then said harshly, ''Yeah, he knows.''

Dean turned away from the window and stared at the picture of his mother on the far wall. ''Does he know how hard you worked to overcome your addiction?''

''Is this why you called? To rip Randy apart?''

Dean sat on the foot of his bed and rubbed a knot from his neck. He'd like to rip Randy apart, but the truth was, although Randy might have provided temptation, the responsibility for staying sober was Carol's. ''No,'' he said at last. ''I called because I'm worried.''

''Why? I love Randy. He makes me happy. I know Tyler doesn't like him, but what am I supposed to do? Tyler will be an adult in a couple of years and I know he won't stay here once he's eighteen. When he goes, I'll be alone. I've devoted my whole life to raising him. Don't *I* deserve a little happiness?''

''Of course you do, but Tyler's not gone yet, and if your relationship with Randy is leading you to drink again and making your son unhappy—''

''My relationship with Randy is the only good thing in my life,'' Carol broke in. ''The *only* good thing. I'm not giving him up just because Tyler doesn't like him.'' She took another drink and set her glass on the counter with a bang. ''I *told* you that Tyler was impossible. Maybe *now* you'll believe me.''

Like she'd done countless times before over the years, Carol hung up before Dean could respond. He replaced the receiver slowly, aching for the agony she insisted on causing herself, the pain and heartache her choices inflicted on her son. In frustration, he picked up the bottle of pain medication he always kept on his nightstand and threw it across the room.

No one, not even Gary, completely understood why he put up with so much pain before he succumbed to the need for a pain pill. But Dean had seen too many lives ruined because of addictions. After the conversation he'd just had, he could almost guarantee that he'd force his threshold of pain up a few more notches. He'd endure almost anything to escape the risk of becoming addicted.

He paced the length of his room for a long time, but no amount of thinking changed the facts. He didn't feel right letting Tyler go home as long as Randy was in that house and Carol was up to her old tricks. But he was the only other family Tyler had left and Tyler obviously didn't want to be here.

Somehow, Dean would have to convince Tyler to stay here—and Carol to allow it. But he knew damn well it wouldn't be easy.

ANNIE DIDN'T GET A CHANCE to think about hiking trails or spending quality time with Nessa until late the next night. Their first guests were scheduled to arrive the following day, and last-minute preparations had taken every spare minute she had. But as she helped Irma clean up after dinner, the need to spend time with Nessa hit Annie with a vengeance.

She enjoyed keeping busy. She was grateful that she hadn't been left with countless hours with nothing to do but think. And she was relieved that Nessa had stopped begging to go back to Chicago. But a whole week had slipped by and they still hadn't spent any significant time together.

When Irma went to find Les, Annie hung the dish towel she'd been using over a cabinet door and stepped onto the porch, trying to remember if Nessa had said anything about after-dinner plans. The lights were still on in the stables, and that seemed the most likely place to check, but there were also half a dozen other places she could have been.

Annie spent a minute trying to decide where to check first. Crickets sang all around her, leaves whispered in the soft breeze, and the sound of water tumbling over rocks in nearby Wolf Creek almost convinced her that everything would be all right. The sounds of nature began to ease the heaviest concerns from her shoulders. Maybe it wouldn't hurt to unwind for a minute before she went in search of Nessa.

She walked to the far end of the porch where shadows would protect her from the glare of the kitchen light. The forest hovered on the edge of the clearing—the pine trees lurked blue-black in the night, the quivering aspen leaves shimmered in the moonlight. The sky was darker than any she'd ever seen, but it seemed brilliantly alive at the same time—as if she could gather a handful of stars if she swept her hand through it.

"They look close enough to touch, don't they?" Dean's voice came from behind her.

She whipped around quickly and found him lounging against the door frame, thumbs hooked into his pockets, one foot crossed over the other. The breeze teased the hair away from his forehead, and the light coming from the doorway bathed him in a soft golden glow.

Her reaction was so strong and unexpected, Annie had trouble remembering what he'd asked her and even more trouble remembering her vow to ignore her attraction for him. "It's incredible," she said after a pause that felt embarrassingly long. "I've never seen anything like it."

Dean stepped away from the door frame and came a little closer. "That's probably because you've always lived in the city where the lights get in the way."

She could feel his voice in her pulse. The woodsy scent he wore drifted across the space between them, filling her senses and making it even harder to hang on to common sense. "Is that what makes the difference?"

"So I'm told." Dean turned his gaze to the sky and Annie was finally able to catch her breath.

He leaned against the porch rail and trailed his gaze toward the two cabins they could see from where they stood. "Whenever I'm outside on a night like this, with the stars overhead and the forest and mountains surrounding me, I always feel small and insignificant."

Annie flashed him a brief smile. "If *you* feel small and insignificant, *I* should probably feel puny."

Dean laughed softly and sent her a sidelong glance that lingered on her face. He looked away again and silence fell, but it seemed charged with something that made Annie's skin tingle. If she was having a similar effect on Dean he didn't show it, but she felt foolish for letting that disappoint her.

"We probably won't have many nights like this after tomorrow," he said. "I'll be glad to finally be bringing money in, but I'll miss this."

Annie leaned her head against the smooth pine pole at her side. "I don't think I've ever been anywhere so peaceful."

"That's what made me fall in love with this country the first time I saw it. And when I was trying to find a place to start over, there wasn't another location that interested me."

Even with Irma's warnings ringing in her ears, Annie couldn't resist asking about his past. "After a career in baseball, what made you decide to open a dude ranch?"

Dean shrugged one shoulder. "I needed something to do."

Relieved that he didn't seem annoyed, Annie laughed softly. "Ask a silly question... It's just that one doesn't exactly seem to flow from the other." He seemed so unconcerned, she found herself relaxing slightly. "Maybe it's because I'm in the middle of making a switch myself that I'm so curious about how you got here."

Dean glanced toward the stables and seemed to be collecting his thoughts. "I came here for the first time about four years ago. A teammate of mine grew up in the area and brought me here. From the very first day, I felt as if I'd come home to Whistle River, and I came here as often as I could after that." He looked out at the trees and his expression grew almost wistful. "This ranch stood deserted for several years after its previous owner died. Gary and I came out here on horseback a couple of times, and I knew I had to own this property." His gaze drifted slowly across the clearing. "When the doctors finally convinced me that my career was over, this was the first place—the *only* place, really—that I thought of. I poured my life savings into renovating it and now I'm holding my breath that other people will feel the same way about it that I do."

"They will," Annie assured him. "Once people see the Eagle's Nest, you won't be able to keep them away. *I* certainly didn't expect to like it so much, and I'd love to come back as a guest."

Annie couldn't read the sudden change in Dean's expression. "You'd be welcome, of course. I hope building the rest of our clientele will be that easy, but I'm not going to hold my breath."

Annie thought about how much work she and Spence had put into taking over Holladay House—the seemingly endless days, the weeks that felt as if they'd lasted a year, and the sleep deprivation she thought she'd never recover from—and laughed at her own statement.

"Well, it might be a *little* harder than that," she admitted, "but the Eagle's Nest has a very nice feeling. I came outside to look for Nessa, but instead I've been standing here and feeling all my cares slip away. That can't hurt business."

Again, that strange expression crossed Dean's face, but he turned his eyes away before she could read them.

"Maybe it's being in the middle of nature that makes me feel that way," she continued. "It's so consistent. I see the mountains that have been here for billions of years, the forest that keeps growing, the creek that keeps flowing, and I feel comforted. They prove that no matter how big my troubles might feel, the sun will still come up in the morning, the trees and the mountains will be here, and the water will still be splashing over the rocks."

Dean focused on an aspen tree at the end of the porch. "Sometimes that constancy is annoying. Your whole world can be falling apart and Mother Nature doesn't even bat an eye. The sun comes out and the birds sing as if you and your problems don't matter in the least."

Irma's warning not to bring up the past echoed through Annie's mind again, but curiosity was stronger. Annie didn't want to spend the entire summer tiptoeing around this man and his moods. "Maybe it depends on the catastrophe," she said. "I like knowing that it would take more than what I'm going through to upset this world."

Dean turned to face her. "You must be talking about your divorce. Or is there something else?"

Annie blinked in surprise. "It's a really *tough* divorce. We've been legally separated for eight months and the judge has granted our divorce, but it won't be final until the end of the summer. I guess he thought we needed time in case we wanted to change our minds."

"And will you?"

"No." The intensity of his gaze made her skin tingle. There was more than idle curiosity in those dark eyes and Annie's heart gave a leap of anticipation. "No, I won't."

"You sound pretty certain."

"I *am* certain." Memories of the day her world shattered tore a shudder from her. "I found my husband making love to another woman. That's a mental image I'll probably never lose, and it would be impossible to climb into the same bed with him or even eat at the same table with him after seeing that. It's hard even to have a conversation with him at times."

Dean nodded in understanding. "Still, I get the feeling the divorce isn't the whole story."

"There's also Nessa," she admitted, running one hand along the polished wood railing. "She hopes that Spence and I will change our minds, and maybe that's why she's fighting so hard not to leave Chicago. I don't want her to be unhappy, but she'll be even more miserable if we tried to put things back together."

Dean leaned forward slightly. "Why do you think that?"

"Because she *would* be. It's pretty hard to be happy when you're living in the middle of tension all the time. And since I could never trust him again, there'd be plenty of tension."

Dean seemed about ready to touch her arm, then caught himself. He fell silent and Annie found herself wondering about his struggles. Since they were becoming friends, she didn't feel right pretending not to know his story.

The moon, the stars, the soft breeze all combined to give Annie courage. Curiosity and the warmth of a budding friendship bolstered it. Wise or foolish, she was beginning to care about Dean and she wanted to know what put a smile on his face and what made him frown. And it was only fair. He'd asked about her life. As the old saying went, turnabout was fair play.

She just hoped Dean had heard that one.

CHAPTER EIGHT

ANNIE LET THE SILENCE linger between them for a few more seconds and studied the night sky while she tried to figure out how to broach the subject of Dean's accident. When she couldn't come up with anything subtle, she decided to just plunge in. "You're going through some rough things yourself," she said, watching him covertly in case he reacted badly. "Irma told me about your accident."

Dean skimmed a glance across her face. His eyes didn't change, but Annie didn't miss the stiffening of his shoulders and the tightening of the muscles in his jaw. "I shouldn't be surprised. I'm sure she thought you deserved a warning."

"Do you mind?"

He shook his head. "It's no secret."

Annie let out a silent sigh of relief. "I know you're probably reluctant to talk about it—"

"I *don't* like talking about it. There's no point."

Annie couldn't agree with that. "I don't know what I would have done after I found Spence with Catherine if I hadn't been able to talk through what I was feeling. My mom listened to me for hours. My best friend listened to me for twice as long." She cautiously added, "Sometimes talking can help a person deal with a tragedy."

"I've *dealt* with mine." His voice sharpened, but he held up one hand and dipped his head while he tried to pull himself together. "I'm sorry," he said after a min-ute. "I didn't mean to snap, but everyone I know has been nagging me to talk about the accident. Doctors, ther-apists and clergy have tried a hundred different ways of getting me to discuss it. But no amount of talking will ever change the facts."

Annie sat on the porch rail beside him. "Maybe that's because they know that keeping your feelings bottled up will only hurt you. I'm a good listener if talking would help you deal with the facts better."

Dean pushed up from the railing as if he couldn't get away from her fast enough. "The fact is," he said abruptly, "my life will never be the same, thanks to a woman who shouldn't have been behind the wheel of a car on a snowy night. She took away my career, the woman I *might* have actually married and eventually my home. In the blink of an eye, she stole my self-respect, my dignity and my future in front of the Mini Mart on Highway 74. Those are the facts, Annie. Tell me how a few conversations are going to change them."

The vehemence of his reaction left her speechless, but Annie had brought it on herself and she knew that if she buckled now she'd have a hard time earning his respect later. She kept her gaze locked with his, even though the glare in his eyes frightened her a little.

"I can't argue with most of that," she said. "I don't know the details of your accident. But nothing can take away your dignity and self-respect unless you hand it away. And as for the future, you haven't lost that. You're still here, still healthy and breathing—"

Dean cut her off with an impatient wave of his hand. "Have you ever been in the hospital?"

"Yes, when Nessa was born."

"Have you ever been hooked up to tubes and monitors

and machines? Or had complete strangers doing things for you that no one should *ever* have to do? Or been patted on the head like a child because you sat up or went to the bathroom by yourself?''

His anger was so fierce, Annie had to fight to hold on to her courage. "No. And I'm sorry you have. But the fact that you survived all that and that you're...well *look* at you, Dean. You're incredibly fit and strong. I would never have known you'd been injured if Irma hadn't told me.''

"I'm functional,'' he snarled. "That's it. I'll never have the physical agility to play baseball again.''

"Maybe not, but that's only one thing. There are so many other things you *can* do. I've seen you doing some of them.''

Dean laughed harshly and turned away. "Making my mark in the Major League was the only thing I ever wanted to do, the only goal I ever had. At times it feels like losing my career is the same as losing my ability to breathe.''

"But—''

"Logically, I know it's not the same at all,'' he said. "I do okay most of the time, I guess. Until something happens to bring it all up again.''

Annie wondered if her questions were solely responsible, or if something else had happened to bring on this reaction. Maybe it was selfish on her part, but she wanted to think there was something else.

Dean wheeled back suddenly, his eyes glittering with some emotion Annie couldn't identify. "Put yourself in my place, Annie. What if someone took away your dream? What if, without warning, you were told you could never cook again?''

"I'd find something else to do—just like you have.''

Dean made a noise and turned his attention back toward the sky. His voice had become more restrained, almost impersonal. "The answers look easy when it's someone else's life. They're not so obvious when it's your own. All I can say is, be thankful you haven't lost your dreams."

He seemed so comfortable with his assumption, Annie felt her own temper flare. "You act as if you're the only person in the world who's ever suffered a setback," she said, trying to keep her tone as cool as his. "Well, this may come as a surprise, but you're not. I not only lost my marriage, I lost my career along with it, so don't think I don't understand what you're feeling."

Dean smiled sadly. "I know I'm not the only person hurting, but you have to admit that losing a marriage isn't the same thing as losing your entire identity. Not in this day and age."

"I can't believe you just said that. You haven't ever *been* married, so you can't even imagine how it feels to find out your life isn't what you thought it was. That the person you've loved and trusted for sixteen years isn't who you thought he was. That everything you believed in was really a lie and the future you worked toward almost as long as you can remember was nothing more than a pipe dream." Her breath was coming hard and fast and her anger had taken the chill off the evening. "You have no idea what *that* does to a person's identity, do you?"

The muscles in Dean's jaw stopped twitching. "No, I don't. Not firsthand. I only know there's a whole lot of damage done in the name of love."

That strange mixture of vulnerability and aggression Annie had glimpsed the first time she met him clouded his eyes again, but she was too angry to care. "There's a lot of good, too. And I believe that you always find what you look for in this life. If you want to believe that life's unfair to you, then you'll find proof of that everywhere you look. I'm starting over on a new career, too. But *I* know how lucky I am to be able to do it. I worked for a long time to get where I was. A *long* time. And then I had to walk away from everything—and not by choice. And in a few months my daughter's going to leave me to live with her father because she doesn't want to leave her friends. But I refuse to make myself miserable by pouting over my bad luck. Just do me a favor. While you're feeling miserable about the life you've got, try to remember that the road the rest of us are on isn't easy, either."

Dean smiled, but there was no warmth in it. "It seems that what I consider a healthy grip on reality turns into self-pity in your eyes. Maybe now you can understand why I prefer not to talk about my past."

He didn't wait for her to respond, but turned away and strode into the shadows. It was only after he left that Annie realized Irma was right. It was pain that brought on his Dr.-Jekyll-and-Mr.-Hyde act, but Annie would have bet everything she owned that physical pain wasn't the only issue.

DEAN STOOD IN A GROVE of trees for what felt like forever after Annie slammed the kitchen door battling a mixture of amusement and irritation, of admiration and annoyance. He was irritated with her for bringing up subjects that were better left alone, annoyed with himself for responding the way he had. He couldn't believe all the admissions he'd made before he could stop himself. He should have kept the vows he'd made to forget baseball and to never talk about the accident. But, then, he seemed to forget a whole lot of things when Annie Holladay was around.

Determined to put some distance between them, he began walking even though he had no place to go. He shouldn't have let his worries about Carol and his inadequacies in dealing with Tyler affect him so much, but he was the only family they had and his sense of responsibility sometimes overwhelmed him. It seemed natural to associate Carol, whose drinking problem had returned, with the woman who'd caused his accident. Dean had been thinking about that fateful night and growing increasingly angry for hours before he had run into Annie.

He definitely owed Annie an apology, but what would he say? That he was sorry, but for the first time in hours he'd been able to stop thinking about the drunk driver who'd ruined his life because Annie's eyes and hair and skin had distracted him? That he hadn't meant to snap, but he'd been thinking about kissing her when she'd blindsided him with questions about his accident?

He laughed, and the sound echoed in the still night air. Oh, yeah. Either of those explanations would really sweep her off her feet. His feet stopped working and his eyes locked on a stand of aspen a few feet away. Did he *want* to sweep Annie off her feet?

She was attractive, he couldn't deny that. And nice. And full of fire. He was starting to care for her. But she was technically still married, and she had a daughter who needed a father figure. Those were two facts Dean couldn't afford to forget. Even if he'd been interested in a relationship, this was about the worst possible time to consider one. The ranch was opening tomorrow and he needed to stay tightly focused on business. His entire future was hinged on making the Eagle's Nest a success.

A burst of laughter from near the stables caught his attention. He recognized Gary's laugh, guessed that the higher, feminine one belonged to Nessa, and knew that Tyler had to be there, too. He fought a pang of envy over the quick and easy relationship Gary had developed with Tyler, another over the relationship Annie shared with Nessa.

He mopped his face with one hand and looked back into the sky, wishing answers would suddenly appear there. Because no matter how much logic he applied, no matter how many times he reminded himself that he'd never been that interested in marriage or family, everything inside him seemed to be turning that into a lie.

DEAN WAS STILL PUTTING off that apology to Annie four days later. He'd gone over it in his mind again and again, but every explanation he could have offered seemed weak or pathetic. Anyway, he didn't want to apologize in front of everyone else. And their days had been so busy since the first round of guests had arrived, an opportunity to get her alone hadn't presented itself.

He didn't want to seek her out for a private conversation. That might give someone the wrong idea. Hell, it might give *him* the wrong idea. He was still trying to decide if he really wanted a relationship at this stage of life or if he'd been under the influence of moonlight, meat loaf and fresh raspberry pie.

One of these days, the perfect opportunity to talk with Annie would come along. When it did, he'd be ready. Meanwhile, he had other things to worry about. Gary had found a leak in the men's shower room before breakfast, and Dean was scrambling to fix it. He was in the shed, measuring a piece of pipe, when the commotion started.

He stopped working and listened to the dull throbbing

that seemed to match his heartbeat. Wondering what else was going wrong, he strode to the door and listened more closely. It took only a second to recognize the rhythmic pulsing as an insistent bass beat coming from a stereo turned up too loud—and he had a good idea whose stereo it was.

Whatever progress Dean imagined he'd made during their conversation by the woodpile had been just that— a figment of his imagination. He'd tried repeatedly to talk with Tyler since then, but opportunities had been few and far between, and he'd been rejected at every turn.

Mealtimes had turned into silent battlegrounds during which Dean sensed an awareness of the tension from their guests. More than once Dean had smelled the lingering odor of cigarette smoke on Tyler's clothes, so it was obvious that the kid still had a supply. It seemed as if Tyler went out of his way to make sure Dean knew he was still smoking.

Just the day before, Dean had confronted him about it, but Tyler had put on an injured expression and pleaded innocence, and since one of his paying guests was a smoker, Dean couldn't prove his suspicions so Tyler had won that round. Dean would be damn sure he had solid proof before he confronted him again.

Luckily, Tyler couldn't feign innocence this morning. That damn music was loud enough, the folks in town could probably hear it. Dean didn't want to engage in a battle where the guests might hear, but the heavy pounding in the still morning air was just another act of aggression. One Dean couldn't ignore.

Swearing, he set aside the tools he'd been using, stepped out of the shed and tried to figure out where the sound was coming from. When he realized that it seemed to be originating from the stables, his irritation took a giant upswing. The Carters had arranged for a trail ride that afternoon. If Tyler spooked the horses, Dean would throttle him.

He was halfway to the stables when Hugh Morrison from cabin three stopped him to ask about a guided fishing trip. Dean tried not to look irritated by the delay, directed him to make a reservation through Irma and kept going. He made it to the stables a couple of minutes later, jerked open the door and stepped inside. A boom box sat on a bale of hay, its volume turned so high the equipment hanging on the walls rattled with every pulse of the rhythm.

Dean looked around for Tyler, fully expecting to see him waiting, watching, smirking. To his surprise, the building seemed deserted. Even the stalls were empty. At least Tyler hadn't turned on the music and left the animals to suffer.

But that didn't make Dean any less irritated. He turned off the music, and the sudden silence was almost as loud as the music had been. He heard running footsteps behind him and turned just as Gary burst through the door.

His friend's face was creased with concern, but when his gaze landed on the long black box beside Dean he propped his hands on his hips and grinned. "All right, young man. How many times have I told you not to play your music that loud?"

"Funny." Dean headed back outside and started toward the paddock. "Did you tell Tyler he could have that thing here while he's working?"

Gary trailed behind him. "No. He didn't ask. But how—"

"Figures." Dean cut Gary off. He rounded the corner and saw that someone had let the horses into the fenced pasture behind the paddock, far enough away to lessen the impact of that so-called music on the high-strung animals.

He ignored the inner near-silent whisper that told him not to overreact. He might have been able to listen if this had been Tyler's only act of aggression, but it was just one in a long string of similar incidents and Dean knew he couldn't keep ignoring them.

"I'd like to know what the hell he's thinking," he grumbled as he churned up the remaining distance to the paddock. "He could have spooked the entire herd with that noise."

"It's not that big a deal," Gary said, matching his stride. "These horses are probably used to noise. And anyway, how—"

"Not *that* much noise," Dean snapped, cutting off Gary's question again.

"I don't know. I've heard some stable hands play some pretty loud music—of all kinds. Actually had a horse once that liked it. High-strung beast. He'd get wound up tighter than a drum, and he'd only settle down to really loud Spanish music."

Irritated by his friend's unflagging optimism and by his growing friendship with Tyler when Dean couldn't even get a civil word from the kid, Dean rounded on him. "Why the hell are you sticking up for him? You know why he did this."

Gary's smile faded and his eyes lost their sparkle. He squared his shoulders as if he sensed a battle coming. "Do I?"

"Are you trying to say you don't?"

Gary propped his hands on his hips and looked Dean square in the eye. "Suppose you tell me."

Dean wasn't in the mood to play games. "It's as obvious as the nose on your face, and if you can't see it, you aren't paying attention." He started walking again.

Gary fell into step at his side. "Why don't you cut the kid a little slack? Even if the music *was* a problem, how do you expect him to know?"

"He knows. I guarantee it."

"Maybe. But let me ask you—"

Before he could finish, Tyler came barreling through the open gate and plowed straight into Dean. His expression went from wide-open and smiling to closed and angry in a heartbeat.

Dean tried hard to keep his grip on his own anger. Letting Tyler see that his tactics were achieving results would make him worse. He jerked his head toward the stable wall. "What's the rush? On your way to check out the mysterious silence?"

Tyler pulled back, muttered something under his breath and turned on his heel. For the first time, Dean noticed Nessa sitting on the top rail of the fence a few feet away. Again, some inner voice whispered caution, but Dean was too angry to let Tyler off the hook without a fight. "Do you want to tell me what the hell you're doing?"

Tyler shot a dagger-sharp look over his shoulder. "Just playing some music. Is that a crime?"

"Do you have any idea how sensitive the horses are to disturbances? Do you even *care* what might have happened to them if they'd gotten spooked? Or to the Carters if the horses are still skittish later?"

Red splotches flamed in Tyler's cheeks. His eyes flashed. "But they're not skittish, are they? Your damn horses are fine."

"Are they?"

"If you don't believe me, see for yourself."

Dean heard Gary mutter something he couldn't make

out and his irritation climbed another level. "Horses are
highly strung, sensitive creatures," he shouted at Tyler.
"No matter how tame they might seem, you can't afford
to forget that they could snap if conditions are wrong.
One alone could kill a person. I don't even want to think
what could happen with that many together."

Gary put a restraining hand on his shoulder. "Come
on, Dean. Back off. He's never worked with horses before."

Dean shook off his hand and glared. "He's sixteen,
not six. That's old enough to think before he acts."

Tyler made a noise of disgust. Gary's eyes narrowed
into thin slits in his face. Dean heard Nessa jump down
from the fence rail, and a second later she was standing
in front of him, her face creased in a frown, her eyes
dark.

"That's *so* not fair. You don't even know what happened."

"I *heard* what happened," Dean argued. "Everyone
in a fifty-mile radius probably heard what happened."

"Okay. So you heard the music. And yeah, it was on
and it was loud and that was probably stupid. But you
don't have any right to get mad at Tyler, because the
boom box is mine. *I'm* the one who turned it up that
loud."

Dean stared at her while her words sank in, and he
swallowed around the lump of embarrassment in his
throat. "You?"

"Yes. Me." She was less than half his age and only
reached the bottom of his chin, but she met his gaze with
the unwavering coolness of an absolute equal. In spite of
the difference in their coloring, she resembled her mother
so closely, Dean couldn't speak.

"So if you're going to yell at somebody," she was saying, "yell at me. But leave Tyler alone."

Dean's fury ran out in waves and left him feeling about an inch tall. He tried to remain angry—after all, the offense was the same. But the truth was that it wasn't the offense that had him so riled, it was the offender. And he hated knowing that about himself.

He couldn't make himself look at Gary and he didn't want to see Nessa's expression, but he forced himself to face Tyler. "I'm sorry. I jumped to the wrong conclusion."

"Don't worry about it," Tyler muttered, his eyes downcast. "I'm used to it."

"It's just that—" Dean broke off, unsure how to justify himself, not even sure that he could. "I was wrong, Tyler. What can I say?"

"Nothing, dude. I said don't worry about it." Tyler turned his back on Dean, and his meaning couldn't have been more clear if he'd painted a billboard. He didn't want to hear anything more Dean had to say.

Dean's stomach cramped and he thought for a few seconds that he might be sick. Slowly, he started back toward the far end of the building. He hadn't gone far when he realized Gary was still at his side, but he didn't speak until they'd turned the corner and the kids couldn't see him any longer.

Then he drew to a halt and scrubbed his face with his hands. "I feel like a jerk."

"You're really pulling for that Mr. Congeniality award, aren't you?"

"I was wrong, okay? I told him that."

"Yes, you did. And to be fair, he *has* been pushing your buttons all week."

"I'll talk to him later—when we've both had a chance to cool off."

Gary nodded and put a brotherly hand on Dean's shoulder. "Good idea. He's one hurt and confused kid."

"Yeah, he is." Almost as confused as his uncle. "I wish I knew what to do for him."

"You're doing it."

"I'm doing nothing," Dean countered. "I'm arguing with him all the time and managing to keep him constantly upset."

Gary squeezed his shoulder gently. "Quit being so hard on yourself, would ya? You're showing him that you care, and from what I've managed to pick up that's not something he's used to. He just has to *get* used to it and then maybe he'll start believing that he can count on you to be there no matter what. Give him time. He'll get there—and so will you."

Grateful for Gary's faith in him, Dean started walking again slowly. "I hope you're right. I already feel like I've failed Carol. I don't want to fail him, too."

"Let Carol take *some* responsibility for her decisions," Gary said. "You can only do so much to save someone else."

Dean wanted to believe that on one level, but it felt like a huge cop-out on another. But now, with the bathroom needing to be fixed and Tony Carter from cabin two looking as if he needed help with something, it wasn't the time to solve all of his family problems.

Remembering that on top of isolating his nephew, he had cut off his best friend, Dean asked Gary, "What was it you were going to ask me back there?"

"When?"

"Right before we ran into Tyler."

Gary slanted a glance at him. "Oh, that? It was nothing."

"It must have been *something* or you wouldn't have tried so hard to ask it."

"You sure you want to know?"

"I wouldn't have asked if I didn't."

Gary shrugged and began to head toward the lodge, walking backward for a few feet so he was still facing Dean. "I was just going to ask why you were so sure the boom box was his."

THAT EVENING AFTER DINNER, Dean made his usual circle of the property. He strolled past the occupied cabins, checked each of the empty ones, made sure no one had started a fire in the fire pit, then turned toward the shed so he could lock it for the night. Crickets sang softly in the still night air and a few lit windows still made it easy to find his way in the dark. Flashlights played along the edge of the forest as folks strolled the paths he and Gary had cut through the trees. The ranch was growing so familiar now, he wondered if he really needed any light to see.

He was becoming used to the human sounds around him, too—a radio playing softly from cabin three, the muted hum of conversation from cabin five. Usually at this time of night he could hear Nessa and Tyler laughing together about something they wouldn't share with anyone else. They must be somewhere else tonight.

He rounded a corner and stopped short when he realized that someone was sitting on the shed's front step.

"Hi." The shadow spoke and Dean recognized Nessa leaning against the rough plank door.

"Hi yourself. What are you doing out here alone? Where's Tyler?"

Nessa shrugged and tilted her face to the stars. "I don't know. He's probably checking the horses with Gary. I just felt like being alone, I guess."

"Well, then, I'll just slip the padlock onto the door and leave you to it."

To his surprise, Nessa scooted over and put a hand on the space she'd vacated. "You can sit if you want to. I don't mind."

Dean hadn't planned on stopping, but something in her voice and the fact that she was speaking to him at all after that afternoon changed his mind. He padlocked the shed, then took the spot she indicated. "So, what's up?"

"Nothing much. Just thinking."

"About anything special?"

Nessa shrugged one thin shoulder. "Lots of stuff, I guess."

Dean linked his hands on his knees and listened to the buzz of a nearby mosquito. "I'm surprised you're still speaking to me," he admitted after a few seconds.

Nessa glanced at him in surprise. "Why wouldn't I be?"

"I overreacted about the boom box."

Nessa smiled slowly. "Yeah? Well, I probably shouldn't have turned it up so loud, and I shouldn't have yelled at you."

Dean grinned at her, liking the way she'd put the incident behind her and wondering if she'd learned to do that from her mother. "You were right to set me straight."

"Yeah, but you *are* an adult, and my dad hates it when kids mouth off."

"If you can forget about it, so can I," Dean said, leaving that subject and moving on to another. "How do you like it here so far?"

"I like it a lot."

"Still think I need to put in a satellite dish?"

She grinned slyly. "It wouldn't hurt."

Dean laughed aloud. "I shouldn't have asked. How does your mom like it?" No matter how much sense it made to ignore Annie, he seemed to grow more aware of her by the day. Her laugh, her voice, her smile, her scent.

Nessa's expression changed subtly. "She likes it fine, I guess."

"You don't think she regrets coming?"

"I don't think so." Nessa swatted a mosquito from her leg, propped her elbows on her knees and her chin in her hands. "I don't know. She hasn't said."

Dean tried to hide his disappointment over her vague answer. "She's a wonderful chef. She's going to be a tough act for my next cook to follow."

Nessa turned her eyes toward him. "This is nothing compared to what she usually does. She's really, *really* good—if you like gourmet stuff, that is. My dad still hasn't found anyone good enough to take her place at the restaurant. I don't think he will, either."

Maybe he should have considered that before he took a mistress, Dean thought. He stretched his legs out in front of him and crossed one boot over the other. "As long as your mom's happy, that's what matters."

Nessa looked at him strangely. "I don't know whether she is or not. She *loves* cooking. I don't know why she suddenly wants to teach." She laughed without humor and trailed her gaze across the clearing. "I can't figure out why she does half the stuff she does lately."

Dean swatted away a mosquito. "Like what?"

"Like moving away from Chicago. Like coming here." She glanced at him and smiled sheepishly. "I didn't mean that the way it sounded. It's pretty cool here, I guess. But she's just acting so different lately.''

"From what I hear, she's been through some rough times.''

"Yeah? Well, she's not the only one.'' Nessa plucked a stalk of wild grass from the ground near her feet, tore it into tiny pieces and scattered them in the breeze. "I *hate* this stupid divorce.''

The conversation was getting a little deep for Dean. He wasn't sure he knew the best way to handle it. But there was no one else to take over for him, and he certainly couldn't walk away just because he was growing uncomfortable. He looked at her out of the corner of his eye and shifted his weight on the step. "I wish I could say that I understood, but I don't. I grew up without a dad, so I never knew what it felt like to live with both my parents.''

Nessa sent him a matching glance. "That's not fair.''

"Yeah, well a lot of things in life aren't fair.''

She rolled her eyes. "Now you sound like my mom.''

Dean laughed and some of his edginess faded. "Well she's right. When I was a kid, I spent a lot of time wishing I had a dad. I wished on stars, fought for the wishbone when my mom fixed chicken, and would have killed for a toothpick in my piece of cake.'' He smiled at the memory he hadn't thought about in years. "My mom always put three toothpicks in her cakes to hold the layers together and she told us they were lucky. There were times I think my sister would've clawed out my eyes to get one.''

Nessa's lips curved softly and the resemblance between mother and daughter made Dean lose his train of thought. She tilted her head and looked straight at him.

"I suppose the point of this story is that all your wishing didn't work."

Dean wagged his head from side to side. "Not even a little bit. My mom never remarried, so I didn't even have a stepdad."

"And you survived."

"We did." He bent his knees again and rested his elbows on his thighs. "I guess there are a few people out there who have picture-perfect families, but most of us don't." He thought about Tyler's situation and felt a strange hollow sensation in his chest. "I wasted a whole lot of time wanting something that didn't exist. I wish now that I'd figured it all out sooner—before my mom died and my sister moved away. Maybe everything would have been different if I had."

"How?"

"Maybe I would have spent more time being part of a real family and less time wishing for a fantasy one. Maybe my mom would have died knowing that I appreciated what she did to keep us together. Maybe my sister wouldn't have had to search so hard for what she already had."

Nessa folded her arms and turned toward him. "So, when *did* you figure it out?"

"About two minutes ago."

Nessa grinned slowly. "Okay. So what do I do about my mom? Do I go with her to Seattle or stay in Chicago?"

Dean shook his head and turned his gaze back toward the sky. "That's the hardest question you've asked me all night. I'd say you have to do whatever you think is right."

Nessa let out a heavy sigh. "Thanks a lot."

"No problem. That kind of terrific advice is what I'm here for."

"I can see why," Nessa said with a grin. "You're good at it."

"Aren't I, though?"

She sobered slightly and nudged him with one knee. "You know what? You're okay."

"Yeah? Well, so are you. Now, if someone would only convince Tyler of that, I'd be happy."

"He knows."

Dean shook his head. "I don't think so."

"Yeah, he does. He just doesn't *know* that he knows. But he'll figure it out one of these days." Nessa stood, stretched and jumped to the bottom of the steps. "Just give him time."

Dean smiled as he watched her walk away. Both Gary and Nessa had offered the same advice. Dean just hoped he had enough time to give.

CHAPTER NINE

DEAN'S CONVERSATION with Nessa buoyed his spirits a little, but he was still reluctant to risk talking with Tyler until the first wave of guests had checked out. He wasn't even sure he wanted to risk it around Annie and the others.

The longer things went on, the more determined Dean became to find a way to reach Tyler and the more embarrassed he became by his inability to do it. He let the needs of his guests create a diversion for him—the guided fishing trip for Hugh Morrison and his son, trail rides with the Carters and Takiyamas, repairing the volleyball net after Andy Takiyama lost his footing and fell into it, and cementing the tetherball pole deeper into the ground when Virginia Carter mentioned that it wobbled a little.

With every day that went by, Dean found himself growing closer to changing his mind about marriage and family. When he would walk in and find Annie, Nessa and Tyler deep in conversation or when he heard them laughing together or saw them sitting on the front porch late in the evening, rockers lined up in a row as they studied the sky, he began to envy that kind of closeness.

Night after night, Dean sat at the table surrounded by people and was reminded of all the nights he'd sat inside his Baltimore apartment alone. Sometimes, as he worked in his office, he listened to the footsteps overhead, the doors opening and closing, the water running—sounds that meant he wasn't alone any longer. At times like these, Dean wondered what it would be like to always have people around. He had almost convinced himself that he could be part of a family again—and do it right this time—but just thinking about it scared him back into his shell.

He wasted two weeks after what he'd started thinking of as the boom box incident before he could make himself talk to Tyler, and the wasted time earned him another two hours of argument before he could coax Tyler to ride into town with him. If Gary hadn't intervened, they'd probably still be in a standoff.

Now, on a warm June morning, Dean listened to the hum of tires on asphalt while he drove in to Whistle River. Tyler sat on the other side of the truck, hands locked between his knees, eyes riveted on the window.

While Tyler glared at the passing scenery, he plucked nervously at the denim of his baggy jeans and shot an occasional dagger-sharp look across the truck's cab just in case Dean didn't understand how annoyed he was at this enforced togetherness.

After about ten minutes of this, Dean turned down the stereo and took a stab at breaking the ice. "I've been meaning to thank you," he said, glancing across the truck's cab so he could watch Tyler's reaction.

The boy didn't move a muscle. At least he didn't throw open the door and try to escape.

"You've been working hard this past month," Dean continued. "I appreciate the help."

"Everybody's been working hard." The words fell grudgingly from Tyler's mouth, but hearing four words in a row made Dean feel like uncle of the year.

"That's true, but everyone else isn't here right now. I'm trying to thank *you.*"

Tyler shifted in his seat so that he was facing even farther away.

Dean pressed on, anyway. "I also want to apologize again for what happened that day by the stables. With the boom box."

The kid's right arm twitched.

"I know it's kind of late to be doing this, but I *was* wrong. And I *am* sorry."

Tyler whipped around to face him, his face tense. "I told you then, don't worry about it. I'm used to being blamed for stuff I don't do."

Dean wasn't quite ready to tackle that subject yet. "Gary says you and Nessa have been a big help with the horses." Tyler fell into another stubborn silence. Dean kept talking as if they were actually having a conversation. "Which is great because that's left me free to take care of other problems as they arise."

Tyler scratched his leg, and Dean let himself believe the kid was actually warming up.

They passed a reduced-speed sign just outside town and Dean slowed as the feed-and-grain store came into view. "Everyone else has given me a list of things they want, but I don't know what you need. If there's anything you want while we're here, let me know."

That brought Tyler's head up in a hurry. "I don't need your charity."

Dean glanced at him in surprise. "I'm not offering charity."

"What would you call it?"

Dean hadn't ever considered how Tyler might feel about that aspect of their living arrangements, but the expression in the kid's eyes touched him deep inside. He made a split-second decision. "If it'll make you feel better, I'll give you an advance on your wages today and then deduct it from your check on payday." How he'd manage paying another person was anyone's guess, but he should have thought of it long before now.

Tyler's shoulders shifted slightly and he seemed almost interested. "What wages?"

Dean gave himself a mental pat on the back for doing at least one thing right. "You didn't think I expected you to work this hard for nothing, did you?"

"You don't?"

"Of course I don't. If you work for me, you get paid."

Tyler's gaze came close to actually touching Dean's face. "Does that mean you're paying Nessa, too?"

Dean supposed he was now. "She's working, isn't she?"

"Does she know?"

"Probably not." Dean stepped on the brakes and waited while a mud-splattered pickup pulled out of a parking spot on the side of the street. "The Eagle's Nest isn't a prison, you know."

Tyler's gaze jumped to Dean's face, then away. "Does that mean I can leave?"

Disappointment replaced the hope Dean had been nursing. "It's not up to me," he said. "Your mom's the one in charge."

Tyler flopped back against the seat. "Oh, yeah, like *she'd* say yes."

Dean would rather have avoided talking about Carol. He was still working through his feelings about her drinking again, still trying to decide what he could and should do for Tyler. "You're right. She probably won't agree," he said as the truck moved out of their way. "I understand how you feel, you know. I used to hate the fact that my mom still called the shots when I was your age. I was eager to leave home and make my mark on the world—and absolutely convinced that I would.''

"You have no idea how I feel about my mother.''

"You're right. But I know you're unhappy with what's going on at home, and I'd like to help.''

Tyler's head shot up. "Why?''

"Because you're my nephew. I don't want you to be miserable.''

"Oh, yeah. Right.'' Tyler laughed with a snort. "You care.''

"Yeah. I do.''

"You care that my mom's drinking again? That the SOB she's shacked up with is doing drugs and that she's probably doing them, too?''

Dean's lungs stopped working for a heartbeat or two. "I suspected about the drinking,'' he said when he could trust his voice again. "I had no idea there were drugs involved.''

"Yeah. Well, that's life.''

Dean gripped the wheel with both hands. All the old feelings about his sister came rushing back again. Dean hoped Tyler wouldn't see the weariness on his face. But he couldn't keep it from his voice. "It isn't life, Tyler. Not everyone lives that way.''

Tyler leaned back and propped a foot against the dashboard. "We do.''

"That doesn't make it right.'' Dean tightened his grip and made a decision he'd already put off too long. "What would you think about staying here in the fall?''

Tyler's gaze whipped to his face. "It's only June. I thought she'd at least wait until August to ask.''

"She didn't ask. This is my idea.''

Tyler studied him for a long moment, then turned away again. "Why?"

"Because I don't think that going back there is the best thing for you."

"And staying here is?"

Dean smiled ruefully. "I know I don't have a lot of experience with kids your age—with any kids, for that matter, but it still might be better than going back."

"Forget it."

"I can't do that."

"You don't have to worry about me. I'll be okay. I always am."

"But I do worry. When I didn't know, I could close my eyes and pretend everything was fine. But I *do* know now, and I can't pretend that I don't."

Red-faced, Tyler rounded on him. "I know you want to look like some kind of hero in front of everyone, but I sure wish you'd stop using me to do it."

The reaction caught Dean so unaware, he didn't even notice that he'd run a red light at Whistle River's only traffic signal until a blaring horn brought him back. Shock turned to anger as he pulled up in front of the general store half a block later.

He turned off the engine and shifted to face Tyler. "Do you want to explain what you meant by that?"

"Just what I said."

"You think I'm asking you to stay here so I can look like a hero to someone?"

"Aren't you?"

"No."

Tyler threw open his door and jumped from the truck. "Could've fooled me."

Dean clambered out and planted himself in front of the kid, who stood almost as tall as he did. "You know what,

Tyler? This attitude's getting old. Why don't you just tell me why you hate me so much? I'm getting tired of trying to figure it out on my own.''

Tyler reached into his pocket and pulled out a pack of cigarettes. He shook one from the pack, stuck it between his lips and flicked a lighter. He lifted the flame to the tip, sneering at Dean the whole time.

Dean snatched the cigarette from Tyler's mouth before he could light it and snapped it in half. ''I told you before, you're not smoking as long as you live with me.''

''Fine.'' Tyler took another smoke from the pack. ''Then let me leave.''

Dean grabbed the second cigarette and broke it into pieces. ''If your mother gives permission, I'll put you on a bus this afternoon.''

Tyler seemed ready to go for the pack a third time, then changed his mind. ''Yeah? Well, *that's* not going to happen and you know it. She doesn't want me back home, so you'll get to keep your troubled nephew and show everybody what a great guy you are. That ought to make your year.''

Tyler turned away, but Dean grabbed him by the shoulders and pulled him back around. ''You have *no* idea how wrong you are.''

Tyler rotated his shoulders to break Dean's grip. ''Say what you want, dude. You might even believe it. All *I* know is what I see. You haven't had five minutes for me my whole life, and suddenly you care so much you want me around forever? I don't believe it.''

Dean recoiled and tried to come up with an explanation or even an excuse. There was no defense he could offer, and the anger in Tyler's eyes grew hotter as Dean groped for a response. ''You're right,'' he said at last. ''I haven't been the best uncle in the world. My career took up a lot of time, and I let it. But I've always cared about you.''

Tyler laughed bitterly. "Oh, I *know* how much you care. You can't fool me.'' He held out a hand and wiggled his fingers impatiently. "So if we're through with this tender moment, how about that advance on my wages?''

Dean suddenly regretted making the rash promise. If he gave Tyler money, the kid would probably try to leave town. If he didn't, he'd make himself a liar on top of all his other sins.

He drew out his wallet slowly and counted thirty dollars—enough to let the kid buy a few things but hopefully not enough to bribe some truck driver or tourist to take on a passenger. "Meet me back here at noon," he said as he put the money into Tyler's outstretched palm. "I'll need your help loading the truck.''

Tyler stuffed the money into his pocket and swaggered off down the sidewalk without answering. Dean watched until he rounded a corner on the next block, then let out a heavy breath. He sank onto the tailgate of the truck and rubbed his face with both hands. He'd always liked thinking of himself as competent and capable, but he was in *way* over his head with this one and he had no idea what to do about it.

He was on pins and needles for two full hours, wondering whether or not Tyler would come back. He watched every car and truck that passed to make sure the kid wasn't inside and argued continually with himself about what he'd do if he was.

He'd have to call Carol, of course, but she was no better equipped to handle Tyler than Dean was. Maybe less. He could alert the police, but he had a feeling that would only make things worse. If Tyler tried to leave,

Dean would have to go after him. No matter how anxious Tyler might be to see the last of him, Dean couldn't let someone else take care of his mess.

He just hoped it wouldn't come to that.

By the time his watch hit noon, Dean was a nervous wreck. He was working on his second cola of the morning and pacing behind the truck bed. When Tyler came around the corner at ten minutes after twelve, Dean's knees nearly buckled with relief.

It didn't matter why he'd come back—whether he wanted to be around Dean or was just afraid of leaving. He was here, and Dean still had a chance to reach him. He didn't want Tyler to think that he had doubted him, so he unlatched the tailgate, hopped into the back of the truck and set to work making room for the supplies.

When Tyler drew closer, Dean climbed out again and nodded toward a small white plastic bag in Tyler's hand. "Get everything you need?"

"I guess."

"Good. Let's get this stuff loaded. Annie said she'd have lunch ready at twelve-thirty."

Tyler sent him an odd look, then shrugged. "Okay. Whatever."

Dean jerked his head toward the supplies on the sidewalk. "Why don't you get in the truck? I'll pass this stuff up to you."

Tyler shrugged again, put his bag on the truck's seat, then scrambled into the bed and waited, hands on hips, for Dean to start handing bundles up to him. So far, Dean's shoulder was feeling pretty normal, so he worked carefully to keep from straining it. They'd nearly reached the end of the job when a woman's voice interrupted them. "Dean Sheffield? Is that you?"

He turned toward the unfamiliar voice and saw Coretta

Bothwell, the mayor's mother, hurrying toward him. Her gray hair glistened in the late spring sunshine and her curls bobbed a little with every step. A smile lit her thin face, fueled by her well-known enthusiasm for life.

Coretta was one of those people who liked having a finger in every pie on the stove. No matter what was happening in Whistle River, you'd find her in the middle of the action—and nine times out of ten, in charge of it.

Dean couldn't imagine what she wanted with him.

She shielded her eyes from the sun as she drew closer. "It *is* you, isn't it?"

"It is. How are you, Coretta?"

"I'm fine, of course. Couldn't be better." She dropped her hand from her eyes and touched his arm. "If this isn't a coincidence, I don't know what is. You're *exactly* the man I was planning to call on this afternoon."

Dean lowered the sack of potatoes he was holding to the ground. "What can I do for you?"

"Well, I'll tell you." She turned a bright smile on Tyler. "Just as soon as you tell me who this young man is."

"Tyler Bell," Dean said, willing the kid to be civil. "My nephew. Tyler, this is Mrs. Bothwell. She's the mother of our mayor, among other things."

Tyler muttered something that sounded like a greeting and sat on the side wall of the truck bed. To Dean's amazement, Coretta's smile almost tugged an answering one from the kid's sullen mouth.

"It's always nice to see new faces in town," she said. "Especially when they're on people who plan to stay awhile. How long will you be with us? Permanently, I hope."

Tyler shook his head and actually managed to appear regretful. "I don't know yet. I'll probably just be here for the summer." Coretta seemed disappointed, but Dean couldn't have been more thrilled to hear the kid leaving the door open on the future and making that much of a commitment with his own lips.

"Well, that's too bad," Coretta said. "We could find lots of things for a young man your age to do." She turned away just in time to miss the roll of Tyler's eyes. "I won't keep you hanging, Dean. You might have guessed that we need your help."

"We?"

"The city's summer recreation department."

Coretta had probably volunteered to organize the annual Founder's Day Pancake Breakfast again. Dean had manned a pancake grill at the last sunrise get-together and surprised himself by having a good time. He nodded and bent to pick up the potatoes again. "I'll be happy to help. What do you need me to do?"

"I don't know if you've heard that Hank and Leslie Miner are leaving us."

Dean shook his head and tried to remember who the Miners were. "I hadn't."

"It's a sad day for Whistle River High School losing two teachers at once, but Leslie's expecting a baby and Hank's accepted a job in Spokane."

That was enough to help Dean place the young couple he knew only by sight. "I'll be sorry to see Whistle River lose another family," he said, "but what does that have to do with me?"

"You must know that Hank has been the coach of our Little League baseball team for the past five years."

Dean's smile froze. He had a good idea what was coming next, but Coretta was headed down the wrong road. He'd been thinking about baseball too much already. "Sorry. You'll have to find someone else."

"I know you're busy at the lodge," she said, "but the team will only take a few hours of your time every week."

"That's not very much," Tyler put in.

Dean sent him a warning glance.

"I'd ask someone else," Coretta continued, "but there isn't a soul in town who doesn't have far too much to do, and you're by far the most qualified for the job."

Dean managed to get the potatoes past her and into Tyler's hands. "Sorry, Coretta. Not interested."

"But you know we play a game on Founder's Day every year against the team from Red Lodge. If we don't have a coach, we'll have to cancel. That's a lot of disappointment for nine- and ten-year-olds to handle."

"Yes, but Founder's Day isn't until August. And I never suggested that the kids should go without a coach." Dean reached past her for the bag of new linens Irma had been expecting. "Just that the new coach isn't going to be me. Now, if you'll excuse me—"

"No, I *won't* excuse you." Giving him a disapproving look, Coretta snatched the bag from his hands before he could react. "You're the perfect man for the job, and you know it."

"You could find a dozen people in Whistle River who'd do a better job than I would."

Tyler took off his cap and ran his fingers through his hair to resuscitate a few limp spikes. He worked up an expression of mock concern. "But Uncle Dean, are you *really* going to let those poor little kids suffer?"

Dean could have throttled him. "They won't suffer."

"How do you know?" Tyler smirked and turned to Coretta. "He *would* be a good coach, you know. He's great with kids. You're just asking him the wrong way.

You gotta tell him what a hero he'll be if he does the job. He can't resist that.''

Dean didn't know which emotion was stronger—embarrassment or anger. It took all his self-control not to grab Tyler by the shirt and drag him out of the truck. ''Whatever I've done,'' he snapped. ''Whatever you *imagine* I've done, it doesn't warrant this kind of hostility.''

Coretta glanced from one to the other, and for the first time since Dean had known her she actually seemed at a loss for words. But she recovered quickly and scowled up at Tyler. ''There's no call for rudeness, young man.'' She swiveled back to Dean. ''The town needs you. The kids need you. If that makes you a hero in some people's eyes, well, so be it.''

''My shoulder's worthless,'' Dean reminded her. ''I can't throw a ball anymore. Can't hit. Can't pitch. I'd be about the worst coach you could get.''

''You don't have to *do,* just teach.''

Couldn't she see that he had his hands full with Tyler? ''You can't teach baseball without doing, Coretta. It doesn't work that way. And it should be obvious that I'm no good with *one* kid, much less a whole team full.''

Coretta waved away his argument. ''You'd be great with the kids. I'm sure of it. We'll just have to figure out how to work around that shoulder of yours.'' She tapped her cheek with one finger, still obviously reluctant to abandon her scheme. After a few thoughtful moments, she brightened. ''And I have it. The *perfect* solution. If you'll agree to coach, we'll make Tyler your assistant.''

Tyler shot to his feet. The dismay on his face was almost comical. ''No way. No *way*. I'm not doing it.''

''Of course you are.'' Coretta winked at Dean as if they'd thought of the solution together. ''The town needs your uncle, he needs you. This will give *you* a chance to be a hero.''

For the first time since Tyler had arrived, Dean felt like laughing. Much as he wanted to avoid baseball, he wanted to reach Tyler even more. He pushed back the brim of his hat and propped one foot on a tire. ''You know, Coretta, I think that's the best idea I've heard in days. You've got yourself a coach—and an assistant.''

Coretta's eyes danced. ''Wonderful! You won't regret it. I'll call you with details in a few days.'' She patted his arm, waved to Tyler and hurried away.

''I'm not doing it,'' Tyler called after her, but if she heard him he didn't give any sign. Tyler sighed heavily and glowered at Dean. ''I'm *not* doing it,'' he said again. ''There's no way. *You're* the big baseball hero.''

''And you're the big baseball hero's nephew.'' Dean hoisted a bag of flour and tossed Tyler's own words back at him. ''Are you *really* going to make those poor little kids suffer?''

Tyler's eyes narrowed into slits as he grabbed the bag of flour out of Dean's hands. He swore under his breath and turned away. ''I thought you said I wasn't in prison here,'' he muttered as he tossed the bag onto the stack of supplies. But there wasn't much heat in his argument.

Dean leaned against the tailgate and grinned up at him. ''You aren't in prison. But you helped get me into this coaching job, so I think it's only fair that you help me fulfill my obligation. And who knows, it might even be fun.''

He reached for a bag at his feet, but maybe he'd relaxed *too* much. He stretched the wrong way, and felt the familiar flash of fire through half his body that meant he'd just made a big mistake. Before he could stop himself, an involuntary groan escaped his lips, his legs buckled, and he felt himself dropping to his knees on the sidewalk.

CHAPTER TEN

FURIOUS WITH HIS WEAKNESS, Dean clenched his teeth and tried to pull himself together. Through the haze of pain, he saw Tyler jump from the truck bed and come to stand beside him.

"Are you okay?"

Dean didn't trust himself to open his mouth. He shook his head and touched his other hand to his shoulder, but even the slightest movement made the pain worse. He closed his eyes briefly and bit back a moan.

"Dude, where are your pain pills?"

Tyler sounded worried. Dean must have been hallucinating. He tried to pull the bottle from his pocket, but the pain was too severe. His hand fell uselessly to his side and he fought to control the sudden stinging of tears in his eyes.

"Don't move." Tyler slipped his fingers into Dean's pocket to bring out the bottle himself. "How many? One? Two?"

Dean managed to lift one finger.

"You got something to take this with?" Tyler shook a pill from the bottle and pressed it between Dean's tight lips. He disappeared for a split second, then came back and held something cool against Dean's mouth. "Swallow, dude. You got it down? You okay?"

Dean nodded, and Tyler stuffed the prescription bottle into his own pocket. He sat back on his heels, glowering as if he really cared. "Dude, what did you do that for? I could've loaded this stuff myself."

The genuine concern on Tyler's face stunned Dean almost as much as the pain had. He tried to answer, but he still couldn't concentrate enough to make his voice work.

Tyler scrambled to his feet and came around behind him. "I'm going to get you into the truck, and you're going to sit there while I finish loading up. And then *I'm* driving us back to the ranch. Where are your keys? In the ignition?"

Dean nodded.

"Okay, then." Tyler slipped his hands beneath Dean's arms and lifted him to his feet. The kid's strength amazed Dean, but not half as much as his gentleness. If Tyler had hated him, this would have been a golden opportunity to make sure Dean knew it. Instead, he was handling Dean with kid gloves. It almost convinced Dean that Nessa and Gary were right.

Maybe Tyler *did* like him a little.

BY THE TIME THEY GOT BACK to the Eagle's Nest, the raw edge of pain had diminished, but it still felt as if someone had thrust a burning log into Dean's shoulder. Tyler didn't even give him the option of helping to unload the truck, and Dean was grateful. Shouting for Gary to take his place, Dean ignored Annie's summons to lunch and headed straight to his room.

When he awoke several hours later, the pain had let up a little. It wasn't gone by any means, and he'd have to be careful for a few days. But at least he was somewhat functional again.

He sat on the edge of the bed and rubbed his face gingerly, slowly becoming aware that he hadn't eaten anything since breakfast. Making himself weak with hunger wouldn't help his recovery, so he padded downstairs in his socks and went to the kitchen. He rummaged inside the fridge for something that wouldn't even require the effort of heating it in the microwave.

Luck was with him. He found some leftover orange-glazed chicken, a block of cheese and some melt-in-your-mouth rolls from dinner the night before. When he saw one lone piece of cherry cheesecake on the top shelf, he claimed it and realized that besides needing to apologize to Annie, he also should thank her for not sticking strictly to the menus he'd planned.

He stuck one chicken leg in his mouth and pulled a plate from a cupboard. Turning back to the fridge, he heaped two breasts and another leg onto the plate, wedged the cheese against his side and took a good, long look at the covered containers lined up against one side of the refrigerator. They were all full to the brim, which meant Annie probably intended them for their weekly campfire dinner the next night.

He was just about to open one, anyway, when the kitchen door swished open behind him. He turned to find Annie watching him, arms folded across her breasts. It was the first time he'd been alone with her since their conversation on the porch, and facing her like this made Dean nervous.

She slid her gaze from his face to his plate and back again. "If you'd asked, I would have fixed you something to eat."

Dean pulled the chicken leg from his mouth and grinned sheepishly. "It's no problem. I can do it."

She crossed the room and faced him across the chopping block. "Tyler told us what happened in town. How's your shoulder?"

Embarrassed at having his weaknesses discussed behind his back, Dean shrugged. "Better."

"Is that true, or are you just saying that so I'll drop the subject?"

He laughed a little and felt some of his nervousness abate. "It's true," he said, and moved his shoulder gingerly as proof.

Annie didn't seem impressed by his demonstration. "I hope you plan to take it easy for a few days after this. You could do some permanent damage if you push too hard."

Yesterday, Dean might have been offended by her comment. Today, it made him grin and wiped away the rest of his jumpiness. "Heaven forbid something permanent should happen to my shoulder."

Annie's frown deepened, but a smile lit her eyes. "You know what I mean. I'm sure you don't want to make it worse."

"You're right. I don't. But I won't lie around playing invalid, either." He leaned on the chopping block and put himself at eye level with her. "I won't overdo it. That's a promise."

Her concern was hard to resist. It had been a long time since any woman had cared how he felt. He ran his fingers through his hair and tackled a subject he'd been putting off too long already. "I've been meaning to apologize for being so harsh last time we talked. I guess now is as good a time as any."

Annie pulled back in surprise, but her lips curved into a pleased smile. "Okay, go ahead. Apologize."

Dean stared at her in surprise. "I thought I just did."

"No. You said you wanted to." She grinned wickedly. "That's not an actual apology."

Dean chuckled and made himself more comfortable. "Okay. I apologize. I was pretty harsh the other night."

"Yes, you were. But I think we should share the blame equally. I wasn't at my best, either."

Dean laughed aloud. "I'm glad to know you haven't suffered irreparable emotional damage." The realization that she was as different from Hayley as a woman could get hit him like a bat upside the head. "But I have a feeling it would take more than me being in a bad mood one day to damage you—especially after what you've been through."

Annie sat on a stool and linked her hands together on the counter. Dean couldn't resist coming around the room to stand in front of her. The sparkle in her eyes turned them the color of the sky. If she wore any makeup, it was invisible. She'd pulled her hair into a ponytail that skimmed her shoulders when she moved. She was far more beautiful in a white T-shirt and cutoff jeans than in silks and linens.

But it was her direct approach, her complete lack of guile, that really got him. He couldn't remember Hayley ever being this direct with him. He couldn't remember her ever taking even part of the blame for one of their arguments. When she'd wanted an apology, she'd manipulated one from him and she'd been slow to forgive. The slightest transgression had required flowers and dinner reservations before she'd even consider granting a pardon. Even then, she'd held his failures over his head until he'd finally grown tired of the games and stopped spending money—at which point the cycle would begin again.

Maybe he'd played the game with her because he'd grown up feeling responsible for his mother and Carol, so it had been an easy step to transfer that accountability for everything to his other relationships.

Could it possibly *be* as simple as an apology?

His smile froze, his throat dried, and his heart began to hammer. Suddenly, there was nothing in the world more important than making sure this woman knew how sorry he was. He took her hands in his and stared into her eyes. "I do apologize, Annie. For everything—including doubting that you could fit in here and trying to direct you in your job when you were more than capable of handling it."

She blinked in surprise and the mischievous sparkle faded to the bottom of the sapphire pool. "Thank you." She touched his chest with the tips of her fingers. "I know how hard it is for you to tell me what's in here."

Dean caught her hand again and held it in place. "There's more if you want to hear it." He lifted her hand to his mouth and kissed her palm gently, surprising himself almost as much as he did her. "You scare the hell out of me, Annie Holladay, and that's the absolute truth. I haven't felt like this in a long time, and I'm not quite sure what to do about it."

Annie turned her hand and cupped his cheek gently. "If it helps, you frighten me, too. I'm still in the middle of an ugly divorce. I'm not ready to have feelings for someone else."

"So, what do we do about this?"

Annie shook her head and dropped her hand from his cheek. "I don't know. If we were smart, we'd agree to be friends and leave it at that."

Her answer disappointed him, but he knew she was right. "I agree, that would be the smart thing."

"Neither of us can afford to get involved," Annie continued quickly. "You have the Eagle's Nest and Tyler to worry about. I have to focus on Nessa while I still have her. And I'm leaving for Seattle in a couple of months. We can't forget that.''

Dean brushed a stray wisp of hair away from her mouth and cupped her chin with his fingers. Swallowing thickly, he traced the outline of her lips with the pad of his thumb.

Annie's breath caught and her lips parted slightly. Her eyes darkened with longing, but that only made it harder for Dean to listen to the logical arguments echoing through his mind.

He groaned low in his throat and forced himself to remember what she'd said. She was leaving. Getting involved with her would be foolish. And yet...

He leaned closer, just inches from her mouth. He ached to hold her and touch her lips with his, no matter how briefly. And he could tell from the look in her eyes, the uneven sound of her breath, the slight shudder when he moved his thumb against her cheek, that she wanted it as much as he did.

She moistened her lips in anticipation, and that was Dean's undoing. He inched closer, hardly breathing, unable to take his eyes from hers until her lids fluttered shut and she lifted her mouth to meet his.

"Mom?"

Dean jerked backward in surprise. Annie's eyes flew open.

"Mom? Where are you?"

Footsteps pounded on the back porch and Dean backed away from Annie just as Nessa burst through the back door. Annie stood quickly, nearly knocking over her stool in the process.

Aching with frustration, struggling to get his brain

working again, Dean crossed to the refrigerator and stood in front of the open door to cool himself off.

Nessa didn't even seem to notice him. "You've got to come see this, Mom. Can you? Please? Or are you busy with dinner?"

Annie's hand fluttered to her chest as if she was having as much trouble returning to reality as Dean was. She nodded hesitantly and sent a silent apology to Dean over her shoulder. "Of course I can come, sweetheart. What is it?"

"You have to see what Gary taught me. It's *so* cool." The door closed behind them and their voices faded away.

Dean stared after them, mopped his face with one hand, then closed the refrigerator door and gathered his lunch from the counter. He made a face at the cold chicken and carried it toward his office. He could stop his stomach from growling, but the other hunger Annie'd awoken in him was a whole lot stronger.

And he had no idea how long he'd have to wait to satisfy it.

DEAN COULDN'T REMEMBER ever being so nervous before in his life. He was forty-five minutes into his first Little League practice, and he was failing miserably. Sweat poured down his back and dripped into his eyes. His head felt as if a brass marching band was practicing inside it. He was edgier than he'd been on his first day at spring training and more nervous than when he'd stepped onto the field to play his first Major League game.

And he was completely on his own.

He shouldn't have been surprised that Tyler had refused to come with him. The softening he'd seen that day in town had disappeared again almost as quickly as

Dean's pain had. But it had been enough to convince Dean that he would eventually be successful. He just couldn't give up.

Right now, he needed to pay attention to the job at hand. He stood on the pitcher's mound with a dozen sets of little eyes watching his every move, painfully aware of his own inadequacies.

Why had he ever agreed to this? Much as he hated doing it, he'd been taking his pain pills more regularly. His aversion to needing the medication was losing ground against his desire to be the kind of man Annie could admire, the kind of uncle Tyler needed, the kind of friend Gary, Les and Irma deserved. Still, his muscles screamed in protest at every movement, and he alternated between a love for the game he'd tried hard to forget and a slight case of envy that these children could do what he couldn't.

He took a slow, calming breath and checked the kids to make sure they'd taken the positions he'd assigned them. The team's ringleader, an auburn-haired, freckle-faced nine-year-old named Rusty, stood on the pitcher's mound.

Rusty's hands were parked on his hips and impatience wrinkled his narrow face. "*Now* what?"

Dean resisted the urge to massage his shoulder. "Now," he shouted loud enough for everyone to hear him, "you'll spend some time throwing the ball from one position to the other. Zachary, Zoe and Nicole need to be able to hit the pitcher's mound from the outfield. Rusty, you need to hit each of the basemen without even thinking."

"I don't want to hit anybody," Nicole protested. "I'm not supposed to hit. And I don't want Rusty to hit *me*."

Dean waved away her concerns. "He won't, Nicole. I only meant that you need to get the ball to them."

"But I can't *throw* that far." Nicole gave her blond curls a toss and sat hard on the ground. "I don't even want to *play* baseball."

Ah, but her parents wanted her to, and so here she was. Lucky for everyone else on the team.

Zoe, a fellow outfielder, made no effort to hide her disgust. "You can, too, throw that far. Quit being such a big baby." She turned to Dean with a roll of her eyes. "She's always such a crybaby."

Nicole shouted something in reply. Rusty snapped at both girls to be quiet. Bobby Baker on second base got into the act by offering his opinion, and Dean turned away to check his watch. This had been one of the longest afternoons of his entire life.

He stepped onto the field and waved his good arm over his head. "All right, team! Let's can it, okay? Nicole, I want you to do your best. If you can't get the ball all the way to Rusty, then throw it to…Pudge at shortstop."

Dean hesitated over the nickname. Why any kid would prefer to be called "Pudge" instead of Chris was beyond him, but that's what the kid said he wanted, and who was Dean to argue? Now, if only Pudge would stand up and stop looking for shamrocks in the grass…

Dean called him once, twice, three times before Pudge glanced up from the great shamrock hunt and blinked in surprise at hearing his name. When he realized that Dean was actually speaking to him, his dark eyes grew wide in his round face and he scratched at the buzz cut on his head. "What?"

"Stand up, please. I need you to be ready for the ball."

"Why?"

"Because we're practicing." Dean pulled a couple of

balls from the canvas equipment bag on the ground beside him, tossed one to Rusty and said a silent prayer for a sudden rainstorm to put him out of his misery.

Rusty caught the ball and hurled it back to Dean without even taking a breath. "Why don't you hit the ball to us? That's what our other coach used to do."

Dean caught it and lobbed it right back. "Because I'm not your other coach and you might have to get used to a few changes."

Rusty wound up and let the ball fly again. "But just throwing the ball around is stupid."

This time the ball stung Dean's palm when he caught it. He held on to it for a few seconds, debating how to handle the challenge from a nine-year-old. He glanced at the other team members, who were watching with rapt interest—except for Pudge, who didn't seem to care about anything but whether or not shamrocks grew behind second base.

Dean turned away from Rusty and tossed the ball to Zachary on first base instead. "Okay, Zach, if Rusty's not ready, we'll let you start."

"*Zach-a-ree*," the boy corrected him. "My name's Zach-a-ree, not Zach."

"Right. I won't make that mistake again." Dean nodded toward the boy's twin sister in right field. "Okay, Zachary, you throw to Zoe. Zoe, you throw to Bobby. Bobby to Nicole, and so on around the field. Pudge, stand up. We're ready." Dean moved toward the backstop and checked his watch again.

Bobby sneezed violently and rubbed his eyes with both hands. "Wait a sec. I need to take a hay-fever pill before we start."

Of course he did. Dean dropped the ball into his glove

and mopped his forehead with his sleeve. "Do you have your medicine with you?"

Bobby started toward the short stack of bleachers at the edge of the field. "In my backpack."

Even so, it took five full minutes to find the box, squeeze out a pill, and choke it down with water. It took another ten minutes to get the team back into order when Bobby returned. But the short break hadn't changed Rusty's mind. He still wanted nothing to do with anything Dean suggested.

He watched the ball go around the field for a few minutes, then threw down his glove and stormed away from the pitcher's mound. "I don't know why they asked *you* to coach," he shot at Dean as he walked away. "You stink at it."

Yeah? Well, Dean could've told him that.

He picked up his glove and worked his hand into it. Watched as the ball hit the ground in front of Pudge and rolled away. Winced when Nicole started crying about a grass stain on her shorts. And sighed softly when another fit of sneezing cost Bobby an easy catch.

He took Rusty's place and spent the last few minutes of practice disobeying doctor's orders. He couldn't do much and his shoulder burned like hell when he was finished, but he thought a couple of the kids had made a little progress by the time practice was over, and in a strange way he felt better than he had in a long time.

ANNIE HUMMED SOFTLY as she put away the groceries she'd picked up on a quick trip into Whistle River with Irma and Les. She'd been lucky enough to find fresh pears and blackberries at a roadside stand, which she planned to turn into individual pear charlottes with vanilla bean crème anglaise and blackberry compote—a hit at Holladay House. She hoped the guests at the Eagle's Nest would be equally impressed by the dessert.

She worked quickly, mindful of the time as she made room in the pantry for the few extras she'd added to the shopping list at the last minute. She had a lot of work to do before dinner, and she'd discovered long ago not to skimp on cooking time or to rush herself through preparations. She did her best to keep her mind focused on the task at hand. But ever since that near-kiss with Dean two weeks before, she'd been having serious trouble concentrating.

She really should be glad Nessa had interrupted. Annie wasn't ready to embark on another emotional roller coaster—and only a fool would imagine that a relationship with Dean, no matter how brief, could be anything else.

Kissing him might have put a salve on her bruised ego, but that's the only good that could possibly have come from it. It was nice to know that someone found her attractive, but that's *all* she felt. It's all she could possibly feel. And using Dean to bolster her spirits would be wrong.

So why was she having such trouble putting that moment out of her mind? Why was she so painfully aware of Dean whenever he was around? And so easily distracted by daydreams when he wasn't?

She forced her thoughts into line and clenched her teeth to help her stay focused. She concentrated so hard that when the phone rang a few minutes later she didn't consciously hear it until the fourth ring. When she realized that Irma must be out, she hurried out of the pantry and snagged the receiver before the caller grew tired of waiting.

"Eagle's Nest Dude Ranch."

"May I speak with Annie Holladay, please?"

Spence's voice on the heels of her thoughts about Dean jerked her firmly into the moment. What did he want now? Determined not to start an argument, she tried not to sound irritated. "It's me, Spence."

"Don't tell me they have you playing receptionist now?"

"It's not like that." Annie stretched the phone cord toward the counter and pulled a few cans from a grocery bag. "I'm a little busy right now, so can we skip the part where you pass judgment on my decisions and go straight to your reason for calling?"

To her surprise, Spence laughed softly. "I didn't call to pass judgment. I called to present a business proposition."

Annie carried the cans toward the pantry and nudged the door open with her hip. "What kind of business proposition?"

"I'm going to ask this again. Straight out. Come back to Chicago. *Work* with me, even if you don't want to *be* with me."

Annie dropped a can of garbanzo beans dangerously close to her foot. She hopped out of the way and leaned against the door while the can rolled to the other side of the kitchen. "Are you kidding?"

"Do I *sound* like I'm kidding?"

"No. But you should be. It would never work."

"Why not? We've worked in this restaurant together for sixteen years. We ran it for twelve. For you to walk away now is just…well, it's foolish, that's what it is."

"Not from where I stand."

"Are you honestly going to tell me that you're satisfied with what you're doing now? Or that you really *want* to spend the rest of your life teaching people how to do the job you love?''

Annie wanted to argue with him, but she *wasn't* satisfied making meat loaf and pot roast. Dean hadn't complained about the items she'd added to his meal plans and she'd received glowing compliments from the guests, but the artistic challenge she loved just wasn't there. And her doubts about how happy she'd be teaching Knife Skills 101 and the Basics of Béchamel Sauce had been growing steadily.

Spence knew her too well.

''That's not the point,'' she managed to say after an uncomfortably long pause. ''I can't do what I was doing before.''

''That's *exactly* the point,'' Spence argued. ''You can. I'm *offering* you the chance to do what you were doing before. I'm asking you to do it.''

''I've severed my ties with Holladay House. I'm not interested in moving backward.''

''What's backward about doing what you were meant to do?''

Annie felt a deep-seated resentment begin to stir. As he had done too often during their marriage, Spence was blindsiding her, leaving her off balance and ill-equipped to fight back. While he presented an argument he'd perfected to a T, she had to scramble just to answer coherently.

''What about the legal agreement?'' She regretted asking the instant the question left her mouth. It sounded as if she was considering his offer.

''The agreement can be amended in court. There's no sane reason not to come back, Annie.''

''There's no sane reason *to* go back, Spence. You can't

really think I could come to work and see you every day, knowing that you're going home to Catherine.''

. ''Look,'' Spence said, sighing heavily as he always did when something began to try his patience. ''I know it wouldn't be easy. I'm not that naive. Believe it or not, it wouldn't be easy on me, either. Facing you every day after what I did to you…?''

He broke off for a minute and Annie could almost see him lowering his head and cradling his forehead in his palm. ''But it's bigger than both of us, Annie. This restaurant needs both of us. We're not children. We ought to be able to get through the rough times, just like we always have.''

Annie opened her mouth to say no again, but Spence kept talking. ''If nothing else, think about Nessa. She's not happy with this arrangement we have, and you know it. She needs you, Annie. You're her mother. Catherine will do her best, but she'll be no real substitute for you.''

Annie bit back the refusal she'd been about to offer. *Damn Spence.* Did he believe that? Or did he know that it was the one argument she couldn't stand up against? She sat at the table again. ''This is all coming out of left field,'' she said uncertainly. ''I'm not sure how I feel about it.''

''That's fair. At least you're listening. Don't answer me right now. Take your time and think it through, okay? If you decide to come back to Chicago, we'll take the fee for breaking your contract with the institute out of the restaurant's profits. It will be worth it.''

''Spence—''

''*Think* about it, Annie. That's all I'm asking.''

CHAPTER ELEVEN

LATER THAT EVENING, Annie sat on a camp stool near the dwindling fire and tried to savor the success of another successful meal. The guests had raved about the Dutch-oven stew and the pear charlottes, but their comments weren't enough to satisfy her and she hated Spence for making her so aware of it.

Earlier, after spending all afternoon caramelizing pear slices in sugar and assembling the charlottes, the blaze from the fire had seemed blistering and unwelcome. Now, with the sun behind the mountains, the temperature had dropped so dramatically, she leaned eagerly toward the flame and held out her hands for its welcome heat.

Four more families had checked in that afternoon, and everyone on staff had spent the evening making sure they had everything they needed. The guests seemed pleased and Dean had been all smiles as they'd reluctantly wandered away from the fire to retire for the night.

But Spence's phone call had left Annie distracted and jumpy all evening—and painfully aware that a full month had gone by and her plans to spend the summer bonding with Nessa were going up in smoke. If Nessa wasn't busy, Annie was. If Annie had a free moment, Tyler was being especially charming and Nessa just couldn't tear herself away.

She glanced at Dean, who stood across the clearing with Gary discussing plans for the next day. Irma and

Les had disappeared, presumably back to Whistle River for the night. She searched for Nessa and found her walking toward the far edge of the clearing with Tyler. Nessa had stopped complaining about boredom, but her growing closeness to Tyler was starting to concern Annie.

What had started as friendship was quickly becoming something more. Annie's feelings for Dean made her even more aware of the sparks flying between Nessa and Tyler, and at Nessa's age, sparks could be dangerous.

Suddenly eager to have some control over some aspect of their lives, Annie called out. Both kids stopped walking and turned back toward her as if they were joined at the waist.

Nessa leaned forward slightly and peered through the dark. "What, Mom?"

"I'm about ready to go back up to the lodge. Do you want to walk with me?"

Even in the dark, Annie could sense Nessa's frown of disapproval. "Not *now*. We're going for a walk."

"In the woods? This late?"

Nessa glanced at the trees behind her. "Um...*yeah.*"

Annie tried not to sound unduly worried. "Would you come here for a minute before you go?"

Nessa hesitated, waited for Tyler's reaction, then trudged back across the clearing with Tyler a step behind. When they reached the flat stone circle Dean had built around the fire pit, Tyler held back.

The fire popped, and sparks flew into the sky. Nessa folded her arms and rested her weight on one leg. "What?"

"It's after dark, sweetheart. Do you really think it's smart to take off into the woods?"

"We're not going into the woods. We're just going to walk down by the creek."

Annie blinked a couple of times and processed what seemed like a convoluted bit of logic. "Don't you have to go through the woods to get to the creek?"

"Not really."

"Yes, you do. And I'd rather you didn't."

Nessa shifted her weight and her expression grew even more pained. "So, what are you saying?"

"That I'd rather you didn't go."

"Why not?"

"Because, honey. It's late. We all have to get up early in the morning."

Nessa gaped at her. "Where did *that* come from? I've been staying up later than this every night we've been here."

"That doesn't mean we have to continue."

Nessa studied Annie closely for a long minute. "What's wrong, Mom? You've been acting weird all night."

Annie wasn't ready to tell Nessa about her dad's offer. Nessa would encourage her to accept it and Annie wasn't sure she could think clearly under the pressure. She focused on the other issue bothering her. "Why don't you sit down for a minute. I think we should talk about this."

"About what?"

"You and Tyler. I'm getting a little worried about how close you're becoming."

Nessa took a quick step backward. "We're friends, Mom. Is that okay with you?"

"Of course. As long as that's all it is."

Nessa darted a glance at Tyler, glowered at Annie and dropped her voice to a whisper. "Would you please quit treating me like a baby? We just want to walk over to the creek."

"I'm not treating you like a baby," Annie said softly. "I'm just asking you to use a little common sense."

Firelight flickered and shadows danced across Nessa's face. "What do you think's going to happen? That Tyler's going to attack me as soon as we're out of sight?"

"No!" Annie glanced over her shoulder to make sure no one could overhear them. "That's not what worries me."

"Oh. So you think *I'm* going to attack *him?*"

"I'm not worried about anyone *attacking* anyone else. But I am worried about you putting yourself into a compromising position and then losing control of it."

Nessa tossed her head angrily. "I'm a lot smarter than you give me credit for, Mom."

"It's not a question of how smart you are," Annie said, struggling to keep her voice level. "Intelligent people get into situations they can't control all the time."

Nessa moved still closer. "We just want to take a walk. Why do you have to make a big deal out of it? Nobody else does."

Annie glanced at Tyler, who seemed as unhappy with her as Nessa. She darted another glance at Dean and Gary. It was true that neither of them seemed even slightly concerned about the two kids wandering off in the dark together—but, then, neither of them was this teenage girl's mother.

"I know you don't understand why I'm worried," she said to Nessa. "Maybe you will when you have a daughter of your own. Until then, you're just going to have to accept my decision."

Nessa's eyes flashed with a mixture of hurt, anger and embarrassment. "That's not *fair*."

"I know you don't think so now," Annie began.

But Nessa wasn't listening. "It's times like these when

I can't *wait* to live with Dad," she shouted. The instant the words left her mouth, her eyes flew wide and regret was written all over her face. But that didn't stop her from bolting across the clearing and disappearing into the trees, or Tyler from following only a step behind.

DEAN WATCHED FROM the shadows as Annie argued with Nessa. He felt the weight of her concern as the two kids disappeared along the path toward the lodge, but he waited a couple of minutes before pulling a camp stool over to sit beside her.

"Are you okay?" he asked softly.

She nodded slowly. "I think so. How much did you hear?"

The hurt on her face was so raw, Dean could almost feel it. "Enough."

"And I thought I was keeping my voice down."

Dean shrugged. "Sounds carry at night."

"I'll remember that." A breeze gusted from the mouth of the canyon and Annie shivered slightly. "I wonder if I ever said anything that hurt my mother like this when I was Nessa's age."

Dean decided to go along with her efforts to lighten the mood. "Of course you didn't. Just like I never had a bit of attitude. We were both perfect angels. I'm sure of it."

Annie laughed and brushed hair away from her forehead. "That helps." They sat in silence for a few minutes before she spoke again. "You're missing your cue. This is the part where you tell me not to worry. That Tyler's a good kid and you trust him completely."

Dean leaned forward and rested his arms on his thighs. "Tyler's a good kid," he said without inflection. "I trust him completely."

Annie glanced at him out of the corner of her eye. "Do you mean that?"

"I hope so." He linked his hands together and smiled to ease the worry on her face. "I don't think they've gone too far yet. And Tyler seems to genuinely like Nessa, so I don't think he's looking for a conquest."

Annie let out a soul-deep sigh. "That's not very comforting."

"I know, but the truth is I hardly know Tyler. I *think* he's a good kid and I do trust him to a point, but we don't have a very long history and I can't offer any absolute guarantees."

Annie stretched her legs out in front of her. "I've noticed that things are a little strained between the two of you, but it's been better the last couple of weeks, hasn't it?"

"Things aren't any worse. That's a definite plus."

Annie smiled softly. "I've been curious about your relationship, but I haven't wanted to pry."

"Afraid I'll bite your head off?"

"You're not *that* touchy," she said, putting more warmth into her smile. "And now that I know what a great apology you offer, I'm ready to chance it—if it's okay with you, that is."

Dean nodded slowly, not at all sure how to explain his family and a little nervous about how she would react. "It's a long story."

"I'm not going anywhere for a while. I don't think Nessa will be waiting to make cocoa over girl-talk right away, and it will probably be smart to let her simmer down before I talk to her again. So tell me about the two of you. Tyler seems so angry with you sometimes, I can't figure out why he's here."

"That makes two of us." Dean was amazed by the

strength and understanding he saw in her eyes. He'd only known her a month, yet it seemed as if he'd known her forever. And the need to share some of the burden they were each carrying—if only for a moment—was almost overpowering.

"Tyler's mom and I are the only kids in our family," he said after a moment. "Our dad died shortly after Carol was born. Mom died when I was twenty-one and Carol was still in high school."

Annie's expression sobered instantly. "I'm sorry. I had no idea."

Dean shrugged. "It was a long time ago."

"Yes, but still—"

Dean wasn't ready to delve *that* far into his emotional waters. He kept his gaze riveted on the fire and tried to stay focused on what he felt comfortable telling her. "Losing Mom was hard on both of us, but I think it affected Carol more than it did me. Before Mom's diagnosis, Carol was a straight-A student. She followed all the rules and never got into trouble. But afterward—" He broke off, remembering. "It was almost as if Carol felt responsible for Mom's cancer. As if losing her proved something horrible to Carol about herself."

The fire popped and a log slid to the edge of the pit. Dean leaned forward and nudged it back into place with the toe of his boot. "Losing Mom was a whole lot rougher on Carol than I realized at the time. I was just getting out of college, full of myself, and determined to *be* somebody. I'd gotten into the university on a baseball scholarship, and coming out, I had a shot at the Major League. I took it."

"And made it?"

He nodded. "And then, suddenly, it was just Carol and me. I was oldest so I felt responsible, but I was scared half to death that I'd fail." He paused, surprised that he'd just admitted that aloud. No one, not even his closest friends, knew how frightened he'd been. "Carol told me she was okay, and it made everything easier to believe her. I poured all my energy and frustrations into my career. Carol poured hers into booze and men."

Annie's gaze drifted to his again. Her eyes reflected the firelight. Her skin glowed from the cool night air and the heat of the blaze. "Sounds like she was looking for someone to take care of her."

"Maybe. Probably." Dean glanced around to make sure Tyler hadn't come back, and lowered his voice just in case. "It was as if she'd suddenly turned into a magnet for every loser on the planet. She got pregnant and had Tyler. And she went through one boyfriend after another so quickly afterward, I never knew who she was going to be with when I called. But I always knew there'd be somebody and I always knew that she'd be drunk."

Annie touched his hand gently. "That couldn't have been easy to watch."

He turned his hand over and closed it around hers. "It *wasn't* easy, so I didn't watch." That admission surprised him as much as the first one had. He smiled sheepishly and dropped his gaze to their joined hands. "I hated seeing what she was doing to herself. Hated wondering if this guy was married, or if that one was on drugs, or if the next one was abusing her. Nothing I ever said made any difference, except to make her increasingly angry with me."

"It's human nature to get angry with people who make us face the truth."

Dean had been guilty of that a few times. He let out a shaky breath and nodded. "Yeah, it is. Things went on that way for a few years and then, suddenly, Carol met this decent guy and actually married him. She seemed happy and settled and he was a good stepfather for Tyler...and I was thrilled. My career was stalled and needed all my attention.''

He relaxed as the conversation moved further away from his own mistakes. ''When Tyler was eleven, Carol's husband left and things started up again. Carol's ex-husband hasn't made contact with Tyler in months. I've never met the guy she's with now, but Tyler doesn't like him. Carol thinks Tyler's stealing from her, but Tyler insists Randy's the guilty one.''

Annie glanced toward the lodge. ''And now Tyler's here, hurt that his mom doesn't trust him, angry because the only dad he knows doesn't want him, and furious with you because you haven't spent enough time with him over the years.''

She'd hit the nail so squarely on the head, Dean let out an embarrassed laugh. ''Sometimes I feel responsible for what Carol and her ex-husband, Brandon, have done. But I can't bridge the gap they've left in Tyler's life, no matter how hard I try. And it wasn't that I didn't want to spend time with him. I just couldn't. The team was on the road for weeks at a time, and Carol and Brandon moved around a lot. There'd be long gaps in time when I didn't even know where to find them.''

Annie squeezed his hand gently and sent him a side-long glance. ''That last part makes a nice story, but what's the truth?''

Dean pulled back sharply. ''That *is* the truth.''

''You *couldn't* spend time with him? Or you used your career as an excuse not to?''

''I couldn't,'' he said firmly.

''Tyler's a smart kid, Dean. Smart enough to understand that people only do what they really want to. We just justify our decisions with excuses to make them more palatable. You can *say* you wanted to see him all you want, but the fact is that if you'd honestly wanted to, you'd have found a way—and he must know that.''

Her observation sliced through every excuse he'd ever created. He tried like hell to come up with a response that didn't sound self-serving but couldn't. ''You're probably right,'' he said at last. ''I could have flown in to see him. I was making enough money.''

''In that case, you could have flown him to where you were.''

Dean acknowledged that with a dip of his head and thought about what Tyler had said in town. ''I never had five minutes to spare for him. That's what he told me the other day.''

Annie tilted her head to one side. ''Well, now we know why he's so angry. What are you going to do about it?''

''That's the problem. I don't know what to do.''

''Of course you do. You're far better with him than you think you are.''

She might never know how much that simple vote of confidence meant to him. ''I guess I'll keep doing what I've been doing, then. I'll try to talk sense into Carol and try to get through to Tyler. But if you have any other suggestions, I'm open.''

Annie shook her head. ''Maybe he just needs you to acknowledge the truth. Tell him just what you've told me.''

''You don't think I've done that? I've told him everything, short of bad-mouthing his mother. That's one thing I won't do, no matter how disappointed I am in her.''

Annie let a few seconds lapse, then shifted on her stool to face him. ''The whole time you were talking I kept waiting for you to say that you love Tyler, but you never did. I can't help wondering if *he's* noticed that you never say it.''

Dean stiffened under the implied criticism. ''He should know I do. He's my sister's kid.''

''When was the last time you told him?''

''That I love him?'' Dean started to answer, realized he couldn't remember and clamped his mouth shut. He remembered how angry Hayley used to get because he couldn't say those words to her, how angry she'd been the night of the accident. He felt the familiar tightening in his chest begin, the way it always did when someone pressured him about his emotions, but this time he tried to overcome the sensation.

''I don't say those words easily,'' he admitted. ''I never have.''

Even now, Annie's eyes held no censure. ''They're important words,'' she said simply. ''I have the feeling Tyler doesn't hear them very often.''

She might be right, but the risk involved in actually saying those words aloud to Tyler was a huge one. ''I'm not sure Tyler *wants* to hear those words from me,'' he said after a long time.

Annie brushed a lock of hair off her shoulder and her lips curved slowly. ''Everyone likes to hear that someone loves them. And it's obvious that you love him deeply, so it wouldn't be a lie. If it makes a difference in his life, isn't it worth the risk? I'd say them a thousand times a day if they'd make Nessa change her mind about living with Spence and Catherine.''

Dean jumped at the chance to move onto a new subject. He released her hand and slipped his arm around her shoulders. ''Is this the part where I tell you that everything's going to work out fine in the end?''

Annie laughed and leaned against him as if she'd been

made to fit there. "That would be nice to hear, even if I don't believe it."

Dean tilted her chin and looked deep into her eyes. "Trust me, Annie. Everything's going to work out fine in the end."

Her eyes locked on his and searched the depths of his soul. More than anything, he wished for the strength to make things right in her world. She sighed softly and her eyelids flickered closed for a heartbeat. "I'd love to believe you."

Dean traced the outline of her lips with his thumb, just the way he'd done that day in the kitchen. Fire burned deep inside his belly, and he wanted her so much he could hardly breathe. "I could try another tactic to persuade you."

Annie's eyes opened wide and her lips warmed beneath his touch. "That might help."

With his heart in his throat, Dean dipped his head and grazed her lips with his. It was nothing more than a feather-soft touch, but scorching heat shot through him in response. She melted against him and ran her hands up his back, holding him tightly and pulling him to her.

Her eagerness sent his desire off the charts, but he forced some restraint. He ran his tongue lightly along the open space between her lips. When she responded by parting her lips to invite more, Dean groaned with pleasure and felt her answering sigh in the very center of his being.

The urge to lower her to the ground and make love to her was almost more than he could resist, but knowing that anyone might find them this way helped him hang on to a little common sense. He could have spent the rest of the night kissing her, but he forced himself to pull away. His breathing was rough and ragged, his heart hammered in his chest. He searched Annie's eyes and face, saw her pulse jumping in the hollow of her throat and had to force himself not to cover it with his lips.

It took a few seconds to pull himself together enough to say, "I thought we were just going to be friends."

Annie slid her hands from his shoulders and grinned wickedly. "That was pretty friendly."

"It was, wasn't it?" Dean's smile was so broad it almost hurt. He tried to look solemn. "I had no idea how rewarding a platonic friendship could be."

Annie snuggled against his chest, wrapped her arms around his waist and trailed her fingertips along his side. "Neither did I. But you know, we really shouldn't do that again."

Dean drew back slightly. "Give me one good reason why not."

"There's Nessa. And Tyler. And the Eagle's Nest. And—"

"I said *one* good reason, not half a dozen." Dean took her hands again and stood, pulling her to her feet with him. "Is that what you really want?"

Annie nodded, wide-eyed and straight-faced. "It is. Nessa's having so much trouble adjusting to the divorce, I really can't throw a new relationship at her. And Gary...well, Gary loves to tease and I'd be foolish to just hand him ammunition."

Dean drew her away from the fire, into the shadows of the aspen. He bent to kiss her again, but Annie stopped him. "Tyler's confused and hurt enough. It would be weird and uncomfortable for everyone if you and I started seeing each other this way."

Dean sighed with regret. "Not to mention the fact that you're still, technically, married."

The shadows bathed her face, but he could see the slight frown that curved her lips. "Only until August."

"Still…"

"You're right," she said with a soft sigh. "We really would be asking for trouble if we got any more involved."

"So we're agreed? No more?"

"Absolutely no more." Before he could react, she stood on tiptoe and caught his mouth with hers for another soul-wrenching kiss and then pulled away to let him see the twinkle in her eye. "Starting first thing tomorrow."

"WHAT'S UP WITH YOU?" Gary demanded about thirty seconds after Dean stepped into the kitchen the next morning.

Dean stopped whistling and glanced at his friend in surprise. "With me? Nothing. Why?"

Gary's eyes widened and his brows winged upward. "*Why?* Just take a gander in the mirror, buddy. You're acting like a different man this morning."

Dean laughed uneasily and tried not to make eye contact with Annie. They might have agreed to be more than buddies last night, but all the reasons they'd discussed for keeping their relationship under wraps still existed—and they were all sitting at the breakfast table behind him. "What's wrong with me?"

"It's not that something's *wrong,*" Gary said, raising one eyebrow speculatively. "Just different."

Dean shut the refrigerator and turned around to find four more sets of eyes watching him intently. Tyler had stopped buttering toast, Nessa held a glass of orange juice halfway to her mouth, Irma held a spoonful of scrambled eggs over her plate, and Les had stopped chewing. In fact, Annie—who'd suddenly developed an intense interest in muffin batter—was the only person in the room *not* staring at him.

"What is it?" he demanded again. "Do I have toothpaste on my cheek or something?"

Nessa recovered first, sipped her juice and set her cup on the table. "No. But Gary's right. You seem different."

Tyler started moving his butter knife again. "You were whistling."

Dean let out a relieved laugh. "I whistle a lot. You know that."

Irma spooned the eggs onto her plate and nudged Les with one elbow to get him chewing again. "Not *that* song."

"What song?" Dean tried to remember, but whistling was such an instinctive thing with him, he rarely thought about it.

Gary pursed his lips and the first few notes of "Take Me Out to the Ball Game" filled the room.

Dean willed away the flush he felt creeping into his cheeks and thought about that old saying—that the two things a man can't hide are when he's drunk and when he's in love. He didn't think his feelings for Annie had gone quite that far, but maybe it was equally difficult for a man to hide the fact that he'd been necking by the campfire.

With a silent promise to disguise his emotions better in the future, he crossed to the table nonchalantly. "It's a great day," he said. "We have three cabins full of paying guests and none of their credit cards were rejected when I ran them through the computer. It doesn't get much better than that."

"Whatever the reason," Irma said with a quick glance at Annie, "it's nice to see you so chipper."

Dean helped himself to two pieces of toast and changed the subject. "Does anybody know if the Jorgensens decided to take that trail ride today?"

Gary nodded and leaned back in his seat. "All four of 'em want to go. And the Feeneys decided to go with them. I thought I'd take Nessa and Tyler along to help out, if that's okay. The more experience they get with small groups, the better it'll be when a large group comes along."

Identical ear-to-ear grins erupted on Tyler's and Nessa's faces. They both seemed thrilled, and Dean's instinctive response was to say yes, but he didn't out of respect for Annie.

He glanced at her for the first time, noticed her trim-fitting jeans and loose denim blouse, and struggled to keep his voice sounding normal when he spoke. "Is it okay with you if Nessa goes along?"

Annie didn't answer until she'd finished filling the muffin pans and joined them at the table. "I don't have any problem with you going," she said to Nessa at last. "Just be careful. You're not used to riding in the hills."

Gary said something about keeping an eye on the kids, but Nessa's delighted shriek drowned him out. She bounded out of her chair, threw her arms around Dean's neck and sent Annie a look filled with a mixture of left-over resentment and imminent forgiveness. She bounded away and Dean took advantage of the moment to put one hand on Tyler's shoulder—casually, as if he did it every day.

Tyler stiffened a little and he didn't quite look at Dean, but at least he didn't pull away. Mentally chalking up his first tiny victory, Dean moved his hand and dove into breakfast as if nothing unusual had happened. But he could tell by the furtive glances Tyler kept shooting at him that he'd either done something very right...or very wrong.

CHAPTER TWELVE

ANNIE KEPT ONE EYE on the door as she pulled her hair into a ponytail. Steam from her shower hovered near the ceiling and traveled outside through a partially open window high over her head. It might have been early July, but the cool morning air drifting past her shoulders drew an occasional shiver as she went through her morning ritual. She hardly noticed.

She had other things on her mind this morning. She hadn't been able to stop thinking about Spence's offer, and she still didn't know how she felt about it. She couldn't deny that the idea of going back to Holladay House was tempting on one level, but that might only have been because it felt safe and familiar. The idea of working with Spence after everything they'd been through still left a bad taste in her mouth.

The glittering appeal of teaching at the culinary institute and relocating to a city where she didn't know a single soul was dulling a little more every day—but that might have been fear talking.

To make matters even more confusing, Annie had started entertaining fantasies about Dean at odd times during the day. She'd be dicing vegetables on the chopping block and she'd imagine him coming into the kitchen behind her and burying his face in her neck. Or she'd be heading toward the showers and suddenly envision him waiting for her at the bottom of the stairs. Or she'd be making her bed and her imagination would transport her to Dean's room at the end of the hall, and images would fill her mind that made it almost impossible to pretend she didn't feel anything for him when the others were around.

And the thing was, she didn't *want* to pretend any longer.

Her reasons for wanting to keep their budding relationship secret seemed to evaporate when they sat at the dinner table together or across from each other at breakfast. She loved watching him with his guests—pointing out the best fishing holes on a map or teaching someone to gut and clean their catch. She took comfort from the sound of his voice and the warmth of his laugh, and loved watching him grow more relaxed and less serious every day.

Annie just didn't know whether she longed to share her feelings with the rest of the world because those feelings were real and right, or because she was still on the rebound after Spence's betrayal.

Scowling slightly, she scanned her face in the mirror and pulled moisturizer from her makeup case. As she dotted some onto her face, the door opened and Nessa came inside.

Annie lowered her hand and turned. "Good morning."

"Morning."

Annie replaced the cap and set the bottle on the narrow counter by the sink. "I was hoping I'd see you before breakfast. What are your plans for today?"

Nessa slipped into the changing room and pulled the curtain shut between them. "The usual stuff, I guess. Why?"

"We only have a couple of families checked in right now, so we could both probably wrangle some free time.

I thought maybe we could try again to spend some time alone together.''

"Doing what?"

"Whatever you'd like. We've both been so busy, I feel as if I hardly see you anymore."

"We see each other all the time."

"Yes, we do. But someone else is always there. I'd like some mother-daughter time." Annie leaned against the counter and rested her hands behind her. "The truth is, I feel like we have a few unresolved issues between us and it's driving me crazy."

"Like what?"

"Like what I said the other day about you and Tyler. Like what you said about going to live with your dad."

Only the sounds of Nessa changing filled the strained silence for several long minutes. Just as Annie was about to give up hoping for a response, Nessa's quiet voice drifted over the curtain. "I didn't mean to say that, you know."

Annie let out a silent sigh of relief. "I know."

"I was just mad because of the way you were acting." Nessa pulled the curtain partway open. "What do you have against Tyler, anyway?"

"I don't have *anything* against Tyler. I like him."

"Then why are you so against him?"

"I'm not against him. That wasn't what I was trying to say, and if it sounded like I was, I'm sorry."

"Okay." Nessa leaned one shoulder against the door frame. "Then tell me again."

"I have absolutely nothing against Tyler," Annie said once more for good measure. "I'm concerned about how close you're getting because I know what can happen. That's nothing against Tyler and it's nothing against you, either. It's simply acknowledging that physical attraction between two people can sometimes feel overwhelming, and it can sometimes overshadow good sense.''

Nessa folded her arms defensively. ''In other words, you don't trust me.''

''That's not true. I think you're spending a little too much time with Tyler, that's all. But I understand what you're feeling and why.'' Maybe even a little too well. She pushed Dean out of her mind and focused on Nessa. ''And maybe that's not the only thing bothering me. It's possible that I'm also feeling a little left out.''

Nessa's posture changed subtly. Her gaze met Annie's squarely for the first time. ''You mean, like, jealous?''

''Maybe.'' Annie stuffed her hands into the pockets of her robe. ''I don't like thinking I am, but it's possible. My mom used to tell me that watching your kids grow up can be really hard and learning to let go is rough. I didn't understand what she meant until this summer. When you were little and you needed me for everything, I was top on your list of important people. Now I fall somewhere lower, and some days I have a little trouble adjusting. I'm glad you like working with the horses and I'm thrilled that you get along so well with Gary. I'm even glad that you and Tyler have each other here. I just want a place in there with everything else.''

Nessa stood up a little straighter. ''Like when?''

''I don't care. Maybe we could fix dinner together one night a week, or you could spend an afternoon talking to me while I'm baking. Or we could actually take that nature walk or drive in to town for a wild shopping spree.''

The corners of Nessa's mouth twitched. ''Now, *that* sounds exciting.''

''It could be. You never know.''

Nessa grinned broadly. ''I *do* know, Mom. I've been to Whistle River.'' She tilted her head thoughtfully. ''I guess your ideas are okay, even though you *know* I hate cooking. But I'll do what you like if you'll do what I like.''

Annie blinked in surprise. ''I didn't know you hate cooking.''

''Well, I do. Why do you think I never offer to help you?''

''I thought it was because you're fifteen.''

''That, too. But I'll do it if you'll come down to the stables and finally learn how to ride.''

Annie let out an abrupt laugh, then sobered just as quickly. ''Are you serious?''

''Yeah.''

Annie ran a hand along the back of her neck. The huge beasts still made her nervous, but she couldn't resist the eagerness in Nessa's eyes. ''I guess I could try, if that's what you'd like me to do—''

''Today?''

Annie took a deep breath and nodded. ''Better to get it over with than to put it off.''

Nessa grinned slowly. ''Cool. Wait until I tell the others. Gary'll be stoked.''

Annie laughed nervously and turned back to the mirror. ''I'm sure he will be. Just make sure he picks a nice, quiet and very *tame* horse for me.''

''You got it.'' Nessa stepped into the shower and pulled the curtain closed. The sound of running water soon followed, and within seconds, steam began billowing over the top of the curtain.

Annie gathered her things and let herself out into the morning. Riding horses sure wasn't how she'd planned to spend the day, but she'd do it gladly if it meant a chance to strengthen her bond with Nessa.

GARY BANGED THROUGH the screen door a few hours later, making enough noise for half a dozen men his size. He gave Annie a quick once-over and pushed his hat back from his forehead. "Are you ready?"

Annie toweled a pan dry and shook her head. "I don't know, Gary. I'm not sure I can do this."

"Oh? And why not?"

"Because I've never ridden before, and I don't know anything about handling animals. The only thing I *do* know is that they sense fear—and I'm terrified."

Gary chuckled and plucked a cluster of grapes from the fruit bowl Annie had started keeping on the counter for snacks. "Trust me, you have nothing to worry about. Old Maisie will be more afraid of you than you are of her."

"I doubt that."

Gary grabbed her hand and tugged her toward the back door. "Come on, 'fraidy cat. Everybody's waiting."

Annie let him lead her, but only because she knew Nessa was waiting. "If I get hurt, I'll never forgive you."

"You won't get hurt."

"You can't guarantee that."

"Near as. Hell's bells, woman," he grumbled as he tugged her down the stairs. "I'm your own flesh and blood. I wouldn't suggest you try this if I thought there was a chance anything bad could happen."

"What if I look stupid?" she asked as they started across the clearing.

"Why would you?"

"Because this is a very unnatural thing for me. The rest of you act as if you were born on the back of a horse."

Gary stopped walking, checked out her jeans, T-shirt

and tennis shoes, and nodded in satisfaction. "You *look* great. Almost as if you belong here."

"It's just window dressing." Annie clasped her hands together and responded to another gentle tug on her arm. "I feel awkward and completely out of place. I stick out like a sore thumb around here."

"Bullroar. I know people who've lived here for years and still aren't as well-adjusted."

Annie laughed softly. "That's a lovely lie, Gary. Thanks."

"No problem." He stuffed his hands into his pockets and settled into the loose-limbed stride he'd picked up over the past few years. "How's everything else? You getting along with everybody okay?"

Annie nodded and fell into step beside him. "I really like Irma and Les. She doesn't mince words, does she?"

"Never known her to."

"Les seems quieter, but very nice."

"He doesn't talk much," Gary agreed. "Doesn't feel the need. How about Dean?"

Annie's cheeks grew warm. She glanced away before Gary could read a reaction in her eyes. "We get along fine. Why?"

Gary shrugged. "No particular reason. I just want to make sure everything's okay since I'm the one who brought you here."

Annie smiled with relief. "Everything's fine." Luckily, it took only minutes to reach the stables, but when Annie saw five horses saddled and waiting in the paddock, she glanced nervously at Gary.

He pretended not to notice and motioned her toward the fence. "Give us a minute and we'll help you get mounted."

Annie's heart pounded and her hands grew clammy

while she waited. Everyone else seemed so comfortable around the horses, she felt foolish. When Tyler held the gate open for her, she slipped inside as if she did this every day. But as she approached Maisie, her fingers grew numb and a strange nervous buzzing started in her head.

Maisie watched her with wide, unblinking eyes. She didn't even move when Gary took Annie's hand and lifted it gently to her broad neck. "See? She's perfectly harmless."

"She could just be biding her time."

Gary laughed and pulled a baseball cap with the Eagle's Nest logo from his back pocket. He shook it to uncrease the folds and settled it on Annie's head. "You're too smart for me, cousin. This is all an elaborate murder plot we schemed up, and we've got the gentlest horse in creation to do the dirty deed. It's the best alibi any of us could come up with."

Annie was nervous, but she didn't pull her hand away from the horse's neck. When she relaxed enough to actually feel the strange bristly softness of its coat, she moved her fingers gently. The strength of the animal's muscles still frightened her, but Maisie twisted her neck to look back and even Annie couldn't deny that her eyes were the gentlest she'd ever seen.

"Hey there, Maisie," she said softly. The horse snorted softly in response and Annie grew a little braver. "Could you do me a huge favor and let me live through this little experience?"

Maisie tossed her head and Annie jerked her hand away. The horse gave her another look and Annie put her hand back where it had been. "Sorry."

"It appears you've made another friend." Dean's voice in her ear brought Annie around sharply, and when she saw him standing there in a pair of faded jeans and a black western-cut shirt, she decided to force herself onto Maisie's back just for a chance to spend a few more minutes with him.

"I don't know if we're friends or not," she said. "I'm just trying to convince her not to trample me."

"Maisie wouldn't hurt a fly, would you, girl?" Dean pulled a carrot from his pocket and held it out so the horse could smell it. Maisie pulled her lips back and nibbled with exquisite tenderness for a second, then snatched the carrot away with a toss of her head and chomped it in half.

Annie shuddered at the animal's brute strength but laughed at the gleam of triumph in her big brown eyes. "Just tell me she can tell the difference between me and that carrot."

Dean came closer and nudged her gently with one shoulder. "You really should stop worrying. I promise I'll keep an eye on you."

His eyes seemed to promise more than just a riding lesson, and warmth spread through every inch of Annie's body in response. "I'll hold you to that."

Before Dean could respond—or do any of the wonderful things she imagined while they were hidden by Maisie's tall back—Tyler shouted something and the moment was gone.

Dean cleared his throat and jerked his head toward Maisie. "Ready?"

Annie nodded before she could have second thoughts and paid strict attention when Dean showed her where to put her hands so she could pull herself into the saddle.

"Put this foot in the stirrup and push off with the other leg. You'll have to use your arms to pull yourself up and swing your free leg up and over while you're on your way up. Do all that and you'll be set. I'll help you get your other foot into the stirrup when you're up there.''

It sounded simple enough, but it was a long way to haul herself. She could barely see over Maisie's back. She gripped the saddle just the way Dean had showed her and heaved with all her strength, but she only made it about halfway up Maisie's broad side before her arms gave out and she came sliding back down to the ground.

Laughing softly, she flicked a quick, embarrassed glance at Dean. ''It's not something I do every day.''

''It will be by the end of the summer. Want to try again?''

Annie nodded and repositioned her hands. But she failed twice more and started wishing that she'd taken time to use the spa membership she'd bought back in Chicago. A little more upper-arm strength would have come in handy.

''Once more,'' Dean said when she came back to earth again for the fourth time in a row. ''I have a feeling that you'll make it this time.''

Annie shook her head. ''I doubt it. I don't think I'm strong enough.''

He came up close behind her and spoke in her ear. ''Once more. You'll make it, I promise.''

His breath caressed her neck and sent a delicious shiver up Annie's spine. Heat emanated from his body and made her long for a minute alone so she could steal a kiss instead of hoisting herself onto Maisie's back. She lifted her gaze to meet his and lost herself for a long, breathless moment in his bottomless eyes.

It would take a lifetime to explore all the hidden mazes inside Dean, all the twists and turns, the ins and outs of his mind and heart. Eventually, some lucky woman would get that luxury, and for a heartbeat Annie wanted to be that woman. But she didn't belong in Whistle River, and Dean would never leave.

Aching suddenly, she turned back to Maisie and gave it one more try. As she lifted off the ground, Dean's strong hands cupped her backside and pushed her up and into the saddle. Surprised, she threw her free leg across the horse's back and clutched the saddle horn with both hands as she landed in the saddle with an *oomph*.

Dean grinned up at her. "You okay?"

"Fine." She shifted to make herself more comfortable, but she felt like a wishbone with her legs stretched across Maisie's back, and she could still feel the imprint of Dean's hands through her jeans.

His eyes roamed her face as he showed her how to hold the reins and how to move them to achieve the results she wanted. His hands brushed hers, whispered against her thighs and calves as he taught her what to do. Finally, he set her walking Maisie around the paddock.

Nessa swung into the saddle as if she'd been riding her entire life. Tyler, flushed with success because he'd convinced Dean to let him ride a slightly more spirited horse, mounted like a pro. Within minutes, Dean and Gary were both in the saddle and ready to go.

Annie held her breath as Gary led the way out of the paddock. Nessa took up the second position and Tyler rode right behind her. Annie clutched her reins tightly and murmured comforting words as Maisie began to walk toward the gate, but she needn't have worried. Maisie fell into step behind Tyler's horse and followed its every move as if she were tied to its rump.

Dean brought up the rear, and Annie was conscious of his eyes on her as they crossed the meadow. Within minutes, the breeze, fresh air and scenery captured her imagination and her self-consciousness began to fade.

Only the sound of hooves striking the ground, the soft snuffle of the horses, an occasional voice broke the stillness. As they crested the first hill and the Eagle's Nest disappeared, Annie could almost imagine that she'd traveled through time to a hundred years earlier.

The scents of pine and soil filled the air. The hush of the forest began to work its magic. The feel of Maisie's muscles working beneath Annie's legs was surprisingly calming and the rhythm began to lull her.

No wonder Gary loved it here. No wonder Dean had chosen this place to help him heal. Annie could almost imagine wanting to stay forever, herself.

TWO HOURS LATER, Dean sat beside Annie on the streambank high in the foothills and watched Nessa and Tyler wading a few feet away. Hot July sunlight sparkled off the water, but this section of the bank was partially shaded by a dense thicket of river willow.

A burst of laughter from the kids echoed in the stillness, Annie moved gingerly on the boulder she'd claimed, and a sensation Dean hadn't experienced since he was a young boy overwhelmed him. It had been years since he'd felt such a sense of belonging, of togetherness…of family.

He gave himself a mental shake and tried to put the feeling behind him, but he wasn't sure he'd be able to. In a few weeks, all of these people would leave. The Eagle's Nest would echo with silence, and he and Gary would be back to living the life of a couple of lonely old bachelors. Not long ago, that life had looked pretty good.

Now it seemed sad and pathetic.

Annie shifted again and stretched one leg gingerly. She was so beautiful sitting on the edge of the creek, the sunlight in her hair, her eyes the color of the water, Dean could have sworn his heart actually ached.

"We never should have stopped," she said with a grimace. "I'm so stiff and sore I don't think I'll make it back into the saddle—even with your help."

Dean tore his thoughts away from the future and forced himself to concentrate on the here and now. "Sorry. To tell you the truth, I'd forgotten how uncomfortable riding can make you the first few times. I should have warned you."

"It's a good thing you didn't. If I'd known, I *never* would have let you shove me onto Maisie's back."

Upstream, Nessa cupped her hands together and scooped water onto Tyler. Tyler responded with a growl, tried to grab Nessa around the waist and nearly lost his balance in the process. Annie smiled fondly at the kids and Dean thought she looked a little less worried about their friendship than she'd been by the fire.

Battling another pang of loneliness, Dean swept a comforting gaze across the scenery. The soft green of willow, the dancing leaves of aspen and the black-green of pines climbing toward mountain peaks still distant enough to appear purple gave him the sense that all was right with the world.

"You could have stayed behind," he said, "but then you'd have missed this."

Annie's expression sobered as she followed Dean's gaze. "That would have been a sin. I'll miss this when we leave."

Words rushed to the tip of Dean's tongue and he almost asked her to stay, but something made him hold back. He'd spent his entire life as a bachelor, and until six weeks ago he'd never seriously considered doing anything else. Annie and the kids made him want to change everything about himself, but he wouldn't do that unless he was absolutely certain that he could live up to the changes. It would be better to let them all leave than to convince them to stay with a bunch of promises he couldn't keep.

Annie stretched again and glanced upriver. "How long do you think Gary will be gone?"

Dean could have kissed her for changing the subject. Hell, he would've used *any* excuse for a kiss. But he didn't dare give in with Nessa and Tyler only a few feet away. Instead, he replied, "He'll be gone an hour—or long enough to catch his limit of trout. Whichever comes first." He watched her testing her muscles for a few minutes and forced away the urge to offer a full body massage. "I guess you won't feel much like cooking dinner tonight, will you?"

Annie bent one leg, then the other, and moaned softly. "No, but I'll do it. I don't want to stop moving or my muscles will freeze. If I take some ibuprofen first, I should be okay."

"We're the ones who did this to you. Let us take care of dinner."

Annie's lips curved gently. "Technically, Maisie's the one who did this to me, and tempting as the offer of a night off might be, I really don't want her fixing my dinner."

Dean chuckled. "Then let us fix dinner on Maisie's behalf."

"And just who would 'us' be?"

"Gary and me."

"Are you in the habit of volunteering him when he's not around to refuse?"

"You know your cousin. That's the best time to do

it,'' Dean said with a grin. "And don't feel too sorry for him. He'd do the same to me in a heartbeat."

Annie laughed and glanced upstream again. "Knowing Gary, I'm sure you're right. But there's one tiny problem with your plan. I'm not sure Gary even knows how to boil water."

"He doesn't, but as luck would have it, we don't need boiled water to cook trout."

Annie finally seemed to realize that he was serious. "You really want me to let you and Gary fix dinner?"

Dean pulled back and raised an eyebrow in mock seriousness. "I'm not sure I like your attitude, Ms. Holladay. Are you implying that you're the only person at the Eagle's Nest who can cook?"

Annie's expression sobered but her eyes danced with mirth. "Absolutely not. I'm well aware that Irma does a wonderful job in the kitchen."

"*Now* you're starting to sound sexist," Dean warned.

"My doubts have nothing to do with gender," Annie said with a lift of her chin. "Some of the best chefs in the world are men. I just don't happen to think you and Gary fall into that category, that's all. And there's no guarantee Gary will come back with any trout, so it might be a moot point."

Dean waved away her argument. "Unless the creek's dried up, Gary'll bring fish back with him. Don't worry about that."

"Well, then, far be it from me to put a damper on the fun." Annie rubbed her legs and grimaced once more. "I'd love to have the evening off."

Another burst of laughter from midstream caught Dean's attention just as Tyler lost his footing and fell into the shallow current. His hand shot out toward Nessa's ankle, but she sidestepped him easily and headed for shore. Laughing, Tyler scrambled to his feet and started after her. He came ashore a few feet away and dropped onto the rock Nessa had chosen to dry off, stretching out beside her, young, innocent and completely relaxed.

Things had been better between Dean and Tyler since that day in town, but the fear of doing something wrong and ruining everything had kept Dean from moving in too close. There must have been something in the air today because Dean couldn't resist the impulse to call out. "I told Annie that Gary and I would cook dinner tonight, but she seems to think we're going to botch the job. What do you say, Tyler? You want to help us prove her wrong?"

Tyler glanced up, his face a mix of emotions while he considered the offer. "What are you fixing?"

"Trout and whatever sounds good to go with it. Do you know anything about cooking?"

Tyler sat up and shielded his eyes against the sun. "Who do you *think* does all the cooking at my house?"

Dean hated hearing that, but he shouldn't have been surprised. If Carol was drinking again she probably didn't think about food much. He forced himself to keep smiling. "Then are you in?"

Tyler nodded slowly, glanced at Nessa for her opinion, and finally managed a half smile. "Sure. I guess. Why not?"

Dean grinned and leaned against the boulder at his back. And this time when that sense of family and connection ran over him, he made no effort to fight it.

DEAN WAS AS GOOD AS his word—or Gary was. He came back with a full string of rainbow trout so fresh Annie itched to get her hands on them. She could have made a basic trout amandine, or broiled the fish and served them with stuffing made from pine nuts, jalapeños, and garlic.

Her mouth watered at the thought of fish served with lemon and capers, and if she'd had cedar planks available, she might have cooked the fish over a fire and served them with avocado-tomato salsa.

Endless possibilities danced through her mind on the ride home, but both Dean and Gary acted insulted by her friendly offers of help, so she had to content herself with teaching Tyler how to create a homemade version of the boxed rice pilaf he was used to making.

She could have taken advantage of the time to spend alone with Nessa, but neither of them was willing to leave the kitchen and miss the fun. Laughter echoed off the walls as Dean and Gary argued good-naturedly over the proper method for cleaning the fish and removing the bones, then launched into a joint—and vehement—tirade about the importance of using real butter instead of margarine, as if they thought Annie might even consider using the latter on fresh trout.

Even Tyler relaxed and joined in the fun, and the joy on Dean's face nearly brought tears to Annie's eyes. She wondered once or twice whether or not she should try to get Nessa alone, but, frankly, it had been a long time since they'd laughed so hard together and even longer since Nessa had seen two cooks laughing together in a kitchen. The evening reminded Annie how important laughter in a relationship had once seemed to her, and she hated realizing how long it had been since she and Spence had laughed together over anything.

So in the end, she stayed in the kitchen and laughed until the tears ran down her cheeks, and she enjoyed the meal more than anything she'd eaten in years—even though the trout *was* a little overcooked, and the rice clumped together in the bowl, and the green beans Gary dug out of the freezer and threw into a pan at the last minute had a touch more crunch than Annie usually liked.

And as she climbed the stairs at the end of the day, she realized that there were times when perfection was highly overrated.

CHAPTER THIRTEEN

FUELED BY THE GREAT EVENING he'd shared with family and friends, Dean slipped into his office the next morning as soon as he had finished breakfast and dialed Carol's number. The phone rang about six times, then someone dragged the receiver off the hook and dropped it to the floor. Dean could hear the muffled sound of a man's voice swearing filled the connection and then, finally, "Yeah?"

The man sounded either drunk or high, and everything inside Dean went cold. "Is this Randy?"

"Sorry. Don't know anybody by that name."

Had Carol already taken up with someone new? Dean took a deep breath and forced himself to speak again. "Is Carol there?"

"Carol?" A long pause followed while the man covered the mouthpiece with one hand. Even so, Dean could hear a woman's voice in the background. "Carol's not here right now," the man said when he came back on the line. "What do you want her for?"

Dean ignored the question. "Where is she?"

"Gone. Out."

Dean checked his watch instinctively. It was only six-thirty in California. A little early for cocktail hour. He leaned forward in his chair and toyed nervously with a pen he'd left in the middle of his desk. "Who is this?"

"A friend of the family. Why?"

"Because I want to speak with either Carol or Randy. I don't care which."

"You a bill collector or something?"

"No, I'm Carol's brother. I need to talk with her about her son."

The man laughed and the tone of his voice changed abruptly. "Well, why didn't you say so in the first place? You're calling about Tyler? How is the little sumbitch, anyway?"

Dean's grip on the receiver tightened. "Tyler's fine. Who are you?"

"Okay, so I lied before about not being me. But hell, man, I didn't know who you were." Randy belched under his breath and Dean would have sworn he could smell the alcohol coming out his end of the connection. "You could've been one of my old lady's friends for all I know."

Dean's hand stilled on the pen and he closed his eyes briefly. "You're married?"

"Naw, but my wife is." Randy snorted a laugh and spent a few seconds indulging in mirth. "Seriously, man, I'm separated. And soon as the divorce is final, you and me'll be brothers, so I guess it's about time we met, isn't it?"

Dean rubbed his forehead and felt as if someone had turned the clock back. Only this time, he couldn't deny that Carol's lousy choices were affecting someone besides herself. "Is Carol there with you?"

"Sure." Randy's voice faded and Dean figured he'd tried to hand Carol the receiver. He heard a bit of frantic whispering, a hand covered the mouthpiece again, and Carol came on the line with an uneasy laugh.

"Dean? Whatsup?"

It was on the tip of Dean's tongue to say something

about her drinking, but he choked the words back. Tyler's future was his only concern this morning, and alienating Carol wasn't smart. "It's been a few weeks since I talked to you. I've been wondering how you're doing."

Carol let out a disbelieving laugh. "You're checking up on me, aren't you?"

"Actually, no, I'm not. I'm calling about Tyler."

"What about him?"

Dean rubbed the bridge of his nose and spoke slowly, knowing that he had to broach the subject in just the right way or he'd lose her. "He's a great kid, Carol. I like having him around."

"Really?" She laughed uncertainly. "He's not lying and stealing and cheating and swearing at you and threatening to run away? Because that's what he does here."

"He did at first," Dean admitted, "but he's settled down a lot."

"How'd you manage that?"

"I don't think it was me. I think the setting agrees with him. The Eagle's Nest is a great place to be a kid his age. He spends a lot of time with the horses and there's plenty of space so it's pretty hard to feel hemmed in."

Carol sighed wistfully and the slur in her words suddenly seemed less pronounced. "Just like what you used to dream about, huh?"

"Did I? I don't remember."

Carol laughed sharply. "You *don't?* Are you serious? You don't remember that summer we spent in Iowa before Grandma died?"

"I remember being there, but not much about it."

"Well *I* do. All you could talk about was how you were going to be a cowboy and live on a ranch someday. I remember because I decided I wanted to be a cowboy, too, but I was too little to get on a horse so Grandma cut a branch from her tree and I rode that thing around for a week.''

Dean sat back in his chair and tried to remember. ''I couldn't have been older than nine that summer.''

''That's about right. I was four or five.''

An image of Carol as a little girl skipping around their grandmother's yard using a tree branch as a hobbyhorse flashed through Dean's mind. Sudden tears blurred his vision and stung his eyes. He wiped them away with the back of his hand and tilted back his head, filled with longing for the children they'd never be again, for the innocence they'd lost along the way.

''I'd forgotten that summer,'' he said when he could get words out around the lump in his throat. ''I wanted to stay at Grandma's forever.''

''Yeah, so did I.''

''Well, the Eagle's Nest is the next best thing,'' Dean told her. ''You can stay here if you want to.''

''I really don't think I'd fit in there now.'' Her voice changed subtly. ''But Tyler's doing okay?''

''Tyler's doing fine, and that's why I'm calling.'' Dean rubbed his eyes and cleared the rest of the lump from his throat. ''I'd like him to stay, Carol.''

''Forever?''

''For as long as he needs to.''

''Why?''

Dean took a deep breath and spoke carefully, trying not to offend Carol with his explanation. ''He seems happy here, and from what you've told me that's unusual for him.''

''Only since I met Randy.''

That was a subject Dean hoped to avoid entirely. ''Whatever the reason, you've both been having a rough time. If his being here takes some of the pressure off your relationship, I'd be more than happy to let Tyler stay.''

''You make me sound like a horrible mother.''

Dean shook his head quickly. ''That's not what I'm trying to do. I'm just…'' He broke off, searching for a way to explain that she'd accept and understand. ''We're family, Carol, and I'm just starting to figure out what that means. Tyler's well-being isn't only your responsibility, it's mine, too. If he's unhappy, I can't just turn my back and pretend not to notice. I've done that for too long and it's not fair to either of you.''

''So you're going to save him?''

The question brought Dean up short. He tried to figure out how to turn the conversation back around. ''That's not what I'm saying.''

''Sure it is. It's Dean to the rescue all over again, isn't it? Just like it was after Mama died. Has it ever occurred to you that we don't *need* you to rescue us?''

''I'm not trying to rescue anyone,'' he protested. ''I didn't come to you and ask you to send Tyler for the summer. You're the one who begged me to take him. And I did. I've spent the past six weeks with him, watching him and learning about him because that's what you asked me to do. So you can't blame me if I have a few opinions about what would be best for him.''

''You know what, dude? If I'm such a pain in your ass, I'll leave.''

The unexpected male voice brought Dean's head up with a snap. Tyler stood in the doorway, arms folded, eyes flashing with anger. Dean had been so intent on his conversation with Carol, he hadn't even heard the door open. He stood quickly, then froze while he tried to decide what to tell Carol and what to say to Tyler. ''That's not what I meant,'' he said earnestly.

"I don't want to hear it. It just pisses me off that I was actually starting to believe you." Tyler spun away and disappeared down the hallway before Dean could move.

Dean started after him, realized he was still holding the phone and that Carol was still on the line, demanding to know what was going on. He didn't waste time on explanations. "Carol? I'll have to call you back."

"Was that Tyler?"

"Yes, it was. And I really have to explain to him what he just overheard."

"Wait a minute, Dean—"

"I'll call you back," he said again, and hung up before she could argue any further. There'd be time enough later for explanations. Right now, Tyler was nursing a misunderstanding that could ruin everything.

THANKS TO GARY, DEAN FOUND Tyler sitting on a rock near Wolf Creek, tossing pebbles into the water. Sunlight streamed through a break in the trees onto the boy's slumped shoulders and spiky hair. He appeared so dejected, Dean could only watch in silence for a long time while he tried to decide what might convince Tyler that he'd misinterpreted Dean's conversation.

Finally, aware that the minutes were ticking by, Dean stepped into the shady copse of trees. "Tyler?"

The boy spoke without turning around. "I wondered how long you were going to stand there staring."

"I should have known you heard me coming. I'm not the quietest person in the world." Dean hunkered down beside him. "We need to talk about what you just overheard."

"What about it?"

"Well, for one thing, you didn't hear the whole conversation—again."

Tyler glared at him from the corner of one eye. "I heard enough."

"If you're thinking that I don't want you here, then you couldn't have."

"Yeah? You said my mom had to beg you to let me come. What's that supposed to sound like to me?"

Dean sat on the rock beside him. "I won't deny I said that, but you didn't hear it in context. I called your mom this morning to ask if she'll let you stay here."

"Why?"

"Well, for one thing, because I like having you here and I'm going to miss you when you leave. We had a great time together yesterday, didn't we?"

Tyler's gaze narrowed, but he didn't say anything.

"The other reason I'd like you to stay is that I'm not comfortable with sending you back to your mom's house while she's drinking and Randy's there." Dean picked up a pebble that had been smoothed by the water and ran his thumb across it. "I had my first chance to talk with Randy this morning."

Tyler's lips curved. "What did you think?"

"He's a piece of work, I'll tell you that much."

Tyler's smile turned into a smirk of distaste. "Yeah, he is. And you haven't even *seen* him yet."

Dean shook his head and kept running his thumb across the stone. "Well, don't feel too sorry for me. If he marries your mom, I might get to see him." He made a face that left no doubt how much he looked forward to it, and Tyler's quick grin warmed him clear through. "For what it's worth, I believe you're right about him."

Tyler tilted his head and regarded Dean intently.

"Is that because you believe *me,* or because you don't like *him?*"

Dean laughed and lowered the pebble to the ground beside him. "Will you be offended if I admit it's a little of both?"

Tyler shook his head and stared at something in the distance. He sat that way for a long time without speaking and Dean forced himself to wait while he worked through his emotions.

"I just don't understand why my mom sticks up for him the way she does."

"Neither do I," Dean admitted.

"If love makes you that stupid, I don't want any part of it."

"That's not love," Dean said sadly. "It's something else. Obsession, maybe. Or weakness. I love your mother, but I'll be the first one to admit that she's not the strongest woman in the world. Part of that is because your grandmother died when your mom was so young and I didn't know what to do afterward. I started a long tradition of hiding from the really tough stuff behind my career, and I'm only now learning how to stop."

Tyler shook his head slowly. "My mom's problems aren't your fault. Neither are mine."

"What made you come to that conclusion?"

Tyler shrugged. "Nessa, I guess. She's pretty smart."

"So's her mother." Dean picked up his stone again and skipped it across the creek, three times before it sank to the bottom. "So what do you say? If your mom agrees to let you stay here, are you interested?"

Tyler shrugged. "What would I do?"

"Go to school. Borrow my truck to go on dates. Get a job in town on weekends during the winter months, or just hang out here after school, do homework in front of the fire, and ask me for money—the usual stuff.''

Remembering his conversation with Annie, he dredged up his courage and said, ''I love you, Tyler, and I want you to stay. If you do, we'll work out the details as we go along.''

Tyler stared at him for a long time before asking, ''You'd let me take your truck to go on dates?''

Dean laughed in relief. ''I don't see why not—unless you give me some reason not to trust you.''

Tyler looked interested for a few seconds, then the sparkle in his eyes died and his smile faded. ''Yeah, but that would leave my mom alone with Randy. I can't do that.''

Dean skipped another stone across the stream. ''Your mom's an adult, Tyler. No matter how much you and I might disagree with her choices, we can't make her do what we think is sensible or right. I don't like admitting this, but she's been on a self-destructive path since she was just a little older than you are now. We can try to get help for her and encourage her to accept it, but we can't force her to get better. And you can't sacrifice your future for something you'll never be able to change.''

''So I'm just supposed to turn my back on my mom?''

''I'm not saying that. But all of our choices come with consequences and sometimes we're not the only ones who suffer. The woman who was driving the car that ran into me chose to drink and drive, and I lost my career because of that. I don't want to see something similar happen to you.''

He shifted on the rock so he could see Tyler better. ''Your mom's making choices that could have a deep effect on your future, especially if you choose to stay on the same road she is. All I'm doing is offering you a detour. If you decide to stay here you can see your mom as often as we can arrange it, and call her as often as you need to. And if things get better at home, you can go back whenever you want.''

Tyler nudged a pebble from the dirt with the toe of his sneaker and plowed both hands through his hair. "Can I think about it?''

"Absolutely. Take as long as you need. I know it's a big decision.'' Dean pushed to his feet and stood looking down at his nephew. "I know you're probably not in the mood for this, but I have a Little League practice in a few minutes and I'd really like you to come with me.''

Tyler lifted his head slightly. "Why?''

"Because I can't do it alone. Believe me, I've tried. I need your help.''

Tyler slanted a glance up at him. "No kidding?''

"No kidding. I think you'd be great with the kids.''

Tyler jerked one shoulder and dipped his head. "I guess I could help.''

Dean grinned and waited for Tyler to get to his feet. "I've got to warn you, it isn't going to be easy. But getting their attention is going to be the toughest part.''

Tyler stuck his hands into his pockets and fell into step beside Dean. And as they walked toward the shed for the equipment bag, Dean knew he'd just had one of the most important conversations of his entire life.

A FEW DAYS LATER, Annie walked slowly along the river path with Gary at her side. The woods were alive with the sounds of nature. A few visitors strolled through the trees, their voices soft as they wound down for the night. Nessa and Tyler were entertaining some of the kids around the campfire, and laughter echoed occasionally through the branches overhead. Dean had gone with Les to check on the wiring in one of the cabins, and Irma was chatting softly in the porch swing with Mrs. Gunderson from cabin five.

That left Annie a rare chance to spend a few minutes alone with her cousin, and she wanted to make the most of their time together. She sighed softly as the night breeze from the canyons set the leaves in motion, and zipped her sweatshirt closed. "I never would have thought the woods would be so peaceful at night. When I first came here, I expected to be nervous."

Gary grinned, a flash of white in the darkness. "Why nervous?"

"Oh, you know. Lions and tigers and bears."

"No tigers in these parts," he said with a laugh. "That leaves mountain lions and bears, but animals rarely come down this low unless it's a drought year. Still, it always pays to be aware. If you see a wild animal, give it respect and a wide berth, and you should be okay."

"Not to worry," Annie assured him. "Distance will *not* be a problem." She took another deep breath and hooked her thumbs in her back pockets. "Thanks for suggesting me for this job, Gary. You may never know what a godsend it was to get out of Chicago."

"It was the perfect answer for both sides." Gary stepped off the path to make room for a young mother carrying a sleeping toddler and tipped his hat as she passed. When they were alone again, he asked, "So everything's okay?"

"Fine. Why do you ask?"

"No particular reason, I guess. Unless you count the fact that you and Dean are tiptoeing around each other lately."

Annie slanted a glance at him, but she couldn't see his face well enough to read his expression. Was that an innocent question, or did he know something? "We're not tiptoeing," she protested. "At least I'm not. I don't know what he's doing."

"Uh-huh. You're forgetting that I know Dean just about as well as I know myself. If something's not going on between the two of you, I'll eat bear grease for breakfast."

Annie laughed, but the sudden urge to talk to someone nearly brought tears to her eyes. Her confusion over Spence's offer, her growing feelings for Dean, her increasing panic over losing Nessa at the end of the summer and her rapidly increasing doubts about teaching at the culinary institute made it difficult to sleep at night and concentrate all through the day.

She could feel Gary watching her, but she was having trouble putting it into words. "It's all so complicated," she managed to say at last.

"Break it down, then. Whenever I have a problem to solve that's what I do. Wipe away all the extraneous stuff, toss aside your preconceived notions and break it down to the basics."

"That's easier said than done."

He lifted one shoulder in a lazy shrug. "At first, but it gets easier with practice. You want to start with Dean or start with something else?"

"What makes you think Dean's the easy subject? He's a pretty complex guy."

"Not really. He's just a man like any other. He's got his strong points and his weak ones, but he's honest. You gotta admire that."

Annie nodded slowly and studied a low-hanging branch. "He certainly doesn't hide anything," she said after a few minutes. "And maybe that's what scares me.

I'm used to peeling away the layers to find the core of a person. Dean's just...*there.*"

Gary chuckled. "He is what he is, that's for sure."

"He's so different from Spence, I don't know quite what to make of him or how to react. Spence always had an angle. Dean doesn't seem to understand angles." Annie shook her head and took a deep breath. "My first instinct was right—let's talk about something else. Nessa seems to enjoy the chores you've given her."

Thankfully, Gary didn't resist the change of subject. "She's good at what she's doing, too."

"Is she?" Annie smiled softly. "I know she's having fun, but it's nice to know that you're pleased with her work."

"More than pleased. She has a way with the horses that's really something to see. She can get 'em to do just about anything she wants."

Annie slowed and glanced toward the stables, even though she couldn't see them through the trees. "Well then, I'm *really* glad we came to the Eagle's Nest. Otherwise, we might never have discovered her hidden talent."

Gary pulled a few leaves from a willow and scattered them in the breeze. "What about you? Any hidden talents lying fallow?"

She laughed softly. "None so far." The breeze swirled around them and carried Dean's voice with it. She couldn't make out what he was saying, but she'd have known his laugh anywhere. She turned abruptly and started walking again. "All right, cousin. I've talked for a bit. Now it's your turn."

He fell into step beside her. "What do you want to know?"

"You came out here when you married Shannon, and

I thought the two of you were so in love. What happened?''

"I don't know. I never thought we'd end up apart. First time I laid eyes on her, I knew she was the woman I was going to marry." Gary's posture changed subtly as he talked about her, and Annie knew that he was still nursing feelings for her. "The changes started happening after her dad died. I guess I wasn't there for her like she needed. I did okay for the first six months or so, but I started resenting the fact that her whole life came to a crashing end when her dad had his heart attack. I guess I thought she should recover quicker than she did, or maybe that she'd care a little bit that *I* was still here, loving her." He laughed without humor and hung his head. "Hell, Annie. At the time I thought I knew what was right, but it's all jumbled up now and I'm not sure which of us was the bad guy anymore."

Annie touched his shoulder gently. "I'm so sorry, Gary. I had no idea. Does she still live around here?"

He shook his head miserably. "No, but I stayed because I kept hoping she'd come back and give me a second chance. That won't happen now unless she divorces her new husband."

Annie felt her stomach knot in sympathy. "I don't think all that news made it to the family grapevine."

Gary tried to grin but managed just a shadow of his usual cocky smile. "I don't tell my mother *everything*."

Annie followed his lead and tried to add a little laughter to the moment, but her voice caught and the words came out thick with emotion. "See what holding everything inside gets you? I hope you'll learn a lesson from this."

"I probably won't."

They strolled for a few minutes without speaking before Gary broke the silence. "Think you'll ever get married again?"

"I don't know. What about you?"

"I think about it, but I'm not sure marriage is something I'm any good at."

"It's not one of *my* hidden talents," Annie admitted. Dean's voice sounded again, a little closer this time, and her step faltered. When she realized Gary was watching her, she gave up trying to be clever and nodded toward the trees. "Why hasn't he ever been married?"

"Who? Dean?" Gary glanced over his shoulder and shrugged. "Why are you asking me?"

"Fine." Annie made a face at him, stopped beside a boulder nearly twice her size and leaned against it. "If you won't gossip about your best friend, I'll ask him myself. Did you know him when he had his accident?"

"I met him while he was still recovering, just before he moved here for good." Gary perched on an outcropping on the boulder. "Tell me the truth, Annie. Why so curious? Tell me what's *really* going on between you and Dean."

Annie tried to regain the teasing note they'd enjoyed just a few seconds earlier. "Is that why you told me about Shannon? So you'd have something to hold over my head?"

"Not exactly. But if it works…"

"Well, you made a bad deal this time, cousin. There's nothing to tell."

Gary made a noise like a buzzer on a game show. "Wrong answer. Evading is acceptable but not encouraged. Outright lying earns you a fifty-point penalty."

Annie smiled. "I'll take the penalty." She tilted her head and studied the stars through the branches overhead, but that brought back memories of that evening she'd shared with Dean on the porch. She closed her eyes for the length of a sigh and wondered why she didn't just tell Gary the truth.

He knew Dean as well or better than anyone else, and he knew her. He might be able to help her understand the conflicting feelings that were raging inside of her.

She opened her eyes again and found Gary waiting, as if he'd read her thoughts and knew she was about to relent. "If you must know, I think I'm falling in love with him."

The twin swags of Gary's mustache twitched. "And...?"

Annie laughed uneasily. "Isn't that enough? I'm not even divorced yet. I'm still working through the issues caused by Spence's betrayal. I've lost the career I've worked my entire life to build. My daughter wants me to put my marriage back together, but there's no way I can do that, even to make her happy. In a few months I'll be single and living alone in a new state. This isn't exactly the best time to be making big life decisions." She let out a breath when she finished and felt her shoulders sag as if something heavy had been lifted from them.

Gary nodded slowly. "Nobody ever said you were standing in a comfortable spot."

"No. No, they didn't."

"And I guess you do have a few things to work through."

"I think that's safe to say."

He slid from the boulder and smoothed the legs of his jeans as the sound of approaching footsteps reached them through the trees. "I can't tell you what to do, Annie. But I *can* tell you that love isn't waiting around every corner. Dean's a good man. One of the best you'll ever find, bar none. He's honest and he's faithful and he's as trustworthy as a person can be.''

The footsteps stopped and Annie knew that Dean had come up behind her. Every nerve was aware of him, every sense picked up his presence. She could smell his aftershave, feel the heat from his body and see his shadow on the boulder.

Gary brushed a kiss to her cheek and whispered, ''Just don't let fear keep you from going after a little happiness. Believe me, nursing regrets is no way to live.''

CHAPTER FOURTEEN

ANNIE TURNED SLOWLY and found herself looking into Dean's curious gaze. He tilted his head toward Gary's rapidly retreating back. "What was all that about?"

"We were just talking about life decisions and regrets."

Dean's smile faded and his eyes filled with concern. "He has a few. But, then, I guess we all do."

"Some more than others, I guess." Annie brushed a lock of hair from her shoulder and tugged the hem of her sweatshirt over her hips. "Gary was advising me to avoid them."

"Oh?" Dean's brows rose and he took a step closer—close enough to hover over her. A tuft of hair peeked out over the open buttons of his shirt. The subtle scents of soap, aftershave and fresh air filled the space between them. He moved close enough to hover over her. "What does he think you'll regret?"

"He thinks I'll regret leaving here."

"Is he right?"

"I won't know for sure unless I leave, but he could be."

Dean took her hand in his and pulled her closer. "So his advice is for you to stay?"

Annie nodded again and tried to shake off the almost mesmerizing pull he had on her. "Yes, but I don't know that staying is the right answer. That's the problem. I don't *know* anything.'' She hadn't planned to tell him everything, but she found herself blurting, "Spence has asked me to come back to Holladay House.''

Dean's eyes darkened. "Is that what you want to do?''

"Yes and no. Holladay House was the project of my heart, my only real success besides Nessa. I poured my whole self into the restaurant, and Spence walked away with everything.'' She shook her head quickly and added, "I don't mean to imply that Spence didn't work hard. He did, and he still does. Maybe too hard at times. But at least he has something to show for his efforts.''

She pulled her hand away from Dean's and turned partially away. "The thought of working with him again isn't very appealing, but at least I could stay with Nessa.'' She turned back quickly. "But if I go...'' She averted her gaze from the flash of pain in his eyes. "I've tried being logical about this, but that's not working so well. I don't think I'm ready to make any big decisions right now.''

Dean reached for her again and she went to him eagerly. "I would never push you,'' he said gently. "You have to do what you think is best. But before you make any decisions, you deserve to know exactly how I feel.''

He was right—even if it made her decision harder. "How do you feel?'' she whispered.

Dean's expression softened and the veil over his eyes dropped completely. "I'm in love with you.'' He moved closer and the air seemed to leave Annie's lungs. She tried to catch a breath, but he was too close, his eyes too dark, his expression too intense. He moved his hand up her arm with agonizing slowness. "I can't stop thinking about you. I want you to stay and run the Eagle's Nest with me.''

"I want that, too, when I'm standing with you at a

moment like this. But if I did stay, I'd be walking into the same situation I had with Spence, and that frightens me. I applied to the institute because I want—no, I *need* to succeed or fail on my own.''

Dean pulled her closer. ''We could work all that out if you stayed.''

''But the Eagle's Nest is only open in the summers. It would never support both of us, and I'd get bored to death working four or five months out of the year.''

''So we'd open in the fall for hunters, and in the winter for snowmobilers. The Eagle's Nest can be anything we want it to be.''

Annie knew what a risk he was taking and how hard it was for him to make this offer. The touch of his hand and the expression in his eyes were almost enough to sway her. But Annie couldn't think of anything more dangerous than letting moonlight and romance affect her decision.

Dean moved closer and she knew he was going to kiss her. She told herself to turn and walk away before they did something they'd both regret, but she couldn't make her feet move. ''Don't, Dean.'' But it was only a token protest, and they both knew it.

He ran his hands gently along her shoulders. ''Don't what?''

''Don't do this.'' She tried to remember every logical reason why she didn't want him to cloud her judgment, but she couldn't summon any of them while he grazed her forehead with his lips. ''I can't think when you do that. I'm not going to make a decision…''

The rest of her objections were cut off as his lips covered hers. Every cell in Annie's body wanted to resist, but the emotions swirling through her had all the power. She knew she should pull away, but didn't move.

A soft moan caught in her throat as his tongue grazed the opening between her lips and when he wrapped his arms around her, crushing her to him, she wanted even more. Heat radiated from the center of her belly and she could have sworn the earth crumbled beneath her feet.

She was riding the clouds with him. Nothing else mattered. No one else existed. She slipped her arms around his neck and worked her fingers into his hair. His tongue probed her mouth gently, giving and taking at the same time. Her hands fell to his shoulders and she gripped them tightly. If one shoulder was damaged, she never would have known it. Muscles bunched beneath the skin, and the solid wall of his chest and back made her feel safe and in imminent danger at the same time.

As his fingers tangled in her hair, she gave in to the sheer luxury of being desired. His hands cupped her head and held her, as if he was afraid she'd pull away. All of her fears evaporated in the intensity of the moment and she clung to him with a fierceness that surprised her.

Too soon, he stilled, released her and stepped away.

She blinked open her eyes, too stunned even to be hurt. He was staring at something just over her shoulder, and the expression on his face chilled her to the core. Annie turned to see what he was looking at…just in time to see horror flash across Nessa's face as she pivoted away and tore off up the path toward the lodge.

All the weight came crashing back to Annie's shoulders, but she couldn't make herself move to follow. "How much did she see?"

Dean shook his head. "I don't know. I just opened my eyes and she was there."

Annie thought she might be sick. She was torn between the desire to stay and the need to go. The fear that Dean

would misread her decision if she followed Nessa, that
Nessa would jump to the wrong conclusion if she didn't.

"She's still too upset over the divorce," Annie finally
whispered. "I'm sorry, but I can't ignore this."

Dean waved her toward the lodge. "No, you can't. Go
to her, Annie. She needs you."

Annie brushed a quick kiss to his cheek, wishing she
could stay but so grateful for his understanding her heart
ached. She ran along the path, searching the shadows in
case Nessa had veered off the trail at some point. She
had no idea how she'd explain what her daughter had
just seen, but she had to try.

She dashed into the clearing and caught a glimpse of
Nessa running toward the stables as if her life were in
danger. Annie turned to follow just as Nessa raced in
through the open doors—straight into Tyler's arms.

Annie ground to a halt and watched, numb with disbelief as Tyler wrapped his arms around Nessa and
brushed a kiss to the top of her head. Obviously, this
wasn't their first embrace, and half of Annie's heart
shrieked in protest. The other recognized the intensity of
feeling behind what she was witnessing.

She bent at the waist and gripped her knees, trying to
catch her breath and thinking frantically. Nessa was too
young to be involved in a serious relationship. *Too
young*. Yet with everything that was going on in Annie's
heart, how could she tell her daughter to ignore the whispers in her own?

She stood there for several minutes while Nessa talked
and Tyler listened. When he slipped his arm around her
waist and led her out of the stables toward the lodge,
Annie pulled back into the shadow of a pine tree. Their
moment was so tender, so real, it brought tears to her

eyes, and she was even less certain what to say to Nessa now than she'd been five minutes earlier.

Not so long ago, Nessa had come to Annie over every problem. Now she was turning to someone else and Annie *was* the problem. It seemed the harder Annie tried, the worse things became.

AT A LITTLE AFTER ELEVEN o'clock that night, Annie tapped softly on Nessa's door. She'd put off talking to her daughter long enough. Sooner or later, she'd have to address the kiss Nessa had seen, and the embrace she'd witnessed between Nessa and Tyler. The discussion wouldn't get easier with time.

When Nessa didn't answer, Annie knocked a second time. When her third knock still didn't produce results, Annie turned the doorknob and let herself into the room. At first she thought Nessa was asleep already, but as she turned to go the undisturbed silence hit her. There was no sound of breathing, no rustle of covers as Nessa moved in her sleep. In fact, there was no sound at all.

Heart pounding, Annie turned on the light just to prove herself right. Nessa's bed hadn't even been touched, and that sent a different kind of uneasiness through Annie. She hurried down the outside stairs through the rising wind. But it didn't surprise her to find the bathroom stalls and showers empty.

The tender embrace she'd witnessed between Nessa and Tyler came rushing back to haunt her, along with a deep pang of guilt that she'd inadvertently pushed Nessa too far by kissing Dean. She raced back upstairs, telling herself with every step that she shouldn't jump to conclusions. But her insistent knock on Tyler's door didn't get any response, either.

That still didn't mean the worst, she told herself. She

should be relieved the kids weren't in one of their bedrooms. It meant they could be anywhere, doing something perfectly harmless. They could be in the kitchen having a midnight snack. Sitting on the porch in the swing. Or walking in the woods.

That possibility didn't make Annie feel a whole lot better.

She considered knocking on Dean's door or Gary's, but she didn't want to seem foolish or worry anyone else unless she had to. Instead, she hurried down the stairs and checked the front porch, then felt her way through the darkened great room into the kitchen. But it was empty, too.

The wind sighed through the rafters and made Annie even more nervous. Tugging the edges of her robe together, she grabbed a flashlight from the pantry and let herself out the back door. She walked carefully across the uneven ground, doing her best to avoid stepping on any sharp pebbles in her thin slippers.

She could have turned back for shoes, but what if she was too late? What if...

A strong gust of wind made her shiver—or maybe it was just the possibility that Nessa could be getting ready to set the course of her future now before she was even old enough to know what she wanted. Remembering what Dean had told her about Carol only made Annie more nervous. She couldn't let Nessa make that kind of mistake.

After what felt like an hour, she reached the stable door, lifted the latch and let herself inside. She stopped on the threshold and trained her light on the hay-strewn floors and wooden stalls.

The scents of dirt and straw mixed with the earthy aroma of horses, tearing a sneeze from her. She froze, listening intently for hurried footsteps or startled whispers. But the only thing she could hear were the snuffs and snorts of horses, who didn't appreciate a midnight visitor.

She walked inside and closed the door behind her. After a few minutes, her eyes began to adjust to the darkness and her ears grew attuned to the animal sounds. Just over the scuffling of hooves, she heard the soft hum of voices coming from a little distance away.

Annie listened carefully, but she couldn't make out what they were saying. She moved toward the sound, steeling herself for the worst and praying for the best. The voices grew steadily stronger as she walked, and by the time she reached the door to the paddock, she could make out bits and pieces of conversation.

"What would I *do* if I stayed?" Tyler's voice rose loud enough for Annie to hear him easily. "After the tourists are gone, there's not going to be much *to* do in a town like Whistle River—except, maybe, ride cows."

"That sounds like fun," Nessa said. "Better than hanging out at the mall."

"Oh, yeah. Sure."

"I'm serious. *I'd* ride cows if you did."

The conversation sounded innocent enough, Annie supposed. But just to be sure, she inched closer and tried to see through a chink in the boards. The hole was too small to let her see more than a faint glow that must have been coming from a flashlight.

Tyler laughed and their voices dropped again. Someone moved, and suddenly Annie could see Tyler standing a little apart from Nessa. She sighed softly with relief and told herself there really *wasn't* anything to worry about. It was late and both kids should come back to the lodge, but at least they weren't in the middle of a tryst.

While she tried to decide how to call them back into the lodge without appearing to spy on them, the wind gusted and a piece of dirt flew through the chink into her eye. Gasping sharply, Annie stepped back into the wall behind her and set metal tools clanging.

Before she could get away, the door flew open, and Nessa and Tyler stood silhouetted by the beam of their flashlight. Nessa gaped at Annie's robe and slippers. "Mom? What are you *doing?*"

Annie blinked furiously and her eye began to tear. "I went to your room to talk to you, but you weren't there."

"So you came *looking* for me?"

Annie put one hand over her eye and struggled to resist the urge to rub it. "I wanted to make sure you were okay. It's late. You should both be in bed."

Nessa's expression grew even more injured. "It's not even midnight."

Tyler shifted uncomfortably. "We weren't doing anything wrong."

The dirt scratching Annie's eye made her want to scream. She tried to keep her voice level. "I never said you were, Tyler. But it's late and everyone else is asleep. It's time to come back inside now."

Nessa pushed past Annie into the stable. "I don't believe this. You were spying on us, weren't you?"

"I wasn't spying. I came out to find you."

"Then why didn't you just open the door and come outside? Why were you lurking in here?"

The argument with Dean, the dirt in her eye and the feeling that she never seemed to please Nessa made Annie's patience snap. "I don't have to explain myself to you, young lady. I have every right to find you if you're not where you're supposed to be at this time of night."

Nessa growled angrily and pushed through the other

stable door. Annie followed, hoping Tyler would come back to the lodge, but too concerned about Nessa to wait.

Halfway across the clearing, Nessa stopped walking and whirled back. The wind whipped her hair straight out from her head and her eyes were wide and wild. "Was I *doing* anything?"

"No, you weren't." Annie kept walking, hoping to close the distance between them. "But that's not the point."

As soon as she got close, Nessa took off again and shouted over her shoulder. "You don't trust me. Do you have any idea how that makes me feel?"

Acutely aware of sleeping guests in the nearby cabins, Annie tried to keep her voice down. "It's not *you* I don't trust. It's not Tyler, either. It's just the situation."

"*What* situation?"

"You and Tyler alone in the middle of the night." Annie drew up next to her and caught her by the shoulders. "I *know* what it's like to be fifteen, Nessa. I remember all too well."

Nessa tried to squirm away. When she realized that Annie wasn't about to let go she stopped fighting, but the expression in her eyes was pure poison. "So what does that mean? That you were sleeping around at my age?"

"No! Of course not."

"But you think *I* am?" Nessa threw an arm into the air and broke Annie's grip. "Thanks, Mom. I feel *really* great now. It's nice to know what you think of me."

"That's not what I meant, and you know it." Annie glanced behind her and caught a glimpse of Tyler hovering a few feet away. Annie appreciated the fact that he wasn't trying to interfere as much as she appreciated his concern for Nessa. "It's just that I know how easily situations can get out of hand. Especially when you're with a guy you really like."

"Yeah? Well, that's obvious." Nessa started walking backward, hands in front of her to keep Annie from touching her. "Tell you what, Mom. When *you* learn how to control *your*self, then you can come and talk to me, okay?"

If the previous question had been a slap, this one was a dagger to Annie's heart. She didn't know if she was more hurt or angry, but she did know she had to clear up the misunderstanding.

"What you saw—" she began.

"What I saw was you kissing Dean. Or are you going to tell me he was just giving you mouth-to-mouth resuscitation?"

Annie clenched her fists at her side and fought to remain calm. "No. It's true. We were kissing."

"Why? You're still married. Or have you forgotten that?"

"I'm separated, Nessa. I'm only a few weeks away from being divorced. And I'm an adult. I agree that it would have been smarter to wait until the divorce is final, but the divorce *will* be final, Nessa. I can't live with your dad any longer and he doesn't want to live with me."

The clouds parted for a moment and Nessa's dark eyes flashed in the moonlight. "Dad does want to live with you. He's still in love with you, Mom. He wants you back."

"I know you love your dad, sweetheart. And you should. Nothing that happens between us should ever affect that. But *he* made the choices that ended our relationship, not me."

"*You're* the one who filed for divorce."

"Because he decided that there were things more important than our commitment."

A light came on in one of the cabins and Annie realized she'd been talking too loud. She lowered her voice again and took a deep breath for control before she went on. "I know you're hurting over the divorce. I'm willing to give you time to work through your feelings. I'm willing to do almost *anything* to help you. But the one thing I won't do is take your dad back. You're going to have to work on accepting that because nothing is going to change it."

"So you're having a thing with Dean now?"

Annie shook her head quickly. "No. What you saw was just a…" Her voice trailed off as she fought to find the right word. "It was a moment, that's all. It doesn't mean that Dean and I are together. I'm not ready to be with anyone yet. It's too soon."

Nessa's lip curled. "But not too soon to kiss him?"

Annie caught Nessa's hand and held on to it. "You and I will be leaving here in a few weeks. We'll go back to our old lives and never see these guys again. That's another reason I don't want you to get in too deep with Tyler."

To Annie's surprise, Nessa gripped her hand tightly. "I don't want to go back, Mom. I like it here."

"Of course you do. So do I. But we've always known that we have to go back to our real lives when the summer's over."

"But I don't *want* to."

"You didn't want to come here at first, either. Remember?"

"Well, I was wrong."

Hope surged, but Annie knew Nessa too well to believe that this mood would last. "When you get back to

Chicago, you'll be glad to see your friends and return to your school.''

Nessa shook her head and sent a wistful glance toward the stables. "I've finally found something I'm good at, Mom. I don't want to leave.''

"There will be plenty of things you're good at. Discovering what they are is what the next few years are for.''

"No, Mom. *This* is what I want to do. This is what I love.''

"It takes *time* to find your passion in life, honey. I didn't realize what I wanted to do until after you were born.''

"I *know* how I feel,'' Nessa shouted, "and I know what I want to do.'' She threw her arms in the air and began to pace the narrow spot in front of Annie. "Do you want to know why I like Tyler so much? Because he *listens* to me. You *never* do.''

"Of course I do.''

"You *don't*. You're so sure that nothing is any good unless it happens your way, you won't even give me the chance to try.'' Nessa stopped pacing suddenly. "When are you going to figure out that I'm not *you?*''

"I know you're not,'' Annie said weakly, but Nessa had already raced up the stairs and the door slammed before she could get the last words out. The only sounds Annie could hear were the soft sigh of the wind and the scuff of Tyler's footsteps as he followed Nessa inside.

THE STORM HIT THE NEXT DAY, and everyone seemed to be feeling it. A few guests roamed the lodge restlessly, others hissed at whimpering children, bickered with their spouses or slumped in chairs in front of the windows watching the downpour.

Gary did his best to lighten spirits, and Annie's respect for his natural way with people grew even stronger— especially now that she knew what was really in his heart. She kept busy in the kitchen all morning, throwing together snacks and making pitchers of iced tea and mugs of cocoa for those who wanted them. Each time she carried something into the great room, she heard Dean or Gary assuring the restless bunches that the storm wouldn't last.

By two o'clock, when even Gary was forced to admit that the storm wasn't going to abate, the tension hung like thick fog in the great room. Irma had taken charge of the children and was reading stories aloud in one corner. Nessa and Tyler huddled together on the far side of the room taking great pains not to make eye contact with anyone else—especially Annie. Gary started a game of hearts for a quartet of willing participants, and Dean carried in firewood while Les set kindling in the massive fireplace.

With everyone else occupied and with a few free minutes to call her own, Annie took advantage of the quiet and slipped into Dean's office to use the telephone. It had been too long since she'd talked to her mother, and after last night she needed to hear a friendly voice.

She shut the office door and sat in Dean's huge leather chair, trying to draw on his strength. She dialed quickly and held her breath, willing her mother to be home. When she heard the familiar voice on the other end, relief almost made her cry.

"Honey!" her mother cried when she heard Annie's voice. "What a delightful surprise." She paused and her voice changed. "Is something wrong?"

"No. I've just been missing you."

"I miss you, too. How's the world at your end?"

Annie leaned back in the chair and began to curl the phone cord around one finger. "Fine. You should see this country someday, Mom. It's breathtaking."

"Have you taken any pictures yet? I'd love to see them."

"Not yet, but I will." The prospect of having photos to remind her of this summer was a bittersweet one. "Pictures won't do this area justice, though. You have to see it to believe it."

"I'm envious. And how's the job? Okay?"

"It's fine." Rain spattered against the window behind her and she huddled deeper into the chair. "It's not what I'm used to, but it has a strange kind of appeal."

"How's Gary?"

"You wouldn't even recognize him. He's a cowboy through and through—and quite a remarkable man now that he's all grown up."

Her mother laughed. "That he is, honey. And Nessa? How does she like living on a ranch?"

Annie couldn't hold back her sigh. "You know how much she fought me about coming? Well, now she's decided she never wants to leave."

"Knowing Nessa, that doesn't surprise me a bit. But what about her friends in Chicago?"

"She doesn't seem to care. She's discovered a new love of horses and she announced last night that she wants to work in a stable for the rest of her life."

"Really?" Her mother's voice changed subtly, but Annie couldn't make out the emotion. "Well. I must say I'm not surprised. She's always loved animals."

"Kittens and puppies," Annie protested mildly. "Horses are a whole different story."

"Yes, well they are bigger, and I think they're probably harder to keep in a downtown apartment. I wonder what the pet deposit would be?''

Annie usually loved her mother's ability to laugh about everything, but she wasn't in the mood for jokes today. ''Can we be serious, Mom? I have a problem here.''

Her mother's voice sobered. ''She really wants to stay?''

''That's what she says.''

''And how do you feel?''

''Frustrated.''

''I meant, do you want to stay there?''

''That's not even an option,'' she said firmly. ''I have a job in Seattle starting in just a few weeks. I've already arranged to have my furniture and clothes shipped.''

Her mother laughed softly. ''Sweetheart, anything's an option if you want it to be. And the way you just raved about the scenery there made me wonder. Do you think your boss would keep you on?''

Annie resented the way her mother was running away with the idea. ''Honestly, Mom, you're talking as if you think staying here is a good idea.''

''I think that whatever makes you happy is a good idea. I'd really like to see you happy for a change.''

''I *was* happy,'' Annie reminded her, ''until Spence decided he couldn't keep his pants zipped.''

''Oh, Annie, you weren't happy.''

''I *was*.''

''You were content, I suppose. But not happy.''

''And how would you know?''

''I'm your mother. I've known you your whole life. I know the way your eyes look and how your voice sounds when you're happy. You *weren't* happy.''

Annie growled in frustration, but she had the sinking feeling her mother was right. ''Fine. But that doesn't mean I should move across the country and embrace a radical lifestyle change.''

''Isn't that what you'd be doing in Seattle?''

''That's different.'' A gust of wind rattled the window. Annie leaned against one side of the chair and draped her legs across the opposite arm. ''Staying here would be just *too* drastic.''

''What's wrong with drastic?''

''I *have* a life, Mom.''

''Yes, you do. Now tell me how it's been working for you.''

Annie opened her mouth to answer, but nothing would come out. She clamped her mouth shut and kicked one leg nervously. ''You know how it's working,'' she said after a lengthy pause. ''But making a huge change is not the answer. In fact, Spence has asked me to come back and work at Holladay House.''

''You told him no, of course.''

''Yes, but he still wants me to think about it.''

''I see.'' Her mother let a moment lapse. ''How do you feel about that?''

''I don't know,'' Annie admitted. ''I don't know if I can work with him, knowing that he's with Catherine. But if I go back to Chicago, Nessa won't have to live with Spence. Besides, I'm not sure that I want to teach. I love *doing* too much.''

''Sounds to me like it's time you figure out what you want.''

Annie twisted the phone cord around her finger again. ''I *know* what I want. I want a normal life. I want a daughter who doesn't hate me and a job I can be proud of.'' *And someone to love.* She pushed that unwelcome thought aside. ''I want to work through the issues of my divorce and get my head on straight before I start making big life decisions.''

"Let's start at the beginning of your list," her mother said with infuriating calm. "Nessa doesn't hate you. She's just a teenager, hopped up on hormones and the agony of growing up."

In spite of her warring emotions, Annie laughed at her mother's choice of words. "*Hopped up?* Really, Mom. You make it sound as if she's on drugs."

"Sometimes that's what it feels like." Her mother let out a sigh and Annie pictured her in her easy chair with her feet up. "Your body just seems to take over at times and your emotions are always running high. Don't you remember being that age?"

"Of course I do."

"Then you remember how much you welcomed my input?"

Annie pulled her finger out of the cord and started winding it up again. "I didn't react the way Nessa does, and I certainly didn't talk to you the way she talked to me last night."

Her mother's sudden laughter rubbed her already raw nerves the wrong way. "Oh, Annie. What universe were you living in? You don't welcome my input *now.* And I distinctly remember a couple of fights we had when you were younger that were real doozies."

Annie frowned at her finger inside the cord. "I don't."

"You *don't?* Think about it, Annie. Remember the argument we had when I was making the macaroni and cheese?"

Annie started to say no, but a flicker of memory came back to her. She sat back in her chair and jerked her finger out of the cord again. "I vaguely remember an argument, but I don't recall any details."

"Well, I do. You wanted to hop on a Greyhound bus and travel across four states with some friends—does that ring a bell?"

Annie bit the inside of her lip and nodded reluctantly. "Vaguely. But—"

"But nothing. You were all of fifteen years old at the time and absolutely furious with me because I didn't want to let you head off with a bunch of kids and no chaperone. And, if you'll recall, the group was co-ed."

Annie laughed and rested her cheek in her hand. "Okay, you win. I remember thinking you were the worst mother in the world."

"So you said…several times."

"Was I really so awful?"

"Yes. And yes, the things you said hurt me—just like some of Nessa's comments hurt you now."

"Why did you put up with it?"

"Because *you* were hurting, honey. You were confused. You were finding your way. Nessa's feeling all that and she has the divorce to deal with, too."

"It would be easier if she'd accept it."

"She will. But I'm sure she's feeling powerless right now. After all, her life's been tossed upside down, too. You and Spence are changing everything and not giving her any say in what happens. Just imagine how that must feel. Her life isn't just an extension of yours, you know."

Being told something similar twice in less than twelve hours made Annie edgy. "I know. I know. But I shouldn't have to reconcile with Spence just so she doesn't have to feel frustrated."

"Of course you shouldn't. I'm not saying that growing up should be a license for kids to do or say whatever they want. But relationships change—even between parent and child—and the growing pains can be very real.

It could be that you're still expecting to see a little girl when you look at her.''

Annie blinked back tears and leaned her head against the chair. "She *is* a little girl."

"No, honey, she's not. She's a young woman and very nearly an adult. She's a whole person who may actually agree with you sometimes, but very probably won't. Your only job is to teach her how to make decisions. Not to make them for her."

In that moment, Annie's own adolescence came back in a rush. She remembered fighting against the constraints of childhood and how much she'd resented her father for holding on long after she thought he should have let go. "Letting go is so hard," she said with a sigh.

"Yes, it is." Her mother's voice grew warm and soft. "But it's also very rewarding to see your child become an adult and to know that you can trust her to do what's right."

There was little doubt what she meant by that. "How did you get to be so wise?"

Her mother laughed. "It's a gift, sweetie. I'm glad you recognize it. I promise that if you'll listen with your heart, you'll find it, too, and you'll know instinctively what to do."

Annie leaned her head against the chair and closed her eyes. And prayed with all her heart that her mother was right.

CHAPTER FIFTEEN

BY MID-AUGUST, DEAN was a bundle of nerves. Things were better with Tyler, but he still hadn't committed to staying, and Dean's last few conversations with Carol had been as unsatisfying as the first two. Irma and Les were making plans to visit grandchildren in the fall. Gary was talking about a visit home after the last of their guests departed. But Dean couldn't make any plans. It felt as if his whole life was hanging in the balance, waiting for other people to make decisions.

His relationship with Annie was no exception. He knew that she was being bombarded from all sides and did his best not to exert pressure on her, but the waiting was beginning to wear on him. Maybe this is what he got for avoiding commitment for so long. If this hell was anything like what Hayley had felt while waiting for him to decide how he felt, it was no wonder she'd walked out on him.

And to make matters worse, he was having trouble breaking even financially. Reservations for the following week were dismally small and the phone calls for new bookings just hadn't been coming in. His former teammates were having a winning season—good for them, not so good for Dean's business, since the chances of them actually being able to come to the Eagle's Nest were growing slimmer with every game they won.

He checked his watch and downed a pain pill on

schedule, then punched numbers on his adding machine and made a face when he saw the total. He tried again and tossed his pencil onto the desktop when the bottom line didn't come out any healthier. If this kept up, he didn't know where he'd find the money to keep the ranch open for a second season. And he had no idea what he'd do if this venture failed.

Maybe Gary was right. He needed a gimmick to set the Eagle's Nest apart from its competition. Fate had tossed a real gourmet chef into his lap, but it was too late to advertise that this year and Annie wouldn't be here next season. Besides, he refused to use Annie to make the Eagle's Nest profitable.

He picked up his pencil again, ready to start crunching numbers, but when he heard the sound of a car's engine through the open window he got to his feet quickly. Gary had taken a small fishing group into the mountains and Annie had gone into town with Les and Irma. It was too soon for them to be back. Maybe it was a family with a wallet full of cash, just looking for a place to spend it all.

Laughing a little, Dean glimpsed a maroon sedan bouncing up the dirt road toward the lodge. It stopped in a cloud of dust a few feet from the front door, and the single occupant stayed inside and waited for the air to clear.

Dean hurried into the great room to check the reservations log. Maybe he'd missed something when he scanned the register earlier. Through the open front door, he saw a man climb out of the car and straighten slowly. He lifted a pair of sunglasses from his eyes, and stared at the cabins for a few seconds before turning back to the lodge.

Something about the guy bothered Dean, but he

couldn't say what it was. Maybe it was the expensive-looking silk shirt, or the casual slacks and polished leather shoes. The man didn't seem like someone who'd be interested in spending a few days at a dude ranch.

The visitor lowered his sunglasses again, reached into the back seat and pulled out a garment bag. Slinging it over his shoulder, he started toward the lodge. Tall and dark, thin and wiry, he didn't seem like the outdoors type at all. But looks didn't mean anything, Dean reminded himself. Mrs. George, the plump middle-aged woman who'd arrived a couple of days ago with four children didn't look like the outdoors type, either.

Dean stepped out on the porch and realized almost immediately what he didn't like about the guy. The other man was studying everything from the yard to the lodge to the dirt as if he found it all distasteful. As if it were all far beneath him.

That only made Dean more curious about why he was here.

He leaned against a post and waited while the man climbed the steps and set his garment bag down on the porch railing and gave him the same once-over he'd been using on the grounds. "You work here?"

Dean dipped his head. "I do."

"Who do I see about getting a room?"

"I can help you."

"Really?" He gave Dean another long appraising stare, as if he didn't believe someone wearing a cowboy hat and boots could actually read the registration form.

"How long do you plan to stay?" Dean would give the guy forty-eight hours before the dirt under his fingernails sent him scurrying back to civilization.

"I'm not sure yet." The visitor picked up his garment

bag again and looked expectantly at the door. "Where do we go?"

Dean pushed away from the post and led him inside. He felt a tingle of satisfaction when the guy's step faltered as they stepped through the doors, and a burst of pride when he glanced over his shoulder and saw him admiring the view.

The man turned toward him slowly. "This is impressive. Surprising, actually."

"Thanks." Dean couldn't be sure, but he thought he sensed a tinge of regret in the man's voice. Was he a competitor trying to check out Dean's operation? If so, he wasn't being very subtle.

Dean found a registration card and put it on the desk. "If you'll just fill this out, we'll find you a cabin."

The man draped his garment bag across a chair and came toward the registration desk. "Sure." He picked up a pen and tapped it on the polished wood surface. "A cabin, huh?" He glanced around the room again. "Do you have anything available in this building?"

"Sorry. We don't have any guest rooms here. Guests stay in the cabins."

"That's too bad. This is quite nice." The man pulled down his sunglasses and met Dean's gaze with a smile. "Not what I expected, to be honest."

Dean forced a smile and refrained from asking what the hell the guy *had* expected. Money was money, and this guy carried himself like a person who had some to spare. "If rustic's what you want, you won't be disappointed with the cabins."

"I'm not looking for rustic," the stranger confessed. "But I'll put up with it if I have to." He glanced over Dean's shoulder as if he expected to see someone else there. "I'm here to see my wife and daughter."

Dean's nerves tingled in warning, but he didn't want to jump to the wrong conclusion. "Are they guests here?"

"Not exactly." He put down his pen and held out a hand. "Spence Holladay. I believe my wife is working here."

It was all Dean could do to shake the man's hand, and it took even more effort to keep the smile on his face. "You're Nessa's dad?"

"I am." Spence filled in the blanks on his registration card and handed it back to Dean. "So, where do I go?"

The temptation to tell him where he *thought* he should go was almost irresistible. Dean tucked the registration card into the desk drawer to keep Annie from stumbling across it before he had a chance to warn her. He grabbed the key for cabin twelve from the strongbox and motioned toward the front door. "I'll show you."

Questions darted through Dean's mind as they walked. Had Annie invited him here? Had Nessa? Or was this a surprise visit? How would Annie react when she found out he was here?

And what would *he* do if she decided to leave with Spence?

ANNIE LOADED HER ARMS with groceries and carried them up the porch stairs into the kitchen. Little by little, she'd been adding new items to Dean's meal plans and he'd stopped putting up even a token resistance. Her work was more satisfying this way, but it still didn't match cooking in her own kitchen, preparing meals that required all of her skill and artistic ability.

The summer was nearly over and Annie was no closer to knowing what to do. Her indecision was making her a nervous wreck. Teaching looked less appealing by the day, and the idea of living without Nessa was harder to face, not easier. But she couldn't make herself agree to go back to Holladay House, and taking orders from Spence again—not to mention running in the same circles as Catherine. On the flip side, she couldn't agree to stay at the Eagle's Nest when she knew that she would wither without a culinary challenge, and she couldn't bear the thought of doing something that could result in her resenting Dean.

She'd talked to Gary a few times, but he'd only offered cryptic advice about the journey being more important than the destination, which only left her more frustrated than ever. She was beginning to believe that he'd eventually land on his feet and even find happiness, but she was having serious doubts about herself.

Since she couldn't seem to put her life in order, she'd spent the past few days focusing on which dishes she wanted to make for the Founder's Day potluck dinner. Now, with the ingredients in hand, she nudged the kitchen door open with her hip and called over her shoulder to Les. "Would you mind bringing in that bag of things we bought at that roadside stand?"

Les sketched a salute and reached deep into the truck bed for the bag she wanted.

Stopping at the ramshackle stand had been the highlight of her day. Imagine finding so many wonderful, fresh vegetables right here in Whistle River. She'd astonished Les and Irma by buying up the poor farmer's supply of jalapeños, but Annie had seen possibilities dancing in front of her eyes and she hadn't been able to resist.

She just hoped she'd remembered everything she needed to make that night's campfire dinner. The drive into town didn't feel long anymore, but it was still a little far to run for one forgotten ingredient. She set the bags on the counter and went outside for more. As she filled her arms again, she realized a car was parked in front of cabin twelve.

Irma came outside for a bag of cleaning supplies and Annie nodded toward the cabin. "Isn't that a new car?"

Irma squinted to see it. "I do believe so."

"You didn't check anyone new in before we left, did you?"

"I didn't." Irma dragged the heavy box of laundry soap toward the tailgate. "Maybe Dean checked someone in while we were gone."

"That must be it. Well, he should be happy, then. Another occupied cabin is always welcome." Annie picked up a twenty-five-pound bag of sugar. "I guess I should find out how many are in their party. I don't want to be short on food tonight."

"And I ought to make sure they have plenty of towels."

Annie trailed Irma into the kitchen and left the sugar on the counter. Together, they walked into the great room and Annie dug through the cubbyhole beneath the telephone for the registration card. "It's not here," she told Irma. "Wouldn't you think he'd follow his own rules?"

Irma laughed. "Honey, Dean doesn't follow anyone's rules—especially not his own." She pulled open the kneehole drawer of the desk and produced a registration card. "Here it is." Irma's gaze shot to hers. "Holladay, party of one."

A strange tingling sensation ripped through Annie's body and a sense of disbelief flooded her. It had to be a mistake—or a horrible coincidence. She took the card from Irma and studied it, but her eyes wouldn't focus on the familiar handwriting.

That was a coincidence, too. A lot of people had similar handwriting. She rubbed her eyes and looked again just as his voice reached her.

"Hello, Annie."

She dropped the card onto the registration desk and felt more than saw Irma stiffen at her side. Her heart slammed against her rib cage and anger got her moving again. How dare he show up here? How *dare* he?

The sun glinted off his dark hair as he crossed the room. The gentle sway of his shoulders, the swing of his arms, the length of his stride were achingly familiar. They should be after sixteen years. She'd seen him in every kind of light, every mood, every situation imaginable. She'd been his wife for so long, there was nothing she didn't know about him.

She felt Irma watching her, asking for a silent indication of whether she should stay or go. "It's okay, Irma. You can get back to what you were doing."

As Irma went into the kitchen, Spence drew up in front of Annie and reached out as if he intended to kiss her hello the way he always had.

Annie jerked backward to avoid him. "What are you doing here?"

Spence's eyes widened slightly, but only for an instant. "No beating around the bush, huh?"

Annie wasn't going to let him pull her into a game of words. She crossed her arms and asked again. "What are you doing here, Spence?"

"I've been worried about you, Annie. I wanted to see where you've hidden yourself away."

Had his eyes always been such a pale blue? And she didn't remember them being set quite so close together. Once they'd dazzled her. Now they were…beady. She shook her head and told herself to stop analyzing. "I'm not hiding."

"Sorry. My mistake." He trailed his eyes slowly around the lodge. "Then I wanted to see for myself that you're okay."

"Your concern is touching, but it's not welcome."

"Oh, come on, Annie." Spence touched her shoulder before she saw his hand move. "I know you're angry, but there's no need to act like this."

"Like what, Spence?" Annie dashed a lock of hair from her forehead and put some distance between them. "Like a woman whose husband betrayed her? Like a woman whose ex-husband is intruding on her new life? Is *that* what you don't want me to act like?" She glanced around the room. "Where *is* Catherine, by the way?"

Spence adjusted his shirt with a twitch of his shoulders. Annie knew she'd touched a nerve. She wished she'd set it on fire. "She's in Chicago, of course. We both thought it would be better for me to come alone."

"How sensitive."

"Okay. Fine. I screwed up and I deserve to be punished. Is that what you want to hear?"

"No, Spence, that's not what I want to hear. You've always been good at saying things, you're *not* so good at meaning them."

"I mean *this*. I've been worried about you. I don't want to see you self-destruct. And I'm not your ex-husband yet. We still have seven days to make things right."

Annie laughed harshly. "Why didn't I realize before what an inflated opinion you have of yourself? Why would I self-destruct just because you don't love me?"

"But I *do* love you. I always have."

"If having sex with another woman is how you show that you love someone, I'm sorry for the people you merely *like*." Looking at him made everything inside her tighten with hurt and anger. He still showed no honest remorse for what he'd done. "Go home, Spence. You're not welcome here. We're doing fine without you."

She couldn't believe the disdain that crossed Spence's face. "You never were a very good liar. You don't really expect me to *believe* that?"

A knot of tension formed between Annie's shoulders and outrage made her head pound. "I don't care what you believe."

"You're being a fool, Annie. Come back to Holladay House."

"And work with you?" Her decision suddenly became crystal clear. "Not if my life depended on it."

"Be realistic. You're too professional to throw away your career over this. At least I *thought* you were."

She glared at him. "You make it sound as if infidelity is something trivial."

"And you make it sound like the end of the world. For God's sake, it was one mistake."

"One? It went on for months before I found out and you would never have told me if I hadn't walked in and found the two of you together. And the affair is *still* going on. Or does your calling it a mistake mean that you're tired of Catherine now?"

"I'll *tell* you what I'm tired of. I'm tired of the way you're keeping all our lives on hold. I'm tired of the way you're making the whole family suffer because of some need you have to punish me."

Annie folded her arms defensively. "If your life is on hold, that's your doing, not mine. I've given you my answer a dozen times. It's just not the answer you want. Now, please leave."

"Not until this is settled."

"It's *been* settled since the day I found you and Catherine together.'' Annie took a deep breath and added, ''Since even before that, and we both know it. What you did hurt me, but you were right when you said the marriage was over a long time before that. There's nothing personal we need to work out, and our professional life is just as dead. Please, can't we end this with what little dignity we have left?''

A shriek from the doorway cut off any response Spence might have made and a second later, Nessa threw her arms around his neck and held on with everything she had. ''Daddy? What are you doing here? When did you get here? Are you staying? Please say you're staying. I want to show you *everything*.''

Spence hugged her enthusiastically and met Annie's eyes over Nessa's shoulder. ''I'd love to see everything, muffin. And I even came prepared to stay for a while just in case. But I don't want to stay unless it's okay with your mother.''

Annie could have throttled him for putting her in that position, but she also realized that he'd been doing the same thing for years. Spence made sure he was the good guy; Annie the one who administered discipline. Spence said yes. Annie said no. Ice-cold resentment made the ache in Annie's head worse, but the smile on Nessa's face froze the words on her tongue.

For once, Annie wasn't going to be the bad guy. Spence would have to fill that role himself. ''You've already checked into a cabin,'' she said as sweetly as she could manage. ''Why would I ask you to leave?''

ANNIE MOPPED THE BEADED perspiration from her forehead as she put the finishing touches on dinner. Even at their high altitude, the early August afternoon had grown uncomfortably warm. She was trying to conserve energy, but the burners she used on the stove kicked additional heat into the room and made her wish she was sitting in the shade of the tall pine trees.

She'd been working steadily all afternoon putting together a meal that would prove to Spence that spending a few months in the mountains hadn't dulled her edge. She'd planned roasted peppers stuffed with feta cheese, parsley and hot chillies. Flank steaks that had already been marinating for hours would be served with her summer salsa made from cantaloupe, jalapeños and blackberries. Side dishes of sage polenta, vegetable slaw with orange cilantro dressing, barbecued quesadillas with lime sour cream, and sweet-onion-and-sage gratin cooked in a Dutch oven over the fire rounded out her choices.

Maybe after seeing what she was still capable of, Spence would tuck his tail between his legs and go back to Chicago where he belonged.

Through the open windows, she heard Nessa's laughter mingled with Spence's and a new battery of mixed emotions bombarded her. She understood Nessa's feelings about the family breaking up, but she'd have to accept the divorce now. Obviously, Spence was still with Catherine. He'd invited Annie back on a strictly professional level. Why couldn't Nessa see that? Why couldn't she understand that Spence still didn't feel any remorse over the affair or what he'd done to their family?

Glancing toward the window, Annie willed Spence to say or do something more in character that would open Nessa's eyes. Something thoughtless or selfish or—

"Got a minute?"

Annie whipped around at the sound of Dean's voice and laughed to hide her sudden nervousness. He stood just inside the doorway, his eyes so penetrating she had trouble catching her breath. "You startled me. I didn't hear you come in."

His lips curved slightly and he pulled out a chair at the table. "Mind if I talk to you?"

That sounded ominous. Annie shook her head quickly, turned down the burners on the stove and joined him. When she realized that her hands were shaking, she clasped them in her lap and tried not to look worried. "What is it?"

He took so long answering, Annie thought she might stop breathing entirely. When he finally spoke, he didn't even make eye contact. "I met your husband today."

"Don't call him that."

"That's what he is."

"Technically, and only for another week. We haven't lived as man and wife for months."

Dean's eyes raked her face as he processed her answer. "Did you know he was coming?"

"No."

"Did Nessa?"

"I don't think so. She certainly seemed surprised to see him."

Dean let out a breath and sent her a lopsided smile. "Can I admit that I'm glad to hear it? I wanted to warn you that he was here—just in case you didn't know—but Mr. Jennings in number seven cornered me so Spence got to you first."

Annie resisted the urge to touch Dean's hand, but only because Nessa could have come through the door at any moment. "I didn't ask him to come," she assured him again. "I wouldn't even let him stay if it weren't for Nessa."

Dean nodded slowly and turned a place mat absently. He ran his fingers along the pattern and studied it as if there was nothing more important in the world. "She misses him," he said at last. "And she needs him."

"Yes, she does. I just wish it weren't true. I wish she and I could just go off somewhere and forget Spence even exists."

"You'll never be able to do that."

"No. Of course not. It's just me being angry and bitter." She smiled sadly. "In my head, I understand why Nessa feels the way she does about Spence. My heart has more trouble. We were a family. He betrayed both of us when he cheated with Catherine. He destroyed our family but Nessa seems to think it's my doing."

"She's a smart girl. She knows that what her dad did was wrong but she still loves him—and she should. She's probably just as confused as you are."

"I know you're right. If it were *my* dad who'd cheated, I'm sure I'd feel the same way she does."

Dean leaned back in his chair and rested an ankle on his knee. He drummed his fingers on the table and glanced at her from the corner of his eye. "He doesn't intend to leave without you. I can tell."

A wave of resentment curled through Annie. "Not because he loves me, though. He just wants his chef back. But he's using some twisted logic to argue his case. He claims that going back to Holladay House would be the right thing for me on a professional level, but he never cared this much about my career when we were together. It was always about his restaurant." She rubbed her temples with her fingertips and let out a deep sigh. "He's going to *have* to leave without me. It's over between us— on every level."

Spence's voice drifted in through the open window and Dean's gaze trailed toward it. "You know, now that he's here and I realize that I really could lose you, suddenly there's nothing I want more than to convince you to stay here with me.'' He smiled without humor. ''Maybe my logic is equally twisted, but I can live with the idea of you going to Seattle, even if I don't like it. Maybe because I think I'll still have a chance if you're there. I *really* don't like the idea of you going back to Chicago, but I'm not sure if it's because I think going back would be bad for you or for me.''

The choices were so hard. She wanted to assert her independence and prove to herself that she could make it on her own. But Gary's warnings about the rarity of love and not living with regrets, along with Nessa's determined announcement that she wanted to stay, kept echoing through her mind.

Tears filled Annie's eyes. Emotion tightened her throat, and she could hardly speak around it. ''Dean, I—''

He held up a hand to stop her. ''Don't, Annie. I don't want you to say anything right now. I want you to be absolutely sure of how you feel. If you go through with the divorce, it has to be because of Spence, not because of me.''

''I *am* going through with it,'' she said fervently. ''And you know why I'm doing it.''

Dean leaned forward and touched her lips gently with his fingers. ''Yes, but I also need to know that if you go to Seattle and the culinary institute it's because that's what you really want, and if you choose to stay here it has to be because of me, not him.''

Annie gulped back the protest she'd started to form while he was speaking. She gripped his hand and held it between both of hers near her heart. ''I know how I feel about you, Dean. I—''

He cut her off again. ''I don't think you do, Annie.

You won't until you've worked through all the issues you have with Spence." Dean pulled his hand away with exquisite gentleness. "His affair is still too recent. The hurt is still too raw. And I'm not sure there'll be room in your heart for me until he's out of it."

His arguments were making her head hurt. Hadn't he been listening? "Spence *is* out of it," she assured him. "He has been for a long time. For years before he took this final step, all we did was go through the motions. We never kissed, never made love, never talked—*really* talked. There were many times along the way when I wondered if he stayed with me because of the restaurant. I know there were times when that's why I stayed."

Suddenly too agitated to sit, she pushed herself to her feet and paced a few feet away. "The marriage is over, Dean. I've filed for divorce and it galls me that *I* had to do it. I'm furious that he probably would have let us go on that way indefinitely if I hadn't found out for myself what was going on."

Dean watched her carefully and listened without interrupting until she'd finished. "The problem is, I don't know how to love halfway. If you get me, you'll get everything I've got. I'm selfish enough to want the same thing in return. As long as you're this angry with Spence, he's taking part of your heart."

Annie shook her head, but Dean raised his hands so he could finish his thought. "Believe me, I know a little something about anger and what it does to a person. You can't give me all you have if you're passionately angry with your ex-husband."

Annie's thoughts were all jumbled up with feelings that washed up and receded like waves. He was right. He was wrong. He was blindly, foolishly unfair. He was a hypocrite. How dare *he* talk to *her* about anger? How dare he tell her to put Spence out of her heart when the woman who'd caused his accident still owned such a huge chunk of his?

But she didn't want to bring that subject into the discussion or they'd argue. She didn't have enough emotional energy for that. "The choice I have to make isn't between you and Spence," she said. "It's between striking out on my own and linking my fate to another person's like I did at Holladay House."

He stood and leaned toward her, close enough for her to smell that scent of soap and outdoors that was uniquely his, and gave her the briefest kiss in history on the cheek. "I know that, Annie. So take your time. I'm here if this is what you want. I'm not going anywhere."

ANNIE WAS ON PINS AND NEEDLES that evening. Everyone could see it. Dean could feel her agitation as if it were his own. Usually, she worked smoothly. Seamlessly. Watching her prepare a meal was like watching an artist create an oil painting. Tonight, she seemed so jittery as she lowered the Dutch oven into the coals, he nearly stepped in to help.

But the anxious glance Annie cast in Spence's direction stopped Dean cold. Her expression was almost impossible to read. But he knew instinctively that she'd resent him implying that she wasn't functioning at full capacity. So he kept his comments to himself.

Dean kept one eye on her as he made his way along each of the tables occupied by the guests. He listened to Mrs. George with half an ear as she chatted about the fish her boys had caught that afternoon, and he made an effort to concentrate when he promised to provide Doug Wright and his son with wading boots and hand-tied flies for an early-morning fishing expedition the next day.

As he left their table, Gary stopped him. "You okay?"

Dean nodded, but he made a face and let down his guard. "Peachy. Why? Don't I look okay?"

"Not exactly. Your face is all scrunched up, the way it gets when you miss taking your pills...but I'm sure I'm the only one who's noticed. You seem fine around the guests."

Dean turned toward the trees and let the plastic smile slip from his face. "Have you talked to Annie since he got here?"

"I haven't had a chance. She's not exactly in the mood to talk." Gary ran his thumb and forefinger along his mustache. "I've gotta tell you, though, she's not the happiest I've ever seen her."

Dean put his hands on his hips and took a deep breath, hoping a little oxygen would help him get his thoughts together or make sense of the emotions warring inside him. He glanced over his shoulder toward the fire. In spite of Annie's assurances, Dean wasn't convinced that Spence wasn't a choice. "Do you think she's going to take him back?"

"Come on, Dean," Gary said with a scowl. "You know her better than that."

"I know they have a lot of history together," Dean said. "And that can be hard to turn your back on." He stole another peek at Nessa. "Especially when there's someone who wants you to put things back together so badly."

"Nessa's just scared," Gary said. "She doesn't want her dad to disappear from her life, and she only knows of one way to keep him around."

Dean nodded and turned back toward the trees. "Have you met him?"

"Briefly."

"What do you think?"

"I think he's okay. I think he made some bad choices and did things backward, but he's not a bad person. I think he's anxious to get Annie back and worried about losing his daughter. But I think he's more worried about what losing Annie will do to his business than anything." Gary clapped a hand to Dean's shoulder. "You're going to have to trust Annie to do the right thing, buddy. What other option do you have?"

Dean wished he could think of one, but Gary was right. What other option *did* he have?

CHAPTER SIXTEEN

AS SOON AS HE THOUGHT he could get away unnoticed, Dean hurried back to the lodge, grabbed a sandwich and some chips, and carried them to his room. He could either mope over Annie and Spence, or he could do something constructive.

He'd been watching Tyler with the Little League team at their last few practices and he'd been amazed by the kid's easy, natural ability. Working with the team seemed to be loosening something inside Tyler. Dean had no idea whether or not Tyler wanted to play baseball, but he thought the kid had a chance to make the high school team and even go on from there if he wanted to.

He didn't intend to push Tyler one way or the other, but he couldn't deny the surge of pride he'd felt when he realized that he and Tyler shared something. As a token of respect—or maybe a means of making amends—Dean had decided to offer Tyler the glove he'd used when he played professionally. Even if Tyler didn't want it, Dean wanted to make the gesture.

Never one to enjoy living amid boxes, Dean had quickly unpacked everything after he'd moved into the lodge. All but one carton. The one Hayley had packed for him shortly after the accident. The things she'd put away just before she left.

It was the one box he'd never been able to make himself open.

He knew, because Hayley had told him, that his glove was inside, but he had no idea what else she'd put in there. He wasn't sure he wanted to find out. But every time the urge came to carry the box, unopened, to the garbage dump, that glove was the only thing that kept Dean from following through.

He opened his closet door and pulled the carton toward him. He spent a minute studying the neat label in Hayley's handwriting and marveled that she'd taken such pains to put his things together when she'd been about ready to walk out on him. Her image floated in front of his eyes for a second, but Annie's face quickly replaced it.

Dean thought back to his first encounter with Annie—she had reminded him so much of Hayley. It was true that the two women shared a few physical characteristics, but Dean now knew they were nothing alike. Annie had helped Dean forget about the pain Hayley caused him. Even better, the animosity he'd once felt toward his old flame had faded to nothing.

Looking at the box she'd taken such care to pack made him feel pretty sure that he'd been a whole lot more responsible for their break-up than he'd ever wanted to admit. Wherever she was now, Dean wished her well. He hoped she'd find someone to love her as deeply as he now loved Annie.

Dean blinked rapidly to clear his eyes and started toward the small desk he kept in the corner of his room. But now that he'd thought of her, Annie wouldn't leave him alone. Her hair glimmered in imaginary sunlight. Her eyes glittered with excitement. Her quick smile and ready laugh seemed to float in through the window on the gentle breeze. He had to find some way to stop thinking about her or he'd go crazy.

Dropping to the foot of his bed, he rubbed his eyes and told himself to *do* something. He slit the tape on the box and began digging through the things Hayley had stored inside. Cards and letters that had been sent to him in the hospital formed a layer on top. A little perturbed with Hayley for keeping them, Dean scooped up the envelopes and set them on the bed beside him. As he turned back to the box, one envelope slipped from the pile and dropped onto the floor by his feet.

He reached down to retrieve it, glancing at the handwriting on the front as he picked it up. When he saw the return address, he dropped the letter as if it had scorched him.

How had *that* gotten here? He distinctly remembered telling Hayley to trash it.

He'd only touched it once before. He hadn't even read the whole letter inside—and why should he? The woman who'd plowed into his car had offered a weak apology and then started in with the excuses. When Dean had reached that point in the letter, he'd told Hayley to burn the damn thing.

No apology could make up for what that woman had done. No excuse could justify it. And the inconsequential legal punishment she'd received as a first-time offender certainly hadn't atoned for it. Compared to losing everything, what price was a suspended driver's license and a fine?

His heart hammered in his chest as he bent once more to pick up the envelope. Holding it in two fingers, he carried it to the trash can across the room. So Hayley had kept it, probably thinking that Dean would change his mind someday. Maybe she'd even believed those things she'd said in the hospital about him needing to forgive the woman.

Well, Dean had no intention of forgiving her. And he would never forget. He stopped beside the trash can and held the letter over it, but for some reason he couldn't make himself drop it. He stared at the small, neat script on the envelope and let the name sink into his fevered brain.

Maria Hillyard.

He'd seen her only once through the haze of painkillers, but once had been enough. He remembered the dark-haired woman standing over him, her face twisted in agony as she'd stammered an apology. Dean hadn't wanted to hear anything she'd had to say, and the nurses had ushered her out of his room before she could finish.

So why was he hesitating about throwing the letter away now? Morbid curiosity? Did some twisted part of his brain, some dark corner of his heart *want* to know what her excuses were?

He crumpled the envelope in his fist and held it over the garbage can again, but the memory of that night on the porch with Annie stopped him. Annie had told him to remember that everyone had a rough road in life, to stop feeling sorry for himself or imagining that his was worse than the next person's.

But he was doing it again.

He walked to the window and glanced at the light from the fire dancing on the trees. Annie was down there in the thick of battle. She couldn't turn around and walk away or shove Spence into a box and pretend he didn't exist.

And Dean had left her out there alone, as if her problems were less painful than his, as if her decisions were less frightening. He uncurled his fist and stared at the handwriting on the envelope again.

If Annie had the nerve to face Spence, Dean had

enough courage to read the letter. He'd told Annie to work through her anger with Spence. What kind of person would he be if he didn't face his own? The consequences of Maria Hillyard's actions were going to be with him forever; he might as well bring her excuses along for the ride.

He sat on the edge of his bed and thought of everything he'd been before that split second when his life had collided with Maria Hillyard's. He spent a long time remembering the joy of walking on to the field for the first time as a professional ball player and even longer reliving the pain of finding out he'd never do it again.

And what had he become since?

A little smarter, maybe. A *lot* more cynical. He ran a hand along the back of his neck and tried to be honest with himself. He was a better friend than he'd once been. And he was learning to be a better uncle and brother.

Before the accident, he'd been too wrapped up in himself to give Hayley what she'd wanted, and he'd lost her. He'd been too self-absorbed to spend time with his family, and he was having to fight like hell to get them back. He'd been too consumed with chasing glory to lend someone a hand. His relationships had all been centered around what he wanted and needed.

So, maybe he *had* learned something. Maybe he was a better person now. At least the potential to be better was there. And he could honestly say that if he was given the choice, he'd turn down the chance to play ball again if it meant going back to the way he'd been.

He couldn't imagine his life without Irma's well-meaning interference or Les's sage advice or Gary's friendship. He didn't want to imagine his life without Annie's smile or Nessa's laugh or the effort Tyler put in to being "cool." And he wouldn't have any of that if not for Maria Hillyard's mistake.

What a strange piece of irony that was.

He rubbed his shoulder gently for a few minutes, then lifted the flap on the envelope and pulled out the letter.

THE NEXT DAY, DEAN PULLED a cola from the cooler he and Tyler had brought to practice and sat down to watch Tyler in the field with the team. Since this was their last practice before the Founder's Day game, Dean had exerted himself a little more than he should have. The muscles in his shoulder burned in protest, but the pain didn't bother him as much as usual.

He'd read Maria Hillyard's letter more times than he could count the night before, and he'd been turning her words over in his mind ever since. If what she'd said was true—and he had no reason to think it wasn't—Maria Hillyard had started drinking shortly after her husband's sudden and unexpected death the year before the accident. They'd never had children, so after thirty-five years together, she'd suddenly found herself alone. Her husband's death had left her bereft.

Amazingly, Dean had felt a pang of understanding when he read that letter. He knew loss, even though his wasn't exactly like hers. As Annie had pointed out to him, pain was pain. Did knowing about Maria Hillyard's circumstances excuse what she'd done? No. Nothing could. Nothing would. But it did help Dean to start the process of forgiving her, of releasing the anger that had kept him locked in the moment of the accident for so long and of letting some higher power decide the consequences for her actions. Forgiving would do far more for him than it could ever do for her.

Maria Hillyard's loss had driven her to alcohol, which

had eventually led to the accident. Angry as he still felt over it, he also began to suspect that he was guilty of letting grief over his own losses affect far too many people. Maybe he hadn't broadsided anyone with a car, but he'd been running over people's feelings for far too long.

It just wasn't easy to admit that everyone else had been right. It *was* time to stop feeling sorry for himself, to leave the accident behind and move forward with his life.

He took a long drink and carried the can to the short rise of bleachers on the edge of the field. Tyler had the team in the field and was gently hitting balls to each kid in turn. He'd even gotten Pudge to stop trying to find shamrocks. Amazing.

It hadn't taken Tyler long to relax around the kids, and Dean had even caught a few glimpses of the boy Tyler had once been during their practices. One of the kids said something that made Tyler laugh, and Dean marveled at the change the kids had wrought in him. He wondered how long it would last after the season was over. Forever, he hoped.

Dean drained half his cola, turned to set the can aside and caught a glimpse of Pudge trudging toward him across the pitcher's mound. The boy's hair was matted from exertion and his cheeks burned bright red. He mopped his forehead with his sleeve and huffed over to Dean.

Dean studied his face carefully. "Are you feeling okay?" Maybe he should have stayed on shamrock detail.

Pudge nodded and dropped onto the bottom row of bleachers. "It's hot."

"Yes, it is."

"You got any sports drinks in the cooler?"

Dean dug one out of the ice and handed it to Pudge with a warning not to drink it too fast.

Pudge took a sip and lowered the bottle to the bench beside him. "Is it true?"

"Is what true?"

"That you used to be a real baseball player?"

Dean chuckled at his choice of words. "Who told you that?"

"My dad. He read all about you in some magazine."

Must've been an old magazine. Dean glanced toward the others and nodded slowly. "It's true, but that was a long time ago."

Pudge took another sip, picked up a ball someone had left in the dirt and tossed it gently in one hand. "He said you quit because you got hurt. Is that true, too?"

"Yes, it is."

"So, do you wish you could play still?"

Dean watched the ball for a few seconds, up and down, up and down. The sound of the ball hitting flesh seemed to drown out everything else. He gave himself a mental shake, caught the ball in midair and dropped it into the equipment bag. "I try not to think about it."

"But why?"

"Personal reasons."

"Like what?"

Dean glanced down at the buzzed brown hair and the sprinkling of freckles on the boy's round cheeks. "Usually when someone says 'personal reasons' that means they don't want to talk about whatever it is."

"Why not?"

"I'm sure there are a lot of different reasons." Dean dropped the bag beside the bleachers.

One of Pudge's eyes closed to block the sun. The

other was open only a slit. "What don't you want to talk about?"

Dean caught himself about to smile and frowned instead. "If I told you that, I'd be talking about it. That would defeat the purpose, don't you think?"

Pudge shrugged and climbed a row higher. He sat on the edge of a bench with both legs dangling off the side. "My dad says that you were pretty good."

"I did all right."

"He says that you would have had your best season ever if you hadn't been hurt."

"Some people thought so at the time." Dean checked on Tyler's progress and saw that the group had moved out to center field. He jerked his head toward them and tried to divert Pudge. "It's about time to get those guys in here, don't you think?"

"No."

Dean checked his watch and realized that the team still had ten minutes of its scheduled practice. He nodded toward a small clump of trees a few feet away. "You want to go sit in the shade until you cool down?"

Pudge shook his head. "I'd rather talk to you. My dad says that I gotta listen to you because you can teach me how to play really good."

Dean pulled himself onto the bleachers a row higher than Pudge. "I suppose I can if you want to learn."

"He says you can turn me into a real jock."

Dean slanted a glance at the boy's earnest expression. "Do you want to be a jock?"

"I don't know. My dad wants me to be, so yeah, I guess so."

Dean had never approved of parents pushing kids into sports for the wrong reasons, and looking into Pudge's innocent eyes made the decision seem doubly wrong.

"What if your dad didn't care? What would you want to be then?"

Pudge's whole face squished while he gave that some thought. Beads of sweat dotted his nose. "I don't know. I like to draw and I like math and science."

Dean felt an unexpected rush of affection for the boy. "Math and science are good. What do you draw?"

"Cartoons and stuff like that." Pudge sipped from his can and mopped his face again.

"Are you any good?"

"My teacher says so."

"What about math and science? Are you good at those?"

"I think so. I want to be an inventor. I like to make up stuff."

"Is that right?"

Pudge nodded. "My teacher wanted me to go to science camp this summer, but my dad says we couldn't afford it. And besides, he says it's better for me to play baseball than learn more about science and junk."

Dean glanced away so Pudge couldn't see his reaction. "There are a lot of good things you can learn from baseball," he said after a few minutes. "Like teamwork and sportsmanship and how to win and lose graciously." He stole a quick peek at Pudge's face. "But science and math are good, too. The world could really use another great inventor. Maybe your dad'll let you go to science camp next summer." He would if Dean could talk some sense into him.

Pudge watched Rusty catch a high fly ball and sighed heavily. "I'll never be as good as him, will I?"

"I wouldn't say that. Rusty has some natural talent, and he loves the game so he works hard at it. You could probably match him if you wanted to."

"I don't think so. I'm not really good at sports."

"Neither was I at first. I worked hard to make it as far as I did."

Pudge gave that some thought. "How much work would I have to do?"

"A lot."

"What's a lot?"

"Several hours every single day—weekends and after school."

"Every *day?*"

"Every day. If you love the game it doesn't seem so bad."

"Do you even have to practice on Christmas?"

Dean chuckled. "No. I think an occasional holiday is okay."

"Oh. Good." Pudge leaned back and grew thoughtful again. "'Cuz I don't think I'd want to practice on Christmas. Or even when it snowed. Would I have to do that?"

"I think it would be okay to skip those days." Dean put a hand on the boy's shoulder. "Look, Pudge, we're here to have fun, not to kill ourselves. Do your best but don't knock yourself out, okay? Baseball's fun, but it's only a game."

Pudge nodded somberly. "Okay."

When he returned to the field a few minutes later, Dean watched him go with a fond smile, then wondered what his former teammates would have thought if they'd heard him offering that piece of advice.

Only a game. Three words Dean had never thought he'd say—much less mean.

SEVERAL HOURS LATER, Dean stood on the rail of the paddock fence and watched Nessa leading Maisie by the reins while a brother and sister whose names he couldn't remember held on to the saddle for dear life. Their father snapped one picture after another while his wife called directions. "Get one now, Chuck. Move to your left a little so you can get their faces better."

He heard footsteps behind him and glanced over his shoulder to find Tyler walking toward him. They'd been getting along pretty well the past few weeks. Tyler didn't turn away when Dean showed up or leave the room when Dean was in it, and the smell of cigarette smoke on the boy's clothes had become nothing but a memory. But Tyler rarely sought Dean out, and Dean still didn't know what the kid planned to do at the end of the summer—even though Carol had finally given permission for him to stay.

Dean smiled as Tyler approached. "That was a good practice today. You're doing a great job with the kids."

"Yeah?" Tyler leaned against the fence and looked out over the meadow. "Well, they're cute kids, you know?" He squinted slightly and flicked a glance at Dean. "I just got off the phone with my mom."

That got Dean's blood pumping a little faster. "You did? How was she?"

"Okay, I guess. I could tell she'd been drinking, but she wasn't too bad...yet." Tyler grimaced and plucked the head off a weed. A thick silence fell between them while Dean waited for Tyler to continue at his own pace. The song of a nearby meadowlark, the buzz of insects, the laughter of the family behind them, and the plodding sound of Maisie's hooves all seemed muted and far away.

When Tyler didn't speak, Dean prodded him gently. "Did you call her?"

Tyler shook his head. "She called me. Can you believe that?"

"That's good, isn't it?"

"I guess so. It's hard to tell." Tyler's lips curved into a cold smile. "She's pissed, though. Randy found out that you redeemed Grandma's ring from the pawnshop and now Mom's pretending like she didn't know you were going to do it. She said to tell you she wants it back."

"And she'll get it—when the time is right."

A touch of amusement warmed Tyler's smile. "I think she's finally starting to believe that Randy's the one who's been stealing from her."

"Oh? How'd she figure that out?"

"Some money disappeared from her purse last week." Tyler looked away again. "The dude's so stupid that when Mom asked him about it, he tried to convince her that she dropped it. The thing is, the money was there when she went to sleep and gone when she woke up." Tyler wagged his head in disbelief. "Stupid, man. Just plain stupid."

Dean suddenly felt like grabbing the kid and hugging him for all he was worth. He settled for a hand on the shoulder. "What is your mom going to do about it?"

"I think it won't be long until Randy has to find a new place to live."

Dean couldn't stop the pleased grin that tugged at his lips. "Gee, that'd be too bad."

"Yeah. That's what I say." Tyler's smile faded slowly and he kicked one foot onto a fence rail behind him. "She said she's going to ask you for money so she can go into recovery again," he said without looking at Dean. "But she's said that before, so I don't know if she really means it."

Dean's heartbeat jumped a couple of times and he squeezed the boy's shoulder gently. "If she's serious about it, I'll come up with the money somehow." He kept his voice and movements carefully neutral, sensing that Tyler needed space. "I don't know if you remember, but recovery can take a while. So if you want to stick around here while she's working through everything, you're more than welcome to." He chanced a glance at his nephew. "I'd love to have you. And your mom, too, when she's ready."

Tyler dragged his gaze away from the mountains and let it settle on Dean's face. "For real?"

Dean shrugged with as much nonchalance as he could manage. "You're my family. I love you. What can I say? Besides, the horses are getting used to that hip-hop music you and Nessa like, now that you've lowered the volume. None of us will be the same if you leave." He put everything he was feeling into his eyes and willed the kid to accept what he was offering. "Me, especially."

Tyler locked eyes with him for what felt like forever, then looked away again. "I guess I could stay for a while if you want me to."

"I'd like that," Dean said, and he couldn't remember when he'd meant anything more.

BY THE TIME FOUNDER'S DAY rolled around, Annie was a nervous wreck. The longer Spence stayed, the more convinced she was that their marriage had been over for months, if not years. But having him around seemed to make Nessa more determined than ever to put things back as they once were.

Dean seemed a little more distant every day. He spent hours in his office on the telephone with Carol and with his attorney, but he rarely gave any but the most vague explanations about what he was doing.

Annie hated being shut out of his life. She'd have given anything for the chance to talk with him and find out how things were for him but he somehow managed to slip away from every conversation she initiated.

Her nerves were shot and her frustration level was at an all-time high when her alarm went off that morning. She wasn't even sure she'd slept the night before.

Since Dean and Tyler were involved in the big baseball game after lunch, they'd informed the guests that the lodge would be closed all day and arranged transportation into town for any who wanted to join the festivities. Annie was hoping to catch a ride into town with Dean. Even a brief conversation would be better than none.

Just as the sky began to lighten, Les and Gary started loading a borrowed van with blankets, hampers filled with the picnic lunch Annie had packed and coolers full of ice and drinks. Most of the guests had opted to get themselves into town or go somewhere on their own. Only the Gunthers from Missouri—a young couple with a six-year-old daughter—came straggling out of their cabin a little before sunrise. Spence showed up freshly showered and smelling of aftershave a few minutes later.

Annie hadn't seen Dean yet, and she found herself trying to search for him inconspicuously as the little group gathered. Irma appeared a few minutes after Nessa, who carried a huge bag filled with sunscreen, a paperback book, swimsuit and towel, her portable CD player and, no doubt, a supply of CDs as well.

When Nessa noticed little Heidi Gunther battling a huge yawn, she scooped the girl up and made her comfortable inside the van with her CD player and earphones. Annie's heart swelled with pride when she realized that her daughter really was becoming a capable young woman and that she had a kind and generous heart.

Spence came up behind Annie and put his hand on her

shoulder as if they belonged together. "She's really something, isn't she?"

"Yes, she is." Annie slipped away from him.

Spence pretended not to notice that she'd evaded him. He dropped his hand and linked both behind his back. "No matter what you think about our marriage now, you have to admit we've done *something* right."

"She's our crowning achievement," Annie agreed. "But we don't get all the credit. She gets a huge chunk just for being who she is."

"Yes, of course. But you can't see her without realizing that there was something good about us once."

"Point taken," Annie said, remaining expressionless. "But I'd rather not discuss our family issues today. I don't want to ruin the day for everyone else."

Spence looked suddenly grim, but he didn't argue. He turned his attention to the bustle of activity in the clearing. "Which vehicle are we going in?" he asked after a second.

"I don't know which vehicle you're riding in," Annie told him, turning away. "But whichever one it is, I'll be in the other one. We aren't going as a family."

He turned a deep frown on her and his eyes flashed with irritation. "Oh, come on, Annie. Haven't you carried this far enough? It's Founder's Day in Whistle River and all three of us are here. Be an adult about this—for Nessa's sake."

"I am being an adult," she said firmly. "Some day you and I will be able to sit down together with Nessa and maybe even share a day with her. But not yet. Not until some of the hostility has faded and you stop trying to manipulate me to do what you want. Until then, we'll only make her miserable." With that, she walked away

before he could do or say something that might test her
determination to stay calm.

Just inside the kitchen door, she found Irma watching
the goings-on and nursing a cup of coffee. Annie did her
best to wipe away the annoyed expression Spence had
put on her face. "Have you seen Dean this morning?"

"About an hour ago." Irma sipped and sighed. "Just
before he left."

"He left? Already?" Annie's heart sank. "Why so
early?"

Irma glanced at her quickly. "You don't know?"

"He didn't say a word to me."

"Well, no. He wouldn't." Irma ran the fingers of one
hand through her short gray hair and carried her cup to
the table. "He didn't say a word to me, either, but I'm
guessing it's because of your husband out there. I'm
thinking he wants to give you time and space to do what
needs doing."

Annie flushed. "What makes you think that?"

"Don't worry. He hasn't said anything to me. Nessa
told me she caught you two kissing and it doesn't take a
rocket scientist to see that he'd like you to stay here—
and not just because you're an artist in the kitchen, either.
He's happier than I've ever seen him. You and Nessa and
Tyler are helping him to find the best parts of himself."

"He's doing that on his own," Annie said joining Irma
at the table. "And that's what *I* should be doing. When
I came here, the most important thing besides Nessa was
proving to myself that Spence wasn't responsible for my
professional success. Now Dean has asked me to stay.
But how will I ever know the truth if I jump immediately
into the same kind of relationship with him?"

Irma shook her head slowly. "I don't know the answer
to that, Annie."

"Neither do I. And what makes this so tough is that it's not even choosing between my head and my heart. It's having to choose between two different pieces of my heart."

Irma leaned back in her chair and crossed her legs. "It's easy to choose between right and wrong. Not so easy to choose between two rights."

Annie sank back a little farther. "You're not going to help me with this, are you."

Irma chuckled. "Tell you what to do? Not on your life, sweetie." She stood and put both hands on Annie's shoulders. "You want to prove that you can succeed on your own? Well, start right here. The answers you need are all inside you. Just listen carefully and you'll find a better answer than I could ever give you—guaranteed."

CHAPTER SEVENTEEN

"ONE TRAFFIC LIGHT in the whole town. Can you believe it?" Laughing, Spence guided Annie and Nessa through the crush of people hovering around the picnic tables that occupied one whole side of Whistle River's only park.

Adult laughter and conversation rose and fell as people cleaned up after breakfast and set up for the next activity. Children darted in and out between tables and feet, shouting and shrieking with glee, and a large circle of teenagers had formed in the shade near the playground equipment. Annie thought it would have been a perfect scene...except for one thing.

"And that movie theater," Spence continued with a playful nudge of Nessa's arm. "It must be a hundred years old. What do you want to bet they're still using the original projector?"

"I don't know, Dad."

Annie had avoided Spence during breakfast, but she'd come with them now because Nessa had pleaded with her to. Since they'd split from the others Spence had done nothing but complain about the small town Annie was growing to love, and she was beginning to regret giving in.

"If you insist on insulting these people and their town," she said under her breath, "would you at least lower your voice?"

"Oh, come on, Annie. I'm not insulting them. I'm just observing. There *is* only one traffic light, isn't there?"

Annie stopped walking. "It's not *what* you say, Spence. It's the tone of voice you use when you say it." He'd always been good at making innocent-sounding comments and dipping them in acid. "You're insulting these people and we all know it. I'd like you to stop."

Spence rolled his eyes at Nessa, no doubt expecting her to agree that Annie was being overly sensitive.

To Annie's surprise—and maybe more to Spence's—Nessa put her hands on her hips and met her dad's gaze. "She's right, Dad. It's okay that you like living in the city, but some people like having only one traffic light."

Spence held up both hands in front of him and laughed uneasily. "Okay. Sorry. I didn't mean anything by it." He glanced at the smattering of booths across the park, at the baseball diamond, and then toward the playground equipment. "At the risk of sounding rude, is this all that's going on today?"

"I don't know," Annie admitted. "We can ask. Keep your eyes peeled for someone wearing a 'staff' ribbon. While we're waiting for whatever comes next, I'd like to see what they're selling in the booths. How about you, Nessa?"

Nessa nodded eagerly. "Gary said one of the biggest western-wear stores in Wyoming would be here today. Can we see if they have riding clothes? My things aren't sturdy enough."

"Of course we can." Annie started walking toward the booths.

Spence held back. "That stuff's going to be expensive, Nessa. At most, you'll only be here another few weeks. Why waste the money?"

Nessa's gaze shot to Annie's, and for the first time in

a long time, Annie saw a plea for help in her daughter's
eyes. Apparently, in all the talking they'd done, Nessa
hadn't told her dad that she'd been asking to stay.

Annie would have loved to see Spence's reaction, but
she didn't think this was the best time to discuss it. She
put an arm around Nessa's shoulders and pulled her
close. "Nessa's in the saddle every day. She deserves
some riding clothes, even if they're just for fun."

Spence shrugged elaborately and started walking. "I'm
not made of money, you know."

Annie studied him curiously. They'd never been
wealthy, but it wasn't as if Spence had to pinch pennies.
She answered slowly, keeping her voice level so she
wouldn't inadvertently start an argument. "I didn't ask
you to pay for anything. If Nessa finds some things she
wants, I'll buy them." She smiled at her daughter and
added, "Within reason, of course."

"Well, I'm glad *you* have money to burn." Spence
shoved his hands into his pockets. "Working out here in
Nowhereville must be more lucrative than it appears."

Annie fought a flare of irritation. Apparently, Nessa's
request had touched a nerve, and Annie was curious
about why. "I wouldn't use the word *lucrative*," she said
with an easy smile. "But we're getting by."

Twin spots of color formed in Spence's cheeks. "And
is that what you want? To *get by?*"

Annie studied his eyes and saw fear reflected in their
depths. She looked at their daughter and realized that
Nessa wanted her to broach the subject she'd obviously
been avoiding, and that stunned Annie. If Nessa was
ready to let Spence leave without her, she must be serious
about staying.

"Actually," Annie said, "getting by is just fine with
me. If we have a roof over our heads and food on the

table, that's all we need. In fact, Nessa and I have been talking about staying.''

Spence roared with laughter. "*Here?* You're joking, right?"

"I like it here, Dad. I don't want to go back."

"Don't be ridiculous. You're not a..." Spence waved one hand at the people around them. "You're not a *cowgirl* for heaven's sake. You're my daughter. You'll take over Holladay House someday."

"I don't think that's going to happen," Annie said quickly. "It seems that Nessa hates to cook. She's happy here, and so am I. I don't need the limelight anymore."

"*You* don't?" Spence raked his fingers through his hair. "*You* don't need the limelight. *You* don't care what you do to your career." He laughed harshly and turned away, but he turned back again after only a step or two. "You don't care what any of your choices do to *me,* do you?"

Annie caught Nessa's eye and motioned for her to leave them alone. Nessa didn't have to be told twice. When she was gone, Annie folded her arms and stood in front of the man she'd once loved. "What's wrong, Spence?"

He laughed again and rubbed his face with one hand. "What makes you think anything's wrong?"

"I know you. I've spent sixteen years at your side, and I know your moods almost as well as I know my own. Something's wrong, and I want to know what it is."

Spence ran his fingers through his hair again, let his gaze follow Nessa's path and planted his fists on his hips. "It's Holladay House, Annie. I'm going to lose it."

"Lose it? *How?* It's an institution in Chicago."

"Not anymore." Spence dragged his gaze back to her face. "Not since you left. The chef I hired to replace you isn't anywhere near as good as you are, but you know how cash-poor I've been since those renovations we made two years ago. I can't afford to pay for someone better.''

Annie's stomach knotted and a heavy weight landed on her heart. When Spence had decided to renovate the restaurant, she'd urged caution for this very reason. But he hadn't wanted her advice or input at the time. He'd plowed ahead without regard for her feelings or her opinion.

She took in the set of his jaw, the thin line of his lips, the furrow of his brow, and realized that he'd never accepted her input on the restaurant, their marriage, or even the steps she'd taken in her own career. One after another, he'd bulldozed his ideas through and put clamps on hers—all the while calling her his partner.

"You're about to lose the restaurant. That's why you want me back."

"I want you back because you and I work well together. We're *great* together."

"And because you need me to save the restaurant."

"We'll save the restaurant," he said, suddenly earnest. He grabbed her hands and held them tightly. "You and me, Annie. *Together.*"

An immense sadness filled her as she realized how long they'd been living the same lie and how often she'd fed it by taking the path of least resistance. She pulled her hands away gently. "No, Spence. I'm sorry about the restaurant, and I hope you can find a way to save it. But I can't help you do it."

His mood changed in the blink of an eye. "Dammit, Annie, how much longer are you going to punish me for falling in love with someone else? Enough is enough. A business that's been in my family for nearly fifty years is going down the tubes.''

"Then I suggest you save it. Holladay House is a wonderful place. I loved the clientele. I loved the staff. It's worth saving, but it's not worth my life—or yours.''

"It *is* my life.''

"Maybe that's part of the problem. If Nessa and I had ever been more important than Holladay House, things might have been different. But we'd be miserable working together under these circumstances.''

"We don't know that we'd be miserable. And Nessa *wants* us to stay together. If we aren't married, isn't working together the next best thing?''

Annie took his hand in both of hers. "Oh, Spence, listen to us. We're already miserable. How long has it been since we laughed together, or talked about something other than the restaurant? How long since we did anything at home but bicker?'' She waved one hand toward the picnic table where Nessa sat watching. "Look at her. She's nearly a woman. She's heading into the toughest part of her life. She needs us at our best, not our worst. She needs us to pay attention to her, not spend all our energy fighting each other.''

Spence seemed to be taking in everything she said, and that gave Annie hope that they'd finally be able to move on. He glanced toward Nessa as she finished. "We're adults. We can put our differences aside for the sake of the restaurant.''

"I'm not going back to Chicago.''

"You can't really mean that you're staying here.''

Annie nodded slowly and felt joy bubbling up into her heart for the first time in years. "That's exactly what I mean.''

"You'll get tired of it. You both will.''

"I don't think so." Annie glanced toward their daughter and the joy multiplied. "I really think Nessa's found herself here—and so have I."

"What about me?"

"That's up to you. You're Nessa's father. You'll always be part of her life, and I hope you make it an active part. For her sake, I hope you and I eventually learn how to be friends. And I hope you can save Holladay House. It would be a shame to lose it. But even if you can't, I know you'll land on your feet."

"You really *don't* want to help me, do you?"

"I can't, Spence. Don't you see that? You and I both need to stop blaming each other for our unhappiness and using each other to find success. We owe that to each other and to Nessa. And we owe her a chance to become who she really is, not who we expect her to be."

Spence's shoulders sagged. He ran a hand along the back of his neck. "Well, then. I guess I should go."

"Now?"

"In the morning. If you're going to turn your back on me, there's no point in staying."

"Nessa would love to have you stay, and I don't mind as long as you're ready to accept my answer and we don't have to have this conversation again."

He shook his head quickly. "If you're not coming back, there's no point." He kissed her cheek quickly. "I'll go tell Nessa that I'm leaving in the morning."

"Yes," Annie whispered, saddened by the realization that he still didn't understand what she'd been saying. He had his answer and he was rushing back to his precious restaurant. Staying an extra day to make his daughter happy hadn't even crossed his mind.

FOR THE SAKE OF THE TEAM, Dean forced himself to stop thinking about Annie during the game. Tyler had chosen to coach along the third baseline, so Dean was ready to take up position along first. Parents filled the bleachers and called encouragement to their children. Dean watched the players' reactions with interest.

Nicole, his most reluctant player, now bounced with excitement. Zoe seemed suddenly nervous. Zachary was oblivious, and Pudge looked about ready to pass out.

Dean motioned for the team to huddle up and put himself at eye level with the kids. "How's everybody doing? You guys okay?"

Pudge nodded. Rusty popped his gum to show his utter lack of concern. Zachary scratched his ankle and Bobby blew his nose.

"We're okay," Zoe said, once again turning into the spokesperson for the team. She glared around the circle, daring someone to disagree—which, of course, no one did.

"I want you to listen to me," Dean said with a fond smile. "You've worked hard all summer and you're good enough to win this game. The key is to work as a team. Pull together, all right? And remember that we're here to have fun above all."

Pudge nodded solemnly, but his poor little face was still flushed with nervous excitement.

"Just do your best," Dean said. "Nobody can ask for more than that." He stood and brushed grass from his knees, then nodded at Tyler. "Now I'm through yapping. I want you guys to listen to your *real* coach, okay?"

Tyler blinked in surprise, then grinned broadly and took Dean's place. "All right! Listen up, you guys..."

For the first time in his life, Dean understood the phrase "bursting with pride." He wondered if he could

have been more proud if Tyler had been his own son.
And he wondered if he'd ever have a chance to find out.

DEAN WAS HALFWAY TO THE TRUCK with the equipment
bag dragging at his shoulder when he glimpsed someone
sitting in a grove of old river willows near the parking
lot. He might have passed by without stopping if it hadn't
been obvious that she was crying. Even so, he was almost
on the grove when he realized it was Nessa.

Dean stopped walking and studied her. She was young
and vulnerable, and so sad his heart ached. The fact that
she was hidden in a grove of trees meant she probably
didn't want company. But Dean couldn't walk away and
pretend he hadn't seen her.

He left the equipment bag on the ground and moved
to stand between two close-set tree trunks. "Hey, kid.
What are you doing in here?"

Her head shot up at the sound of his voice, and the
tears in her eyes made him glad he hadn't turned away.
She dashed her hand across her cheeks and straightened
her shoulders. "Sitting."

Dean nodded as if she'd given him a meaningful answer. "Sometimes sitting is good." He shifted a little
closer. "Sometimes not so good. If it'll help to talk about
it, I'm a pretty good listener."

She let her gaze drop to her feet. "I don't think so."

"Okay." Dean knew she wanted him to leave, but he
still couldn't walk away from the pain etched on her face.
"Mind if I sit, then?"

Her gaze flew back to his. "If you want."

He made himself reasonably comfortable on a rock
next to hers. "I'm sure you're dying of curiosity about
the game. Our team won."

"Oh. Congratulations."

"Tyler deserves the credit. He did most of the work. I just showed up. The kids really like him."

That seemed to connect with Nessa. Her brow furrowed and her eyes didn't seem so vague. "Did you really ask him to stay here?"

"I did, and I think he's going to take me up on the offer."

Nessa took another swipe at her cheeks with the back of her hand. "He's lucky."

Dean stared at her in surprise. "Do *you* want to stay?"

"More than anything." Nessa glanced at a couple of loudly shrieking kids running past the grove of trees. "I like working with the horses, and I like living at the Eagle's Nest." She sent him a little half smile. "I even like you."

Dean laughed aloud. "Is it that painful?"

She shrugged and bit back a grin. "Not really. Especially now."

"Why now?"

"Because my dad's leaving." She glanced at him from the corner of her eye. "I'll bet you're glad to hear that."

"Yes and no," he said honestly. "I don't like seeing your mom unhappy, and for personal and selfish reasons I'd like to see him go. But your dad seems like an okay guy, and I really don't like seeing you sad." He shifted on his rock to make himself more comfortable. "When did he decide this?"

"A few minutes ago, I guess." Nessa blew her bangs out of her eyes and rested her chin on her knees. "He's going home because my mom won't go back to Chicago with him. So I guess *she's* the only reason he came."

Good thing Spence wasn't anywhere around. Dean could have belted him for hurting his daughter like this.

"Don't jump to conclusions too quickly. Maybe he has to get back. Maybe—"

Nessa rolled her eyes at him. "Maybe he just can't stand being away from his restaurant."

"I'm sure it takes a lot of time and energy. Until this summer, I never understood how much work it is to run your own business."

"Yeah, but you at least put it aside from time to time." Nessa waved one hand toward the crowd in the park. "Like this. My dad would never have done this."

"Come to a community event?"

"He might go, but he wouldn't close down the business so everyone else could." Nessa sighed softly and sent him a sad smile. "He probably wouldn't have gone, either. It's all about the restaurant for him."

"I used to be like that," Dean admitted. "Nothing in the world was more important than baseball. Not my family. Not the woman who was in love with me. Not my friends."

"So you're saying there's hope for my dad?"

Dean grinned. "There's always hope. Unfortunately, it took an accident and losing my career to put things in perspective for me. Let's hope your dad isn't as hardheaded as I am."

"Fat chance of that. Look how hard he's been trying to get my mom back."

Dean didn't trust himself to comment on that subject.

Nessa didn't seem to expect a response. "You know why he wants her back so badly?"

"I could name about a hundred reasons why I would," Dean said. "You want me to start?"

Nessa tilted her head and scrutinized his face thoroughly. "You really like her, don't you?"

"Yes, I do. More than like, actually."

"Are you serious about her?"

Dean thought about dodging the question, but the moment was too special. Nessa deserved the truth. "Yeah, I am. But don't worry. I've been trying to stay out of the way in case your parents decide to patch things up."

"They're not getting back together." Nessa unwrapped her arms from her legs and straightened each leg tentatively. "I think I always knew that, but I was hoping...you know?"

Dean nodded slowly. "I think so."

"So, you want to know why he came after her?"

"Why?"

"So she could save the restaurant for him." Nessa curled her lip and stood. She placed her hands on the small of her back and arched her spine. "I told you that's what it's all about for him. You know what else?"

Dean was having a hard time not grinning like a kid. He wanted to find Annie and ask her if it was true, hear it from her own lips. He held his ground and shook his head again. "What else?"

"He's going to marry Catherine."

Dean's smile faded. "How do you feel about that?"

She shrugged. "I don't care, I guess. I think maybe deep down I always knew that he would."

"Does your mom know?"

"I don't know, but I hope *he* tells her. I don't think I should have to."

"Neither do I," Dean agreed. His heart pounded and his hands grew damp. "So is it okay with you if I ask your mom to stay here? Maybe even to marry me?"

"You'd better. She smiles a lot more when she's around you, and I've started thinking that's pretty cool."

Dean grinned from ear to ear. "There's just one other

problem. If your mom and I do get together, what will that do to you and Tyler?''

Nessa tilted her head thoughtfully. "What do you mean?''

"I mean, you two like each other. That's pretty obvious to the rest of us. If you and Tyler both live here and your mom agrees to marry me, you're going to be family—in a way. I just wonder if that will make it uncomfortable for the two of you.''

Nessa laughed and shook her head. "You haven't been paying attention lately, have you? Tyler and I liked each other that way for a while, but we're more friends now than anything else. It'd be cool to be like cousins or something.''

"Do you think Tyler feels the same way?''

"I'm pretty sure he does. He's out there right now chasing some blond girl around the park and trying to get her phone number.''

For the first time in a long time, Dean felt joy in every cell of his body. Unbelievably, it seemed as if his life just might work out after all.

DEAN SAT AT THE DINNER table and watched the stairs long after all the guests had retired for the night and the lodge had grown quiet. He listened to the sounds of the building at night—to the creak of boards, the hum of the refrigerator coming from the kitchen, the brush of leaves against the window, the muted chirp of crickets outside.

Overhead, he heard a door open and close again, the soft sound of footsteps coming toward the stairs. He forced himself not to move until Annie had reached the bottom of the staircase, then leaned forward, struck a match and touched it to one of the candles he'd set up earlier.

She wore a pair of short pajamas under her robe. She'd pulled her hair up on her head, but loose tendrils escaped and danced around her neck and shoulders. She was more beautiful than anyone Dean had ever seen in his life.

Annie's step faltered and her gaze flew toward the table. She smiled slowly when she saw him sitting there in his pajama pants and slippers. "I got your note. What's this all about?"

Dean blew out the match, struck another and finished lighting the brace of candles so that the light caught the bottle of champagne and fluted glasses. "Contract negotiations. I need a chef next season, and the season after that, and the season after that. I've decided to start looking now."

Annie's quick smile made his heart race. "Is that right?"

Dean nodded and removed the cork from the bottle. He filled both glasses and held one out to her. She took it, letting her fingers linger on his in an unspoken answer before he could ask the questions hovering on his lips. He forced his eyes from hers and made himself continue with his game plan. "I've talked Gary into becoming a limited partner next year. He's done more than half the work around here, but he still won't accept more than that. He recommends you highly—and besides, the guests won't stop raving about the food. So are you interested in hearing my offer?"

She took the seat he proffered and crossed her legs. Her robe fell open to expose the long, slim expanse of silky skin. "What offer?"

Dean dropped into his own chair and tried to keep a straight face. "I'll warn you first that my terms aren't open to negotiation."

Annie sipped and set her glass aside. One sculpted eyebrow winged upward. "Go on."

"I think you'll agree that they're quite generous," Dean continued. He slid to the floor and assumed the position on one knee. "In short, I'm prepared to offer you anything you want if you'll agree to marry me. I love you, Annie. I want to spend the rest of my life with you."

She touched his cheek tenderly and her eyes shimmered. "And I love you. More than you'll ever know."

Joy practically knocked Dean off his knee. "So tell me, what do you need? I'm prepared to do anything you want."

Annie traced the line of his jaw with one hand. "I need to be with you. Besides, I've already turned down Spence's offer and I called today to cancel my contract with the institute. I really don't want to teach, and finding success at something I don't want to do would be a hollow victory. And I can't ignore what Nessa wants, or the needs of my own heart. So the bottom line is, I need a place to live and work and someone to share those things with."

Dean took both of her hands in his, lifted one to his mouth and kissed her palm gently. He reached under the table for the leather case he'd left there earlier. "You drive a hard bargain. So here's my final offer. In here is the Eagle's Nest's new restaurant—at least it's all the legal documents creating it and everything necessary to make it yours. Name it whatever you want. Do with it what you want. Cook whatever you want. It's yours, and I'll contract your services for the dude ranch. I'm not asking you to hitch your star to mine, Annie."

Annie's eyes filled with tears and one slid onto her cheek. She touched the case reverently and her eyes filled with such love and gratitude, he thought he'd burst. "Are you serious?"

"I've never been more serious."

"You'd give part of your business to me?"

He grinned wickedly. "Well, you *would* have to contribute a couple of things to the partnership. Conjugal visits, for one thing. I'm not sure I can survive having separate bedrooms much longer."

Annie's grin matched his. "Ah, *now* the negotiations are getting interesting." She stood and tugged him to his feet with her. Wrapping her arms around his waist, she buried her face against his bare chest and kissed the scar on his shoulder. "What else?"

"Absolute permanence." He slid his arms around her back and murmured against her hair. "You need to know that I'm not even slightly interested in a temporary arrangement. Good, bad or indifferent, this is for the rest of our lives. It's you and me. No third parties. No lying or cheating allowed."

Smiling softly, she lifted her chin and met his gaze. "I can live with that. But Nessa—"

Dean cut her off with a kiss. "Is fine with the idea of us getting married and ready to tell you so first thing in the morning." He trailed one finger along her cheek. "I know this is sudden, Annie. And if you don't love me, I can live with that." He pulled back and tried to smile. "I won't like it, but I'll get used to it. But if you love me, then say yes. Life's short and uncertain. We could wait and hope for a better time, but there's no guarantee that we'll ever have this chance again. You and I both know how quickly life can change. I don't want to lose this chance to uncertainty."

"Neither do I," she whispered. "Or to fear." She kissed his chin gently and shivers raced along his spine.

"Do you really think we can make it?"

"As long as we're together? Absolutely."

"Then you'll stay?"

She smiled up at him and kissed him thoroughly. Her hands caressed his shoulders and trailed down his back to his waist. "Until the end of time."

HARLEQUIN *Super* ROMANCE

CREATURE COMFORT

A heartwarming new series by

Carolyn McSparren

Creature Comfort, the largest veterinary clinic in Tennessee, treats animals of all sizes—horses and cattle as well as family pets. Meet the patients—and their owners. And share the laughter and the tears with the men and women who love and care for all creatures great and small.

#996 THE MONEY MAN
(July 2001)

#1011 THE PAYBACK MAN
(September 2001)

Look for these Harlequin Superromance titles coming soon to your favorite retail outlet.

HARLEQUIN®

Makes any time special ®

Harlequin invites you to experience the charm and delight of

COOPERS CORNER

A brand-new continuity
starting in August 2002

HIS BROTHER'S BRIDE
by *USA Today* bestselling author
Tara Taylor Quinn

Check-in: TV reporter Laurel London and noted travel writer William Byrd are guests at the new Twin Oaks Bed and Breakfast in Cooper's Corner.

Checkout: William Byrd suddenly vanishes and while investigating, Laurel finds herself face-to-face with policeman Scott Hunter. Scott and Laurel face a painful past. Can cop and reporter mend their heartbreak and get to the bottom of William's mysterious disappearance?

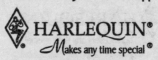

HARLEQUIN®
Makes any time special ®

Visit us at www.cooperscorner.com

CC-CNM1R

Princes...Princesses...
London Castles...New York Mansions...
To live the life of a royal!

In 2002, Harlequin Books lets you escape to a world of royalty with these royally themed titles:

Temptation:
January 2002—*A Prince of a Guy* (#861)
February 2002—*A Noble Pursuit* (#865)

American Romance:
The Carradignes: American Royalty (Editorially linked series)
March 2002—*The Improperly Pregnant Princess* (#913)
April 2002—*The Unlawfully Wedded Princess* (#917)
May 2002—*The Simply Scandalous Princess* (#921)
November 2002—*The Inconveniently Engaged Prince* (#945)

Intrigue:
The Carradignes: A Royal Mystery (Editorially linked series)
June 2002—*The Duke's Covert Mission* (#666)

Chicago Confidential
September 2002—*Prince Under Cover* (#678)

The Crown Affair
October 2002—*Royal Target* (#682)
November 2002—*Royal Ransom* (#686)
December 2002—*Royal Pursuit* (#690)

Harlequin Romance:
June 2002—*His Majesty's Marriage* (#3703)
July 2002—*The Prince's Proposal* (#3709)

Harlequin Presents:
August 2002—*Society Weddings* (#2268)
September 2002—*The Prince's Pleasure* (#2274)

Duets:
September 2002—*Once Upon a Tiara/Henry Ever After* (#83)
October 2002—*Natalia's Story/Andrea's Story* (#85)

Celebrate a year of royalty with Harlequin Books!

Available at your favorite retail outlet.

HARLEQUIN®
Makes any time special ®

Visit us at www.eHarlequin.com

HSROY02

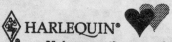

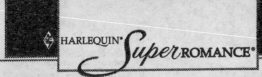

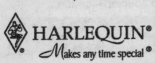